SWEET FIRE

Josie's temper flared. "If this is another of your lectures, doctor, save your breath. I'm not leaving this town until justice has been done!"

They stared at each other in cold, stark silence. Then Rafe grabbed her by the shoulders and, without uttering one word, he bent his head, his mouth claiming hers.

Though startled, Josie did not make any effort to pull away. Instead, she found herself pressing against him, giving herself up completely to the pleasure of his kiss. "Mmm."

The jolt of sweet fire that swept through her veins, the warmth emanating from his muscular body, and the tension of the moment were too much to resist. Wrapping her arms about his neck, she stood on tiptoe and kissed him just as fiercely as he was kissing her. Danger beckoned. Danger and a tantalizing promise of ecstasy . . .

RENEGADE LADY

KATHRYN HOCKETT

ZEBRA BOOKS
KENSINGTON PUBLISHING CORP.

ZEBRA BOOKS are published by

Kensington Publishing Corp.
850 Third Avenue
New York, NY 10022

Zebra and the Z logo Reg. U.S. Pat. & TM Off. The Lovegram logo is a trademark of Kensington Publishing Corp.

First Printing: August, 1995

Printed in the United States of America

Author's Note

The word "duel" is defined in Webster's dictionary as "a combat between two persons." Since the fifteenth century, duels have taken place, first with swords and rapiers, then with pistols and six-shooters. The turmoil that followed the Civil War intensified the incidence of duels. Violence rose to a high-pitched crescendo of gunfire. The anarchy and emotional scars caused by the chaos of the Reconstruction, the hatred for carpetbaggers and Northern-imposed authority, added a new brutality to these combats and spawned killers who took up the gun with one purpose in mind, the murder of their fellow man.

Though the West had been opened to exploration and settlement years before, now there were displaced war veterans moving in that direction. To this often-harsh environment was now added the barbarous lack of proper law and order, and the killing of a man was condoned as long as he was armed and had been warned an instant before the trigger was pulled.

Whether they were lawmen, bandits, or wanton killers, gunfighters shared a purposefulness in being men who frequently resorted to "the gun." Some were hired for their expertise, a few were ready to kill at the slightest provocation, others drew their six-shooters with the purpose in mind of making a reputation for themselves. But fame is fleeting. These same men who killed with profligate ease soon met their demise either by a bullet or the noose.

The list of casualties was staggering. The public hardly knew how to react to those who were capable of such violence. Gunfighters soon came to be regarded with a cautious awe. Many found their place in legend for deeds that were greatly exaggerated. Men, however, did not have a monopoly on making a reputation with a gun. Several Western women became legends in their own time, for good or for ill. They issued a defiant challenge to their male counterparts— anything you can do, we can do too. And they did, shooting with deadly accuracy.

It is just such a woman who is the heroine of this story. Coming out west with one thought in mind, she learns how to shoot a gun so that she can take revenge for a most brutal act. Seeking out the services of a once-famous gunfighter who has become a doctor, she finds love where she least expects to find it.

Part One

A Score to Settle

Spring, 1883— Showlow, Arizona

The patient search and vigil long,
of him who treasures up a wrong.

— Lord Byron, *Mazeppa*, Stanza 10

One

There was going to be a gunfight. It was inescapable. Inevitable. A pulsating, spine-tingling silence paralyzed the onlookers. They froze, watching as the dark-garbed figure stealthfully walked down the middle of the street.

"Tanner! Clint Tanner!" the voice shouted.

Tanner had a well-earned reputation, one so overwhelming that most men went out of their way to avoid an argument. Few wanted to force him to draw his gun. But this antagonist did.

This one was either one of the brave ones or, more probably, one of the stupid ones, Dr. Rafe Gardner thought as he watched from the boardwalk right in front of his office. No doubt this was some fool who wanted to make a name for himself by tangling with a man of Clint Tanner's reputation.

"Did you hear me, Tanner?"

Clint Tanner had heard. Slowly, carefully, he turned around, hands poised at his guns. Tension crackled in the air.

"I heard you."

The sound of scuffling boots on the dirt broke the quiet as the onlookers disappeared, scamper-

ing away to find cover, be it a barrel, the horse
trough, or the greater safety of a building. Everyone sought a place to hide, occasionally peeking
out from concealment to see what was going to
happen next. Only the doctor held his ground. Before this was over he was going to be needed. Now
was no time to play coward.

Stopping in their tracks, neither gunman moved
for a long, long time; they merely eyed each other
across the distance. Tanner was famous for taking
his time. The doctor knew a gunfight was rarely
decided by trick shooting. The man who won a
gunfight was the man who didn't allow himself to
be pressured. A gunfighter had to have confidence
and patience. Both were indispensable traits of the
gunman's breed. That and sheer luck!

"I've been dreaming about this for a long time,
Tanner," the voice cried out again. Beads of sweat
broke out on the challenger's forehead despite the
bravado. It was a hot day. The sun blazed down
like a huge candle.

"You don't say. . . ." The grin that spread across
Tanner's face gave proof that far from being frightened, he was relishing the idea of waiting and
watching his opponent sweat.

Dr. Rafe Gardner squinted his blue eyes against
the bright yellow sun as he watched. Like two roost-
ers in a cockfight, he thought. Slowly he reached
up and tugged his hat down to shade his face,
watching as the stranger in town, the other gunfighter, strode toward Tanner. Damn, he seemed
little more than a beardless boy. A naive, impetuous youth.

"Draw, you bastard!" The voice was high-pitched, as if Clint's poise was irritating. "Let's get it over with."

"You're going to end up dead."

"Yeah?" There was a long pause. The tone was scornful, yet Rafe detected a slight tremor. "Well, I'm not afraid!" As if to prove it, the young gunfighter took one step and then another, closing the distance between them.

A muscle in the doctor's jaw ticked as he studied the scene. Some men still lived by the old creed that the gun was law and whoever was the fastest was in the right. He knew otherwise. A lot of men who were wrong had won plenty of shoot-outs.

"I'm a reasonable man," he heard Clint Tanner call out. "Just turn around and walk back down the street and I'll forget this ever happened."

Well, at least he was giving the kid a chance. Not many men would do that. He had to hand it to him there. He doubted the young challenger would listen, however. They never did. Rafe felt sick at heart. It was all so senseless. What did a thing like this prove? Nothing. Absolutely nothing.

"Turn around? And hightail it out of here. Not on your life. You killed someone close to me and for that you are going to pay!" The voice was shrill. Tanner's poise was obviously irritating. "Let's get it over with." Stealthfully the challenger faced off with Clint, waiting for the first move.

The moment has come, the doctor thought. Hurrying inside his office, he grabbed his black bag. He had best be prepared. One of the gunfighters was going to need him. Or the undertaker.

It happened and happened quickly. The challenger's hands moved downward, Tanner went for his pistol, and with the speed of a lightning bolt his guns cleared their leather holsters. There was a flash of metal and an explosion from the hip as Tanner got off the first shot, aiming for the right arm. A piercing cry of pain rent the air as the sharp staccato blast shoved his assailant backward, but despite being hit the challenger got off a shot. The bullet whistled by just an inch from Tanner's ear.

Thrusting his gun back into its holster, Tanner cursed. Grumbling beneath his breath he came upon his young opponent in three long strides. Reaching out, he grabbed the youth, disarming him before he could fire again.

"I could have killed you, you young fool!" Rafe heard Tanner say as he hurried toward them, "but I didn't. But by God, if you try this again, I won't be as lenient!"

"I will try again." Blazing green eyes glared at Tanner and touched on the doctor. Pretty, long-lashed eyes.

Rafe stared back. The upturned nose dusted with freckles, the round, rosy-cheeked face, looked unnervingly feminine despite its grime. "Who are you?" he asked, bending down.

"Josie. Jo . . . se . . . phine." There was such pride in the voice.

"Jos— " Slowly Rafe bent closer, peering into a very defiant face. For a moment all he could do was to stare in surprise, but Tanner found his voice.

"No! It can't be!" But just to make sure, he grasped his challenger's hat and yanked it off. Two short, wheat-colored braids came tumbling down. "Not a woman . . ."

Rafe slowly unbuttoned Josephine's shirt to get access to the wound that was now bleeding profusely. Though he was careful to protect his patient's modesty, his motions nonetheless bared just enough well-rounded flesh to give undeniable proof. "She's a woman all right, Clint." While dabbing at the wound, Rafe took the time to eye her appreciatively. "And a pretty one at that."

"Goddamn!" Tanner was deeply disturbed at the thought that he had just shot a female.

Rafe took a bandage from his black bag and tied it tightly around the young woman's arm to slow the bleeding. "Not a serious wound," he said, trying to reassure her. "Still, I think it would be a good idea for you to let me take you to my office. I want to prod around and make certain the bullet passed on through."

Josephine bit her lips against the pain. "Your office?" Just who was this man?

"Yes, ma'am, my office." Rafe hurried to explain. "I'm a doctor." His long-fingered hand moved to her forehead to gently smooth the hair back from her eyes.

"A doctor?" He didn't look like the kind of doctor she was used to, bespectacled and elderly. Tall, dark, and broad-shouldered, he cut an awesome figure. He wore a pair of jeans that clung to his muscular legs, a blue flannel shirt beneath a fringed brown leather vest, a red-and-black checked cotton handkerchief knotted around the strong, corded column of his neck, and brown leather boots. His black Stetson was tilted back on his head, its brim curled upward. She couldn't keep from staring. "You don't look like one—"

"And you don't look like the usual gunfighter we see around here," Rafe answered quickly.

As the residents of the town slowly came from out of hiding to crowd around them, Tanner hastily explained that he hadn't known at the time that she was of the feminine gender. Even so, it was obvious by the expression on the ladies' faces that they thought him to be a brute. No doubt what he had done would be the topic of gossip for days. As for the men, they either winked at Tanner slyly or guffawed behind their hands.

"Tanner wins again," one man said. A chorus of laughter echoed his words.

Tanner ignored the sarcasm to inquire about his victim's injuries. "How is she, Rafe?"

"It's nothin'." Josie made great show of acting brave, but her wince of pain and the slow ebb of color from her face gave her away. She didn't resist as Rafe picked her up in his arms and carried her down the boardwalk to his office.

Two

The wooden planks creaked noisily as the doctor strode boldly down the boardwalk. What a strange sensation it was, Josie thought, being whisked up and carried as if she weighed nothing at all. For a moment she stiffened, her fingers clenching Rafe's shoulder as she fought against a stab of pain, then just as suddenly she relaxed. She was in good hands now, and had to admit that she liked feeling the strength of this man's hands as he held her. He was so big. She liked the sensation of feeling small and fragile, she, whose height was usually so intimidating to men.

"We're almost there." His voice was a low rumble that touched every nerve in her body.

Josie didn't answer. She was mesmerized as she found herself looking directly at the chiseled strength of his lips. Though they were firm, she sensed they would be soft when he was moved by passion.

As he walked down the boardwalk, the doctor tightened his arms around her waist and under her thighs, pulling her closer to him, so close that her breasts were lightly brushing against the firm muscles of his chest. The heat from his body was enveloping her. It had been so long since she had sought comfort from anyone. Not since Charlie's death.

Oh, Charlie, she thought. Nothing in this life, not even being shot, could ever rival the gut-wrenching agony she had felt when she had learned of her brother's murder. And murder it was. A senseless killing at the hands of a gunfighter. Clint Tanner. Was it any wonder she was determined to seek revenge?

"I'll get Tanner next time," she mumbled. Her words were muffled by a loud thump as the doctor kicked open a door.

Josie attuned her senses to the room they entered. The doctor's office was cozy and smelled of leather and antiseptic. A large desk in the middle of the room, a huge black chair, and a brocade settee dominated the majority of floor space. Though her experience with men had taught that they were all slipshod in their housekeeping, there wasn't one thing out of place. The office was immaculate, in fact. Only the ominous-looking instruments that hung on the wall marred the tidiness of the room. Josie shuddered.

"You're shivering." His tone was sympathetic, tender.

Josie wanted to snuggle up against him, collapse into his arms, but she didn't and she wouldn't. Instead, she was quick to say, "You can put me down now!"

Slowly, carefully, he lowered her onto the black chair, his hand sliding around her waist and down to her hip as he did so. The touch of his fingers sent her senses spinning with a mingling of pleasure and alarm. Her heart was beating at a furious pace. It was a primitive attraction she had for him, based merely on lust, she thought, but recognizing it for what it was didn't lessen the impact he had on her. Nevertheless, her voice was gruff.

"I'm not a doll, you know. I won't break. . . ."

"I didn't suppose that you would," he countered. "I merely wanted to make sure I didn't hurt your arm."

"Yes, my arm!"

Josie flexed her wounded limb and grimaced. The pain was excruciating. She would never have let the doctor know that, however. She would have endured pain a hundred times worse before she would have confessed such a weakness to him or anyone. She had never wanted sympathy in her life and didn't want it now. Still, she had to admit that it was strangely comforting just being in the doctor's presence.

Josie watched as Rafe washed his hands. "What's that?" She grimaced at the smell.

"Chlorinated lime," he answered. "We've learned a great deal about healing since the days of the Civil War. I want to make sure you don't get any infection."

He pulled up a stool and sat beside her. There were all kinds of wounds to deal with, Rafe thought to himself. Clean wounds, such as those inflicted by knives, or dirty wounds caused by gunshot. Gunshot wounds were the most dangerous because bullets shattered bone and often stayed in the body. If left in the flesh, they could become a source of putrefaction that more often than not caused complications. But he didn't want to scare her.

"Infection?" The way he said the word sounded threatening.

"It would complicate your arm's healing," he answered as he pulled the shirt off her shoulder. He couldn't help but notice that she had very smooth skin. Just like velvet. The deep gash the bullet had left marred the perfection. "You could have been killed today," he said matter-of-factly, trying hard to ignore her femininity and professionally concentrate on what he was doing.

"Yeah, I suppose I could have been," she snapped. By some miracle she had come out of that fight with her skin. Still, it rankled Josie that Tanner was still alive. She would be better prepared next time.

As the doctor poked and prodded at the wound, Josie clenched her jaw, trying to take her mind off the pain by concentrating on his face. He was a handsome man, all right, with his thick, dark hair, straight nose, and firm, square jaw. The mouth beneath his neatly trimmed dark mustache was slightly open, showing perfectly even white teeth. His blue eyes, however, were much too bold. There was a hard look within their depths that bothered her, though she couldn't say why.

"Well?" Josie raised her eyebrows in question as the doctor shook his head. Something was wrong.

"A piece of the bullet is still in there. I'm going to have to get it out. It will hurt."

Josie took a deep breath. "Do what you have to

do!" Brave words that nearly came out in a croak as she watched him take one of the instruments from the wall. Quickly she closed her eyes.

"Would you like a shot of whiskey?"

Though she was tempted, Josie shook her head.

Rafe picked up the long pair of tweezers. Maneuvering them as gently as he could, he stuck them into the open wound. He fully expected the young woman to scream or faint, but her courage was astounding. She winced and clenched her teeth but didn't make a sound.

"There, the worst is over." With a final tug he pulled the bullet fragment free, then washed out the wound with warm water. "You can open your eyes now."

Josie did, to find his gaze riveted on her. The way he was staring was nearly more than her composure could bear. "You through?"

"Almost," Rafe answered. Leaving her for just a moment, he came back with a clean bandage. "My name is Dr. Rafferty T. Gardner, but you can call me Rafe if you'd like to drop the formality," he said in an attempt to be friendly. "And you?"

"Josephine M— " She started to tell him her real name, then hesitated. "Smith. Josephine Smith," she said cautiously. "But you can call me Josie."

"Josie," he repeated. He had the feeling that although she reveled in showing how strong she was, there was a softness deep down inside her somewhere. And when she was soft, he had no doubt that she would be absolutely captivating.

"I was named after my grandmother. A compliment, since she was quite a woman." For just a minute she let down her guard, smiling sweetly, deliciously, at him, showing the indentations in her cheeks when she did. Rafe had always been a sucker for dimples. But just as quickly the moment was gone and she returned to her scowling demeanor.

"Josephine. A pretty name." He finished bandaging her arm and rebuttoned her shirt.

Now that the emergency was over, Rafe took the time to really study this young woman. She was tall and slender, her figure rounded in all the right places. Her face had a delicate perfection, but the determined expression in her eyes hardened her appearance. Her mouth was pretty, he thought, but its downward pull was pouty and spoiled its shape. She was a very pretty girl who was obviously trying to show by the garments she wore and her actions that she was tough and worldly. Too bad, he thought. No doubt when she took more pains with her appearance, found a more feminine style for her hair, she could be quite stunning. In a dress she would be quite beautiful indeed. Shaking his head, he chased such thoughts from his mind.

"Something wrong?" Her eyes flashed angrily, her mouth tightened. She didn't like the way he was staring. Critically, not complimentarily.

"Just wondering about a few things," Rafe answered. "Like what brought you all the way to Showlow." He was curious about her motivation. It wasn't every day a woman strapped on a gun and marched down the street to call a man out.

"I came here to kill Tanner and I will before I am through," Josie threatened.

"Why you?" With all the gunslingers wandering about, why had she taken the vendetta upon herself? "Why would a young, seemingly sensible young woman come all this way to be so foolish?" It would be such a pity for such a lovely young woman to meet her end by being struck down by a bullet. Clint had been lenient this time, but he could be provoked only so long.

"I tried to hire someone, but they were all cowards. No one wanted to tangle with Tanner. Therefore I knew if I wanted him to be punished, I had to do it myself," Josie answered honestly.

"Punished?" The way she said it made her sound more like a preacher than someone out for revenge.

"Tanner killed someone. Someone I loved." Charlie's face flashed before her eyes, but she didn't cry. She had gone far beyond tears. "So now it's only right that he meet the same fate."

"I see. . . ." His tone held scolding and censure. "An eye for an eye."

There was total silence in the room, a quiet that made Josie very uncomfortable. She knew she was right in what she was doing. She wouldn't let anyone convince her otherwise. Not anyone. She was right! Even so, she moved her focus over the room to avoid looking at the doctor, whose self-righteous expression was beginning to get on her nerves.

"You might say that I am a collector," Rafe said dryly, noticing her interest.

"So I see. . . ." Guns hung upon the wall, all kinds of guns, from rifles to revolvers. Josie thought how strange it was that they should be in a healer's office. "Are all these yours?" she asked.

Rafe nodded. "Reminders to me of how senseless violence is. All these guns belonged to the *losers* in gunfights. Some are alive still, but unfortunately most of them are six feet under, pushing up daisies."

Josie tossed her head. "If you are trying to scare me, it isn't working."

"Well, it should!" Rafe put his hands on his hips. "All a gun brings is death!"

"Or justice . . ." Josie returned him look for look, frown for frown.

"Killing a man in a gunfight is hardly justice," Rafe said coldly. "It's murder."

His words held Josie speechless for a moment but then her anger came back to rescue her. Squaring her shoulders, tilting up her chin, she rasped, "It's none of your business!" What did he know about such things? She would bet her bottom dollar he'd never lost a loved one to some gunfighter's bullet.

"Ah, but it is," Rafe countered, though he wondered why he should care. She wasn't anything to him. Why was there something about this young woman despite her bravado and surliness that brought out his protective instincts? His tone softened as he said, "Miss . . . Josie."

Josie refused to talk about it. The time for words had died with Charlie. "If I want to kill or be killed, why should you care?"

"Why? Because . . ." He started to explain, to exhume the ghosts of his own past. She reminded him so strongly of another time, another place, one he wanted so much to forget.

"Well, forget it, doctor! Nothing you can say will make me change my mind." Tanner killed Charlie and she was bound and determined to make him pay.

Rafe was quickly losing patience. It was obvious that the only way to stop her was to tie her up and forcibly haul her out of town. But even then she would undoubtedly come right back. "You are that determined to be stupid!"

"Stupid!" That really riled her. Ignoring the pain in her arm, she jumped up. She was stupid all right. Stupid to ever think he would understand. "To hell with you!" Before he could talk her into coming back, Josie was at the door, but she threw over her shoulder, "Tell your friend Tanner that he was lucky this time. I was only practicing. Next time our gunfight will be for real!"

"And next time you'll end up on boot hill. You can't win, you young fool!" Oh, what was the use in talking to her? She was a headstrong, ungrateful little chit who seemed to want to put herself in the pathway of danger. As Rafe watched her leave, he thought to himself that she was right, it wasn't any of his business.

Three

The land looked like a golden-brown muffin
fresh from the oven. There was dirt, plenty of it.
Atop that dirt huge saguaro cactus stood like
guards over shrubs. Arizona Territory. From the
boardwalk in front of the doctor's office, Josie
stared at the grandeur of it as she tried to calm
her temper.

"The bastard!"

He had called her stupid. A fool. Well, she
would show him a thing or two. He would be eating his words when she brought down Clint Tanner. And she would. Somehow.

"Clint Tanner!"

Josie tensed as she said the name, clutching at
her injured arm. Always a winner, never a quitter,
she was humiliated by her failure. Perhaps this
time she had bitten off more than she could chew
and was not as well prepared as she had at first
thought. Or was it just that Clint Tanner had been
faster on the trigger than she had ever imagined
he'd be?

It didn't matter. The fact that her brother's murderer had escaped unharmed annoyed her. She
had a stubborn streak, or so her father had always

told her. That obstinacy made it impossible for her to leave until the score was settled. By hook or crook she would find a way to carry on. Tanner would pay for the misery he had caused by taking Charlie's life. It was an important vow, the only thing that kept her going.

"Charlie . . ."

Just the sound of his name on her lips wrenched her emotions to the bone. Oh, how she had loved him. And now he was gone, struck down by Clint Tanner's bullet.

Josie remembered her first look at her beloved younger brother. It had been on the day that he was born. She, a quarrelsome six-year-old, had wrinkled up her nose at the sight of the tiny red baby with fuzz on his head. She had been jealous and angry that she would now have to compete with this usurper. She had been certain he would steal her parents' affection. But her feelings had changed in such a short time and Charlie had become the center of her life. Now he was dead and her head swam with angry questions that for a moment blotted out her physical pain.

Why did it have to happen? How could anyone have murdered her brother so heartlessly? Having done so, why hadn't he been punished?

Josie's eyelids closed. She took a deep breath, all the while remembering how excited Charlie had been about his life out west. His letters had abounded with vivid descriptions and enthusiastic stories of people he had met and places he had seen. Who could have foreseen then what fate had in store for him. Fate and Clint Tanner's ruthlessness.

It took Josie a long, agonizing time to get her composure. Looking out again toward the horizon, she saw the landscape through Charlie's eyes. He was right; it was so different from the green, heavily populated East. It was rugged, dry, raw, huge. A land of sagebrush, saguaro cactus, red rocks, and gravel.

Even the buildings looked different. Now that the blinding anger had cleared from her eyes, she could see that they were smaller and more rustic than those in Ohio, but the town was pretty ordinary just the same.

There was a pharmacy, a general store, several saloons, a barbershop, two hotels, a feed store, a newspaper office, a dressmaker, a dry goods and clothing store, a baker's shop, a blacksmith, and a laundry, all made out of adobe or wood and set against a backdrop of desert grassland, dry hills, sagebrush, and cactus. What made it particularly important to her, however, was that it was Clint Tanner's town.

"And now it will be my town as well. Until I accomplish what I set out to do," she mumbled as she suffered the hostile gawks of those who passed by. Men mainly.

It was a man's town. They thronged the dusty streets. Ranchers in denim pants and plaid shirts, miners in baggy pants held up by suspenders, storekeepers wearing big canvas aprons, bankers in well-tailored suits. Some men rode horses, some led mules piled with provisions, a few sat atop wagons, still others walked. All were assaulted by the powdery dust that rose around them, coating everything in its way. A choking dust that made Josie cough.

There were women too, though far fewer in number than men. Dance-hall girls staring at Josie from saloon doors, ladies in faded calico and big bonnets trudging the boardwalk, haughty spinsters in somber brown or black dresses with high starched collars, schoolteachers in all probability. As they walked by Josie, their voices were carried by the wind.

"Why would any young woman be gunnin' for Tanner?" a graying woman in blue asked.

"Unless she had a hankerin' to die," said another in a breathless whisper.

"Hell, he's the best shot anyone has seen around here in a coon's age," another woman said. "She had to know she'd be no match for him."

"None of the men are," a woman with a high voice exclaimed. "Even my Joe."

"He never misses. Never. I swear he has eyes in the back of his head," the woman in blue insisted.

Josie listened to the chatter concerning the gunfight. From the conversation, it seemed everyone liked Clint Tanner, or at least looked up to him, for God's sake. Oh, how that rankled her, more so since that admiration seemed to make her the townspeople's enemy. Or was it that they were afraid of him? She didn't know. She didn't care. It wouldn't be the first time she was friendless, nor possibly would it be the last.

And yet Josie realized that she hadn't been as

clever or as careful as she should have been in seeking Tanner out for revenge. Now everyone knew why she had come, and by the expression in their eyes, they weren't at all sympathetic. Well, it didn't matter. Josie had intended to get the matter of Clint Tanner over with quickly, but now it appeared that what she had in mind was going to take longer than she had first thought.

Meanwhile she needed to find a clean room in a boardinghouse, one that didn't cost an arm and a leg like that hotel room did. She had to buy herself a set of practical clothes too. Blue denim pants, a cotton shirt without a hole in the arm, and perhaps another hat. With that purpose in mind, Josie strode off toward the general store.

Pushing through the door, Josie saw that a variety of provisions were heaped and bundled inside. The usual. Various kegs and barrels brimmed with sugar, flour, molasses, and vinegar. From the rafters slabs of ham and other meat hung, along with cooking pots and pans. From foodstuffs to tobacco, from cotton materials to candy, from medicines to mining equipment, everything necessary for daily life was just inside the door, stacked so neatly as to be able to make full use of every inch of space.

On one side was a counter for groceries, on the other a counter was piled high with dry goods and hardware. It was there that Josie headed, rummaging through a pile of canvas pants. Finding a likely pair of dark blue denims, she held them up, then turned her attention to a shirt, a light blue one.

"The green one would look better. It would match your eyes."

Whirling around, Josie was stunned to see Dr. Rafe Gardner regarding her intently. What was he thinking? She could only wonder. Certainly she didn't intend to talk with him, not after what he had said. Turning her back, she tossed the blue shirt aside and picked up a black and tan plaid, pretending the doctor wasn't there.

Rafe was not the kind of man to be ignored. After several awkward attempts at conversation, he stepped right in front of her, holding out his choice from the stack. "And then again, perhaps the red one is best."

"To match my lips?" Josie shot back sarcastically, breaking her silence. She was infuriated when he smiled.

"To match your temper," he answered, remembering how angry she had been as she stalked out of his office. Though she was the one being rude, he found himself wanting to make amends. "But then, after what happened, I suppose you have a right to be irritable."

"You're damned right I do," she insisted. Still, her anger was beginning to thaw. It was Clint Tanner who should really bear the brunt of her wrath and not the doctor, thus she added, "But thanks for patching me up." She recalled his touch, how gentle his hands had been, and something tense and hard inside her began to melt.

He took off his hat, repressing an overwhelming desire to reach for her hand. "It was my pleasure."

Hesitant, she stood staring, not really knowing

what to say. Although shyness was not something Josie was plagued with, it seemed she was tongue-tied now. Her heart began to hammer with a strange feeling, so different from the anger that had consumed her emotions.

The doctor must have just been to the barber. She could smell the fresh scent of soap on his skin, a pleasant, spicy odor that she detected as she stepped toward him.

Rafe was equally at a loss for conversation. All he could think about was the warm softness so close. How in the devil could anyone have mistaken her for a man, even for a moment? He couldn't help but wonder, his expression turning meditative. "Have you done any more thinking about what I advised?" he asked, feeling protective of her. He could only hope she had.

"If you mean about Tanner, no." Suddenly Josie felt rebellious again. Gone were any womanly feelings. Something in the doctor's eyes goaded her. A look of self-righteousness. She wondered if he had followed her just for the purpose of continuing their discussion. If so, he was wasting his breath. "As a matter of fact, I'm making plans to stay here. At least until my business is finished," she said.

"Business." He knew exactly what she meant. "If you aren't ridden out of here on a rail, you mean."

"Ridden out." Something in his tone had sounded threatening. "By you?"

He shook his head. "No. But if you aren't careful, there will be others. No one wants trouble in this town." And there were those who would go to any length to avoid it. Men who needed Tanner.

Toe to toe and nose to nose, she faced him. "Trouble?"

"You know what I mean." Rafe shook his head. How on earth was he going to get through to her? The damn little fool was going to bring the town crashing down around her head, but she just wouldn't listen. "Look . . ."

Josie didn't reply, didn't even say a word. With a toss of her head she merely moved past him. Without buying even one of the items she had come in for, she strode from the general store.

Long shadows stretched out before Josie as she walked past the center of town on her way back to the hotel. Unfriendly shadows. She ignored them.

She returned to her hotel room as quickly as she could and found a note pinned to her door. Yanking it down, she uttered a sharp gasp of surprise as she opened it and read, "If you are going to act like a man, we will treat you like one. Get out of town. You are not welcome here.

"Get out of town. . . ."

The note brought a sudden chill to her entire body. What would the note writer do if she failed to follow directions? She had never been threatened before and didn't know quite how to react. Still, she wasn't running. She had come to Showlow for a reason.

"Tanner." Her plans had to be modified somewhat now, however. Josie knew she had to find someone to teach her how to be a dead shot with a gun. A sharpshooter. Then she could hold her own with anyone. Indeed, it seemed now that her very life depended on it.

A childish sketch of a gravestone with a grinning skull at the bottom of the note only reinforced Josie's determination. Crumpling the piece of paper, she clenched her jaw, bucking up her courage. If Tanner thought he could frighten her by such an idiotic thing as this, he just didn't understand her kind of woman very well.

"If he thinks this kind of antic is going to send me packing, then perhaps he needs to learn otherwise."

Ignoring the constant stab of pain in her arm, she walked with a swagger as she retraced her steps and ambled along the boardwalk once again. Her intent was to find Tanner. With that thought in mind, Josie weaved in and out among the pedestrians mulling about in front of the stores, her eyes searching for a particular hat. Alas, it soon became apparent that Tanner was not among them.

"If I were a skunk, where would I hide out?" she muttered beneath her breath. The answer came to her in an instant. The saloon.

It proved to be an admirable hunch. As she passed by the Golden Cactus's small front window, she saw him sitting at a table in the corner, glowering at the jovial-looking man who sat across from him. Certainly he didn't seem to be in a very good mood. In fact, if his temperament could be measured by how loudly he was tapping his fingers on the table, it seemed he was steadily getting angrier. At last she heard him blurt out, "What the hell are you smiling about, Daniels?"

"What?" The other man cocked his head quizzically.

"You're laughing at me. Admit it. Smirking inwardly because I was set upon by some little hellion wearing britches." He pointed toward the window, where several people were meandering by, likewise in amiable moods. "Look at them. They all think it's amusing. Well, I don't!"

The other man picked up a discarded newspaper, then rolled it up as if to use the paper "club" in his own defense if need be. "Now, look here!"

"No, you look." The table reverberated as Tanner hit it with his fist.

"Easy. Easy." The other man seemed eager to placate Tanner. "It's your imagination. No one is laughing at you. You're a hero in this town. Always have been, always will be."

"I was until she sauntered in as big as you please." Clutching a bottle of whiskey in one hand, he raised it to his lips. His Adam's apple bobbled as he drank a goodly portion. Putting the bottle back down, he wiped his lips with the back of his hand. The whiskey seemed to have given him courage, for he said, "I'm not beaten. Not by a long shot. You'll see." It was then that he turned around, startled to see Josie standing there, her nose pressed against the glass.

"Howdy, Tanner!" Despite her anger at him, Josie forced a smile, then tipped her hat.

"I'll be damned!" Bolting up from his chair, Tanner didn't even try to hide his anger. Shaking a fist at her, he turned his back, heading for the swinging doors.

Josie was there to meet him. "Got your little note, Tanner."

"Note?" He feigned innocence.

Reaching into her pants pocket, Josie retrieved the evidence. Unfolding it, she held it up. "Can't say much for your drawing. As to your scribbling, I must admit I wouldn't have expected a man like you to know how to read, much less write."

His countenance was that of a thundercloud. "I don't know what you are talking about."

"You're a liar!"

A tense silence crackled in the air as the two adversaries stared each other down. At last Tanner looked away. "Look, lady, I don't want any kind of trouble. Showlow is a peaceful little town. I try to keep it that way." Suddenly he grinned. "Why don't you stop all this nonsense and . . . and go bake a cake or somethun'."

"Bake a cake?" The very idea was ludicrous. "The only thing I'm interested in cooking, Tanner, is your goose." Her eyes glittered with barely suppressed anger. "Meanwhile I'm staying in Showlow, so you can get any ideas of frightening me away right out of your head."

"You're staying?" His voice was a growl.

"I'm staying." As Tanner stepped through the swinging doors, she boldly blocked his path. "We have a score to settle, you and I. I'm not leaving until it's been done."

"Says you!"

"Says me." She felt the pounding of her blood, the fluttering of her heart as she challenged him with her cold stare. Shaking her head to clear a sudden wave of dizziness, she said boldly, "And just to remind you that I'm here, I intend to follow you around. As closely as your shadow." It was a vow she was determined to keep.

Four

The steadily burning light of the lamp illuminated Rafe's office, which, despite it being daylight, was dark. The drapes had been drawn due to the need for privacy for this particular kind of "treatment."

"Jumpin' Jehoshophat, doc. Hurry!"

"Patience, Hollis. Patience."

Slowly, carefully, Rafe took the wooden box that contained his smaller surgical instruments out of his upper desk drawer. Sorting through the pliers, turnkeys, knives, and scalpels, he touched upon just the right tool.

"All right. I'm ready."

Hollis Holmes stretched across the table, his pants and drawers down around his ankles. From his exposed backside protruded a seemingly endless number of cactus stickers.

"Take them out. It hurts, doc. It hurts."

"I'm certain that it does," Rafe answered, trying to suppress a smile. This wasn't the first time old man Holmes had gotten himself into trouble. "But I want you to tell me how they got there in the first place."

"Well . . . well . . . ya see, it was like this." Hollis winced as one of the stickers was plucked out. "I . . . I was out riding."

"Riding?" The white-haired old man wasn't even supposed to be on a horse. Rafe's orders. Because of his arthritis, poor hearing, and bad eyesight, he was an accident waiting to happen, but pure stubbornness seemed to goad him into proving the doctor wrong. Now he was paying the consequences.

"Chasing down a herd of wild horses, doc. Prettiest animals ya ever did see. I wanted to rope one of them."

"Rope one of them?" Rafe shook his head, finishing the story for Hollis. "And you got so rambunctious that you didn't pay attention to where you were going."

"Yep. Fell right off my horse and into that damned cactus patch." He shuddered. "They're in deep. I couldn't budge them, though I tried. Worse yet, my horse got away. I had to walk all the way back into town." Hollis jumped as Rafe pulled out two more stickers. "Did my feet hurt!"

"I'm sure they did." In fact, it was surprising the old man had the stamina to make it all that way. "Nearly as much as your— "

The door banged open. Pausing with tweezers in hand, Rafe looked up.

"Well, when you're finished with that delicate operation, I have some real problems," Clint Tanner grumbled snidely, sweeping his black hat from his ginger-colored hair and tossing it on the hat rack.

"I'll be through in a moment." Rafe didn't like

being interrupted. Still seeing that his friend was agitated, he asked, "What's wrong?"

Tanner's brown eyes flashed. "She's still here. Following me everywhere, for Christ's sake."

"Josie Smith?" Her pretty face flashed before Rafe's eyes.

"The hellion who tried to kill me, that's who." Clint plopped down in a chair, impatiently drumming his fingers on the chair's arms while Rafe proceeded with his patient.

"Following you, ya say?" Hollis Holmes chuckled. "Don't rightly seem to be a problem, if ya ask me. As I recall, she was mighty pretty. Wish she wanted to follow me."

Tanner wasn't amused. "So do I, you old coot. Then I'd be rid of her."

"Old, am I? Why, you! You ain't gettin' any younger, Tanner."

"Peace, gentlemen." Rafe shook his head, remembering his meeting with Josie Smith in the general store. Certainly she could be stubborn. Pity she was so damned pretty. So much so that he hadn't been able to get her out of his mind. "So the little fool is still making trouble. Too bad. Too bad!" Removing the last cactus thorn, he dipped a piece of white sheet in Cuticura antipain plaster and dabbed it on Holmes's backside. "You can pull up your pants now, Hollis."

Looking in Tanner's direction, Holmes made it very clear that he didn't like being called a coot, then, fastening his trousers, he started for the door. "Thanks, doc," he shouted out. "I've got a plump laying hen I'll give ya to pay my bill."

"No need." Rafe put up his hand. "A few of the eggs will suffice." As Hollis reached for the knob, he added, "In the meantime, stay away from cactus."

Hollis Holmes grinned, rubbing his sore parts. "Don't worry. I will." Opening the door, he couldn't keep from jibbing to Tanner, "And you stay away from that gun-toting female, else she beats ya to the draw next time. From what I could see of that so-called gunfight, ya ain't as fast as ya used to be, Clint ol' boy." With that said, Hollis Holmes was gone.

"Not as fast as I used to be. Ha!" Clint Tanner reached for a bottle marked Hostetter's Stomach Bitters, poured himself a glass, and drank it down.

"Clint!" Rafe admonished his friend for helping himself to the indigestion medicine, for he suspected that it was the fifty-proof wallop it packed and not the healing effect Tanner was after.

Putting down the glass, Tanner shrugged. "Okay. Okay!" There was a slight pause, during which time Tanner amused himself by pulling his pistol out of his holster and putting it back in, a pattern he repeated again and again as if to prove something to himself. "I'm still quick on the draw, see," he exclaimed with bravado. The expression in his eyes, however, clearly told that he was worried.

"You're still faster than me," Rafe placated him, then asked, "now, tell me what brings you here?"

Tanner picked up the glass again. "I need your help in getting that . . . that trouble-causing female out of my hair and out of town." He stared at Rafe, his fingers so tight around the glass that it seemed he might break it. "Looks as if she's settling in for a long stay, and I don't like that one damned bit."

"No, I suppose not." Rafe sat down in the chair next to Tanner, coming right to the point. "What is it you want me to do?"

Tanner expelled a harsh breath, retreating behind a mask of pure anger. "I don't care. Just get her the hell out of Showlow, out of Arizona Territory, for that matter, and quick." That said, Tanner made his exit.

Laying his head back on his hands and looking up toward the ceiling, Rafe thought about the matter for a long, long while. No matter how attracted he was to that girl or how protective he felt, he had to defend his longtime friend despite his arrogance and quick temper. He and Tanner understood each other, and why not, they had grown up together in Kentucky.

Rafe chuckled softly to himself as he recalled some of the early days when they had gone swimming at the swimming hole together. As boys, they used to do nearly everything together— hunting, fishing, and even wooing the girls. And the pranks they used to play . . .

He could hardly control his laughter when he thought of the time the two of them had stuffed the chimney of Leona and Ivy Collins's playhouse full of rags to smoke them out just so they could kiss the girls. How were they to know that Leona and Ivy would get so angry at them that they wouldn't speak to them for weeks?

Leaning forward and tapping the glass Tanner

had used, he thought of the bucket of water the two girls had rigged over the stable door to get even for the smoke-out. Clint had looked so silly standing there with that bucket over his head and the water pouring down over his Sunday-best suit. Talk about trouble. He had gotten into plenty of it over that. But Rafe had to pat himself on the back. He had been the one to straighten the matter out with the girls and with Clint's mother. Although Clint had taken the credit for patching things up with the Collins sisters, Rafe knew it was because Ivy had simply adored him. He had had a way with women even way back then.

"A way with women, sure . . ." Certainly his charm hadn't worked on Josie Smith, quite to the contrary, it seemed. Perhaps he'd have to try another way.

Rafe let his thoughts wander, touching again on the past, wondering what might have happened if there hadn't been that war. Certainly it had changed all of their lives. Everything had been so good for them before the War Between the States had brought devastation and heartache to both the Gardner and Tanner families.

"That damned war!" If only.

Kentucky at first hadn't been concerned with the way the fighting was going. The state had tried to remain neutral. Rafe and Clint had sighed with relief, thinking they had escaped becoming soldiers. Eventually, however, they were drawn into the conflict when their friends and companions had joined, some with the army of the North, some with the army of the South. Families had been divided in their loyalties. Families like his.

He and Clint had tried to stay together in the same outfit and had until Rafe was taken into the hospital unit. There he had learned about illness, suffering, and the need for a comforting hand. He had become familiar with healing potions and herbs used to relieve a variety of ailments from toothache to ague, medicines that would be beneficial to him when he became a doctor.

"Someone who comes face-to-face with life and with death," and with the wounded. Wounded that had all too soon included his impetuous friend. But that was another time, another place. Rafe quickly pushed it far from his thoughts, concentrating on other matters. Like Josie Smith. "The stubborn— "

Alas, call her what he might, she was doing exactly what she had intended— making Clint Tanner a nervous wreck. But not for long. As Rafe stood up and walked to the front window, opening the drapes, he knew exactly what he was going to do.

From the shadows Josie, feeling somehow betrayed, watched Clint Tanner leave the doctor's office. Had she wanted Rafe Gardner to be on her side? Perhaps. Or at least to be neutral in the matter. Instead, it was quite apparent where his loyalties rested despite his pretense of being concerned for her welfare.

"So, just like always, I'm on my own." In a town where everyone she met either greeted her with a hostile stare or looked right through her, pretending she was invisible.

Cursing beneath her breath, Josie clutched her arm, unable to ignore a sudden stab of pain. Leaning against the building, she closed her eyes, willing herself not to feel it. She had hoped that the doctor would be able to give her something to ease her discomfort, but after seeing Tanner pushing through the door, smiling like the cat that ate the canary, she was damned if she would reveal her vulnerability. She had to be strong if she was going to survive. There was no one she could count on here. That much was quite evident.

"I don't care! I don't need anyone's help. Most of all his," she exclaimed, looking toward the doctor's office. Still, she had to admit that she needed to rest. Her knees were a little weak, and she felt more than a bit light-headed from loss of blood. It was hot. She needed to rest before returning to her hotel. Spying an old rain barrel, she tipped it over, sat down, and closed her eyes.

"Bet you can't find me, Josie. . . ."

From days long past, her brother's voice seemed to come from out of nowhere, reminding her of happy times. They had played hide-and-seek, retreating behind barrels like this one. Barrels that were just large enough to hide a five-year-old boy.

"Bet I can." Putting her hands over her eyes she had slowly counted to ten, knowing very well where his favorite hiding place would be. One of the barrels. Nevertheless, she had always taken a long time to find him.

"Oh, Charlie . . ." The memory deeply touched

her. Despite her resolve to be strong, Josie buried her face in her hands and cried.

It was a long time before she returned to the hotel. Climbing the stairs slowly, she seemed to take forever to reach her room. Her eyelids felt heavy as she poured water into the basin and washed her face and hands. Picking up a hairbrush, she unbraided her hair, staring into the mirror as she stroked it through the thick blond waves with crackling strokes.

"All a gun brings is death!" she seemed to hear Doctor Rafe Gardner say. "You can't win." Can't win! Can't win! Can't win! His words echoed in her ears.

"No!" He was wrong. Somehow justice had to win out in the end. Or would it?

She didn't know. At the moment all she could think about was that she was so tired. So deathly tired. Without bothering to undress or take off her boots, Josie flung herself across the bed in her room, sighing with exhaustion. She had to leave, had to find a much cheaper place. And yet, for at least the moment all she wanted to do was to sleep and to forget.

Five

The boardinghouse sign with a laughing donkey holding up a knife and fork read IF YOU CAN'T WASH DISHES, DON'T EAT. IF YOU ARE HUNGRY, GRAB A PLATE. YOU HAVE MY BEST WISHES. BUT JEST BEFORE YOU PUT ON YOUR HAT, BE SHORE TO WASH YOUR DISHES. Josie looked at the name of the proprietor: S. R. Howard. Hopefully the man would find her a room that was not too expensive. With that thought in mind, she knocked at the door.

The door was answered, not by a man, as Josie expected, but by a plump, dimpled, dark-haired woman with an engaging smile. "If you're looking for a room, we're full up." She started to close the door in Josie's face, but Josie was too quick for her, using her carpetbag to keep the door from closing.

Damn, Josie thought. Another of those judgmental types who had heard gossip about her. Either that, or another friend of Tanner's. "Full up, or just particular about who you let in?" she asked, adding, "No matter what you might have heard, I'm not dangerous."

"Hmmm." Eyeing her up and down, the woman assessed her.

"Please. I need a room." Josie glanced at a poster attached to the wall and discovered that the rooms were usually rented a week at a time. Therefore, she was prepared to answer, "For at least two weeks."

"Two weeks." The woman thought a moment.

"In which time I promise not to initiate a gunfight. At least on the premises," she added. It was a promise Josie intended to keep. Taking off her tan Stetson, she tucked it under her arm.

"There . . . there is a small room, not much bigger than a linen closet." The woman laughed. "Come to think of it, it *was* a linen closet. It might be stuffy."

"How much?"

"Two dollars a week, lunch and dinner included."

Josie didn't hesitate. "I'll take it." She picked up the carpetbag that held just a few clothes and all her money.

"Come in."

Inside, the boardinghouse smelled of strong soap, beeswax, and cooking. Even at that, Josie thought to herself that she would be comfortable there. And at a reasonable price.

"The room is up the stairs on the second floor."

"Thank you."

The woman pulled a pad and pen from her apron pocket. "Your name."

"Josie. Josie, uh . . . Smith." She reached into the carpetbag for the money due.

"Josie Smith." The woman wrote it down. "Most of the people staying here don't eat breakfast, but

if you want to, that will be fifty cents a week extra."
She waited, then said, "Toast, bacon, and eggs."

"Fifty cents more, then." After paying, Josie
started up the carpeted stairway. She would get
settled in, then go about taking care of the things
she had come to Showlow to settle. The first item
of the day would be finding a teacher who could
help her improve her draw.

"The number is twenty-one."

Josie laughed. "Sounds lucky." She hoped it
would be. When she opened the door she was
pleasantly surprised. Small but cozy, the room had
a bed, table, small dresser upon which was a wash
basin and pitcher, and a chair. Moving toward the
dresser, Josie intended to stash her money in the
second drawer, then changed her mind. The best
place would be under the mattress.

Closing and locking the door, Josie opened her
carpetbag and took out her underwear, socks, one
dress, shoes, an extra pair of pants, and the new
shirt she had recently purchased. A green one.
The shirt was put in the drawer, the dress hung
on the window frame, and the shoes placed on the
floor next to the bed.

Pulling out her money pouch, she walked to the
bed, lifted the bedspread, then peered at the mattress. There were two thin ones piled one on top
of the other. No one would even guess if she was
to slip her money pouch in between.

"Right here." Feeling pleased with herself, and
more secure, she walked to the door and made her
way to the street to go in search of a man to teach
her the skills necessary to beat Tanner.

The boardwalk was crowded with townspeople going to their jobs. Josie spotted a man whose apron and blackened clothing identified him as a blacksmith. She stopped him and inquired as to the whereabouts of the local gunsmith It seemed logical that the gunsmith would know who in town was quick on the draw.

"You want to know about the gunsmith?" For just a moment the blacksmith looked as if he feared trouble, then he shrugged. "He's down the road a spell. Past the drugstore and doctor's office."

"Thank you." Tipping her hat, Josie proceeded on, past the billiard hall, the saloon, the meat market, the general store, Bennett and Jones Land Attorneys, and the drugstore. "Dr. Rafe Gardner's domain," she murmured beneath her breath.

In addition to being the town's doctor, Rafe also owned the drugstore, filling prescriptions and selling soap when he was not taking care of the sick and infirm or repairing gunshot wounds. Though at first she was tempted to cross the street lest she see him, Josie's curiosity got the best of her. Was he there?

Taking a cautious step, she peeked in the window. All kinds of items were on his shelves. There was a stone mortar and pestle, a cork press, a balance scale, and patent medicines, which if the label could be believed, could handle any complaint. An amber-colored bottle in the shape of a fish contained cod liver oil. What was not visible was the doctor.

Which is just as well, Josie told herself. She didn't

need any more of his advice. Even so, she turned her head several times to look behind her as she walked on to the gunsmith's. A sign in the shape of a rifle made it difficult to miss. Colts, Winchesters, Remingtons, and Derringers, it said, as well as specially made guns.

"Can I be of help?" A thin, gray-haired man with spectacles eyed her from behind the counter.

Josie peered in the glass case at a Colt double-action .38 revolver. The pulling of the trigger automatically cocked the hammer, therefore eliminating the need to cock with the thumb between shots.

"This one looks interesting." Another caught her eye, a Buntline Special. It was a long-barreled variant of the two most popular pistols, the .44 and .45 Colt single-action revolvers. It had a detachable metal stock that enabled it to fire like a rifle.

"You interested in buying, or just browsing?" His tone was gruff.

"Browsing." Josie came right to the point. "Who around here would you say is skilled at shooting these guns of yours?"

Folding his arms, he shook his head. "I wouldn't know."

"Wouldn't know or just won't say?" Josie's face flushed, for she knew what he was doing.

"Let's just say that I'd feel mighty guilty siding with someone aiming to shoot my friend Tanner."

"I should have known!" Angrily Josie stalked out. Damn the whole town. And damn Tanner! Wasn't there anyone here who knew what he really was, a cold-blooded murderer!

Josie's booted heels clicked on the boardwalk as she ran back to the boardinghouse. She took the stairs two at a time, fumbling for the key that she kept in her pocket.

It was strange, but as soon as she opened the door she had an eerie feeling that something was wrong. She sensed it in every nerve and sinew of her body. It was a feeling that was quickly proven to be justified as her eyes scanned her room. It had been ransacked, as if a tornado had struck. Her few items of clothing were strewn about. The drawers of the little dresser beneath the washbasin pulled out and emptied of their contents. But it was the sight of the bedclothes dumped in a heap on the floor that caused Josie the greatest alarm. Her money! Frantically she ran to the bed, thrusting her hands inside the mattress. The money was not there.

She panicked. Who would have done such a thing? Who could have so cold-heartedly ruined her? Tanner, of course. Who else would have cause to search her room? Tanner had stolen her money pouch in retaliation. Mumbling every swear word her brother had ever taught her, she straightened up the room, then slipped from the boardinghouse to the stables.

Six

The town was buzzing with activity. Spotting the only place that seemed to be left to hitch her horse, Josie threw the reins over the post and securely tied them. Damn! What was she going to do? Go to Tanner and confront him? Call him out for the thief that he was?

Her mind was a muddle, her emotions in turmoil as she started toward the boardwalk. For the first time in her life she was at a loss. What was she going to do? For just a moment all she could do was stand and stare, but then the chestnut mare next to her horse began to whinny, snort, and paw the ground. Knowing horses could be trouble, Josie stepped back.

"Sorry, ma'am." A young man with curly brown hair beneath a large tan hat approached in quick strides. His smiling face was a pleasant change from all the scowls she had been receiving lately. "Sometimes my horse ain't too friendly." He patted the horse's mane to calm her, then held out his hand. "My name is Parish. Parish Harper. My mom owns the laundry over yonder." He nodded with his head.

She really wasn't thinking much about what he

had just said. Her mind was elsewhere. "Oh." Josie shook his hand and thanked him for calming the horse. Where can I find work? she wondered. If she were a man, there would be dozens of jobs she might do. But only a few types of jobs were available to a woman. Among them were cook, schoolteacher, or, she grimaced in disgust, prostitute.

"I recognized you right away," he said with a smile. "I saw the shoot-out day before yesterday. Everyone was sure surprised to find out you were a woman."

Josie didn't say anything, she just looked down at her boots for a short time. She didn't much care what he thought about her being a woman. She was trying to sort things out in her mind. She needed money. She simply had to get a job. That was all there was to it. Surely someone in this town would hire her. Luckily she had already paid for her room and board, but she would need other necessities. Just what was she going to do? She didn't have the qualifications to be a schoolmarm. Hell, she could read, all right, but she wasn't any good at her sums. And the kitchen? Hell, she was all thumbs.

"Ma'am?"

And the other option? Josie stubbornly shook her head. She would never, never work in a whorehouse. Even if she had to starve. What then?

"Ma'am, are you all right?"

Josie lifted her head to look into the young man's smiling face. Damn, he had been talking to her, yet she hadn't heard a thing he'd said, except that his name was Parish, that his mother owned a laundry, and that he had seen her greatest humiliation.

"Well, never mind." Thinking that she was embarrassed about the gunfight, he quickly changed the subject. "How's your arm?" he asked with a tone of real concern.

"My . . . my arm?" She winced as she touched it. "It's a little stiff, but it's getting better. And I can manage all right."

As they talked, Josie noticed that the laundry seemed to be the most popular business in town. A steady stream of people kept coming in and out of the door.

"So, your mother owns that laundry?"

"Yep!" It was obvious that he was very proud of her.

Well, if it was good enough for his mother, maybe it would be good enough for her. Besides, it seemed to be easy work. "Think your mother could use some help at that laundry?"

"Well, maybe . . ." He thought a moment, then with an attitude that said he was eager to please said, "Tell me your name. I might take you over and introduce you to her."

"I'm just Josephine." She figured that would make a better impression on his mother.

"Glad to meet you 'just Josephine.' " He tipped his hat, blushing a little as she smiled. "I really think Mom could use some help. Since Ted went out to run the ranch, she has been a little short-handed."

"Ted?"

"Ted is the oldest, Ed is next, and I'm the youngest." His brow furrowed. "My pa deserted us after I was born."

"Ohhh." She sympathized with him, having lost someone herself. "I'm sorry to hear that, Parish." Josie looked down at her boots, the talk of brothers reminding her of her own. Would she always feel this deep sadness, this physical ache in her heart? Probably. How could she ever forget?

As usual, her thoughts of her brother also brought on thoughts of Tanner and the anger.

"I didn't come all the way down to Arizona for nothing," she said between clenched teeth.

"Oh?" He sounded disappointed. "A fiancé?"

Josie's laugh was hollow. "Hardly."

"What, then?" He acted as if he really didn't know.

"Business. Personal business," she answered, thinking to herself how naive and sweet he seemed to be. And helpful. Maybe. "But I don't have much money, and now it appears I'll have to stay longer than I planned. And . . . and—"

"And you're broke." Parish patted her on the shoulder. "Well, perhaps that won't be for long." Taking her by the arm, he led her across the street, chattering amiably to her all the while. By the time they came to the laundry, Josie knew she had made a friend.

"I appreciate your kindness more than you know," she said.

"Awww?" He flushed, then turned his head. Opening the laundry room door, he called out, "Mom. Mom?"

Peeking in, Josie noticed the large-boned woman with perspiration on her brow. So, this was "Mom." Well, she appeared to be just as amiable as her son.

"Mom."

The woman did not hear them enter, and kept right on scrubbing.

Meanwhile Jose was assessing the situation, thinking to herself, from here I could learn a lot about this town and the people in it. Maybe even find a way to work my way into their presence. She had to soften the townspeople's hostility if she was going to stay.

"Mom . . . Mom, I have someone here I'd like you to meet," Parish was insistent. "She needs a job."

At last the big-boned woman turned around, smiling. "I heard you, dear. She needs a job." Her critical eye looked Josie up and down, then she said, "Parish, introduce me."

"Oh." He flushed again. "Mom, this is just Josephine."

She looked at Josie quizzically for a moment, then recognition set in. "Aren't you . . . ?"

"Yes!" Josie blurted out. "I am." Here it comes, Josie thought. She won't hire me because of Tanner. She'll make judgments. Won't even give me half a chance.

"How did that fight start?"

"What?" Josie was unprepared for the question since no one had asked before. "You mean why did I go gunning for Tanner?" Josie knew she would have to do a little explaining if she wanted the job.

"Yes." The woman's eyes softened.

"Well, you see, ma'am, my brother Charlie and I were very close," Josie began, thinking that honesty really was the best policy. "Charlie was murdered by that man."

"Oh, no!" Putting down a shirt she was cleaning, the woman came to Josie's side and reached for her hand. "I'm sorry."

For a moment Josie feared she would cry, but she chattered on. "My father tried to get a lawyer back home, but no one wanted to bother with the case. They seemed to be afraid. So Tanner just walked. No one would even track him down."

"I see."

"And I just can't live with that. So . . . so it seemed there was only the Western way of solving problems. I can't let up until Charlie is resting in peace and his killer is out of the way."

"An eye for an eye, is that it?"

Josie could hear a note of scolding in the woman's voice.

"I have to do what I have to do, Mrs. Harper." If she didn't understand, well, so be it.

"Well," Nora Harper sighed. "I suppose I have to try to understand, even if I don't agree. As to the job, I'm willing to give you a chance. Can you start tomorrow morning?"

Josie's smile was sincere. "Yes." All the while she was thinking that perhaps in reality things weren't as bad as they had first appeared.

Seven

Dr. Rafe Gardner sipped the aged bourbon and leaned hack in his leather office chair, wrestling with his conscience. What he had done he had done not only for Clint but in the best interest of a certain feisty little blonde as well. If she stayed in town much longer, she was going to get into some kind of trouble that might well ruin her entire life.

So I took matters into my own hands. Maybe someday he could make Josie understand.

Rafe turned his head at the knocking. Rising from the chair, he set down his glass, opened the door, and greeted the plump, dimpled, dark-haired woman standing there. "Did you get it, Gwen?"

She nodded. "Though I felt guilty using my key to slip into her room. She's a boarder in my boardinghouse. I'm supposed to be trustworthy."

"And you are. Usually." He shut the door, then ushered the woman away from the window, where they wouldn't be seen making their transaction. "And besides, I paid you well." He shrugged wishing he could dispel his feelings of guilt. It wasn't like him to be so underhanded, or to interfere in such matters. Too bad it had been necessary.

"Not as well as I would like." Flirtatiously Gwen batted her lashes at him, a gesture that went unnoticed.

Taking the money pouch from her hands, he hefted it. "Not much here. Only enough to last her a week or two at most." Feeling uneasy holding it, he quickly put it into his safe.

"She didn't look at all as if she were well-to-do. That's why I felt doubly troubled pilfering her money from the room." She clucked her tongue. "Shame on you for putting me up to it, doctor."

Rafe immediately bristled. "I didn't steal this for profit, but for her own good." Without money she would soon get discouraged. He was certain of that. "I didn't want to take the chance of another gunfight."

Gwen's eyes opened wide. "Do you think . . . she would really . . . really shoot him? Clint, I mean." Without being asked, she plopped down in a wooden swivel chair.

"There is a good possibility that she might." Picking up his glass, he stared at the amber-colored drink reflectively. "A good possibility." He was eager to soothe her mind. "Look at what you did as a good deed, Gwen. Suppose she engaged Clint in another fight and this time got killed. Or shot Clint and got herself hung for murder?"

She studied him a moment, then grunted, "I suppose so. But you know, Dr. Rafe, I do sort of like her. She's got spunk. I like that in a woman."

Rafe was thoughtful. "So do I." If only that spirit could be routed in a different direction she might have been a valuable asset to the town. As it was, she was a one-woman vigilante group.

"Hmmm." She pouted. Rising from her chair, she helped herself to the bourbon. "From the tone of your voice it sounds as if you like her more than you'll admit. Are you certain you really want her to leave?"

Rafe tensed in every muscle, bothered by her question, one he had asked himself a hundred times or more. The truth was, there was a part of him that didn't want her to go. The soft-headed part.

She looked at him through her lashes. "Just as I thought."

Expelling a gasp of exasperation, Rafe retreated behind a mask of indifference. "Don't be foolish. Of course I want her to leave. I had you take her money, didn't I?" His fingers tightened around his glass. Hurriedly he changed the subject. "So, how is the boardinghouse business, Gwen?"

She licked her lips, then smiled. "Fairly profitable considering . . ."

"That you have to pay off your late husband's gambling debts," Rafe finished for her. "I'm sorry it's been so hard for you." And sorry that he hadn't been able to save her husband. What the poor man had thought to be indigestion had turned out to be a heart attack. The fatal kind. Rafe hadn't had a chance of saving him. Now Rafe fully suspected the widow was after *him*. Certainly the way she was staring at him seemed to tell him so.

"And lonely." Bending over, she offered him a view of her breasts.

"Of course it would be," he answered tersely. He, however, did not intend to offer comfort or companionship no matter how much she flirted. To put it bluntly, he just wasn't interested in what she had in mind. Friendship was all he had to offer.

"Aren't you ever lonely, Rafe?" It was a pointed question.

"I'm alone, yes. Lonely, no." His life was just too filled up with memories for him to open his heart to any woman just yet. Even so, he smiled. "Don't worry about me."

"I do. I can't help it." She cocked her head, admitting honestly, "It just doesn't seem right for a man like you to remain a perennial bachelor. Every man needs a woman to mother him and care for him and—"

"I'm not the right suitor for you, Gwen. I'm not the man to fill your late husband's bed." He didn't know how he could make it any plainer than that.

She paled. "I see." Squaring her shoulders, she swept past him. "Well, I guess you could say that our business is completed, thus it's time for me to go." She hesitated for just a moment, as if hoping he would tell her to stay. When he did not, she walked to the door. "Good night, Rafe."

Gently her touched her arm, pausing for a moment as if to find the right words. He ended up saying simply, "Good night." He opened the door for her, stepping back suddenly so that he would not collide with the shadow that stood on the other side. "You!"

Josie put her hands on her hips. "Me." She nodded her head in the direction of the woman who owned the boardinghouse, watching for just a moment as she moved gracefully through the doorway. She turned her attention back to the doctor. "I didn't mean to interrupt anything." She raised her eyebrows suggestively.

He grimaced. "You didn't. Gwen was just leaving."

"Oh," she said lightly, her tone belying the slight twinge of jealousy she felt. Oh, but he was a handsome man. Comely enough to make any woman want to make a late-night office call. Just the kind of man it would be easy to fall in love with, that is, if such a thing was on a young woman's mind. "Which it isn't!"

"Isn't what?" Rafe's gaze moved to the safe. Did she suspect? If so, how?

Realizing she had spoken aloud, Josie was huffy. "It isn't going to work. That's what I came to tell you."

So, she had put two and two together. Even so, Rafe played it cool. He leaned against the door, his eyes searching her face. "Precisely what are you talking about?" Mentally he prepared his denials.

"That weasel of a friend of yours stole some money from me. I know it, so does he." Angrily she jabbed her index finger into his ribs. "You can tell him for me that despite what he did, I'm going to stay right here in Showlow."

"Stay?" Silently he swore. So much for his well-laid plans.

"Yes." Turning, she started to leave, but the doctor didn't allow her a hasty retreat. Taking her by the arm, he drew her into his office.

"Sit down." He pushed her none too gently onto the black leather chair he had recently vacated.

Josie was up like a flash. "I prefer to stand, thank you." Her mouth twisted in anger. "But if this is another of your lectures, doctor, I can tell you right now you should save your breath. I'm not leaving this town until justice has been done."

"Justice!"

They stared at each other in cold, stark silence. An angry stare and a defiant one. Then something altered in Rafe's subconscious. Before he knew what came over him, he grabbed her by the shoulders, not to propel her toward the door but to pull her up against him. Without uttering one word he bent his head, his mouth claiming hers.

Startled, Josie nonetheless did not make any effort to pull away. Instead, she found herself pressing up against him, giving herself up completely to the pleasure of his kiss. "Mmm."

The jolt of sweet fire that swept through her veins, the warmth emanating from his muscular body, the tension of the moment, evoked a deep sense of excitement within her. Wrapping her arms around his neck, she stood on tiptoe and kissed him back just as fiercely as he was kissing her. Danger beckoned. Danger and a tantalizing promise of ecstasy that filled her with a pleasurable tingle.

"Damn!" In the end it was Rafe who pulled away, stunned by what he had done.

A smile tugged at the corners of Josie's mouth. "Well, now. I'm certainly of the opinion that was much better than a scolding." She moved toward him. "Care to try that again, doctor?"

"No!" All too quickly he recovered his senses, appalled at his lack of restraint. Despite his resolve, he really was taken by the little hellion. Tonight had proven that.

"No?" she was disappointed.

"You'd better go." His body tensed, his nostrils flared. *And quickly, before I lose my head.* Swallowing, he regained control. Still, his voice was harsh. "Leave, before I give you the spanking that you deserve."

"Spanking?" For just a moment her expression dared him, then with a shrug she turned toward the door. Opening it, she started to leave, then paused. "See you around, doc." With a bounce to her step Josie walked through the doorway and down the wooden steps.

Rafe lay in bed, staring up at the ceiling. Dammit all, why couldn't he sleep? Why couldn't counting sheep lull him into slumber tonight as it always had before when he was troubled? What was wrong?

"Wrong?" Guilt, that's what. The truth was that for whatever noble reason he had told himself he had stolen Josie's money, it bothered him nonetheless.

Because of me she's penniless. Condemned to work in the laundry, of all places. The twittering gossips had quickly spread that news around. Rafe couldn't help but feel that it was a terrible punishment for a young woman of Josie's spirit. Backbreaking, tedious work. Rafe knew he didn't want that for her.

"I have to help her." But how? He certainly couldn't give her the money back. That would be an admission, a confession. Rafe's pride wouldn't allow him to do that.

"Oh, damn her!" A normal woman would have given up, would have done the sensible thing. But not Josie Smith! Oh, no. Stubborn to the end, she had stuck right in there. Oh, but she was so exasperating. So irritating. And yet for all that he had to admit, she was quite a woman. One who couldn't be intimidated, even by a bully like Clint Tanner.

Dammit, though. If only she weren't so headstrong. If only she would pack up her bags and leave town. If only . . .

Leave? Was that what he really wanted? No! Slowly, as his thoughts gained coherency and he sorted out his emotions, he knew that a part of him definitely wanted her to stay. Tonight's kiss had convinced him of that.

Putting his hands behind his head, Rafe reflected on that brief, passionate moment when their lips had touched. How had it happened? How had he suddenly lost his self-control?

He shifted his body slightly, answering the question truthfully. He was as attracted to the pretty, gun-toting miss as a mouse was to cheese. Truth was, ever since he'd first swept her up in his arms and acted as Sir Galahad he had been smitten.

He'd secretly fantasized about holding her, giving vent to the hunger her nearness inspired. And so tonight he had kissed her, little realizing what a soul-stirring experience it would be. An experience he couldn't put out of his thoughts no matter how much he wanted to.

"Oh, no!" Bolting up from the bed, Rafe put his hands to his face. He didn't want to feel this way, not about any woman. Not about her. Women were all trouble. All they wanted in their lives were white picket fences, fences that would quickly put an end to a man's freedom. They were as unpredictable as the weather. Bothersome. Quarrelsome. And Josie Smith? She was much worse. Rafe was determined he wouldn't care about the "hellion," as Tanner called her. She was trouble. She was . . .

Beams of moonlight danced through the window, casting figured shadows on the wall. Two entwined silhouettes conjured up memories of the embrace they had shared. Her mouth had been so soft. Her hair had smelled so fragrant. Her breasts had felt so good against his chest.

A rush of blood spread through Rafe's veins. His throat went dry. Despite his efforts at self-control, an unwanted arousal spread through his body, desire that could be quenched only once he had risen from the bed and splashed his face and arms with cold water.

"Tanner's right," he said to himself, staring out the window. "She is dangerous." The kind of dangerous that went way beyond her just carrying a gun. If he allowed Josie Smith into his heart, into his life for even a moment, Rafe knew she would completely upend him.

Eight

The laundry room was hot and steamy, not at all the kind of place Josie would have wanted to work in had her circumstances been different, she thought as she paused in her washing to look around the huge, bleak room. There were no windows, no chairs or stools on which to sit, no pictures on the wall, nothing at all of interest to look at. Around here each woman earned her wage. There was always something to do.

Along one wall were drying racks and ironing boards; along the adjoining wall were stoves with flatirons heating on top and big oval copper boilers filled with steaming water bubbling on the burners. On a shelf near the boilers were the copper kettles used to fill the washtubs from the boilers. A stack of firewood in the corner by the stove looked as if it might topple at any moment.

In the middle of the room were the washtubs. A huge rectangular tub that resembled a horse trough was used for washing bedding and blankets. Each laundress had two tubs in front of her on a wooden stand, one of soapy wash water, the other of rinse water. Her other tools were a washboard, a hand wringer between the two tubs, a wooden

table with a large laundry basket on top, and a
plunger used to agitate garments up and down in
the water. Beneath each washtub was a floor drain
where the dirty water was poured to flow underneath the building and empty into the alleyway.

Adjacent to the washroom was a small entryway
with a desk, a pair of scales where overlarge garments and bedding were weighed, as the customer
was charged so much per pound. A sign that listed
the prices of single items was posted next to the
scales. A shirt was ten cents, a pair of socks a
penny, a pair of trousers fifteen cents, a dress
twenty cents, petticoats and drawers ten cents each
depending on the size. Customers could either
take these items home and iron them themselves
or pay a nickel to have that done at the laundry.

The smell of lye soap permeated the air, so
strong that it made Josie cough. Her hands were
red and itchy from contact with the strong laundry
soap, her knuckles blistered from rubbing the
clothing on the washboard. Worse yet, the constant
up-and-down motion of her scrubbing irritated her
wounded arm. As she stood over the washtub, her
back ached and her temperament was anything but
cheerful. If she had thought that working in the
laundry would be an easy job, she had been dead
wrong! It was horrible. Still, she was determined
not to utter a word of complaint even if it killed
her.

"This is almost as bad as being in purgatory,
don't you think, dearie?"

"Purgatory?" Turning her head, Josie looked
down the row of washtubs to see which one of the

five other laundrywomen had spoken and decided it was the tall, lithe blonde the second from the left. "I suppose you could say that it is," she answered.

"Oh, well." The young woman wiped her soapy hand across her sweat-beaded brow. "At least Mrs. Harper pays a decent wage."

"And she is an honest woman," piped in another of the laundresses, "who works just as hard as we do."

It was true. Josie had found that Nora Harper was not the kind of woman who let others do the work for her. Taking the afternoon shift, she did more than her share. What's more, she had been very good to Josie, giving her an advance on her weekly wage.

Well, I will not disappoint her. Nora Harper and her son Parish were the only friends Josie had in Showlow, the only ones who had been at all kind or friendly. Everyone else seemed to view her as an intruder in town and seemed only too eager to offer her a one-way train ticket out of Showlow. Well, as Josie had informed the doctor over and over again, she just wasn't leaving.

So there, Dr. Rafe Gardner, she thought defiantly, taking out her anger for him on the unfortunate shift she held in her hand. That is, until she heard a high-pitched voice giving her advice.

"Take it easy, dearie. You're scrubbing that collar so roughly, you'll either make holes in it or wear out the washboard."

Looking down at the shirt, Josie could see that the warning came just in time. "Thanks, Sarah," she said with an embarrassed grin. "I . . . I was just pretending that the shirt was someone I know."

"A man, no doubt." Sarah giggled.

"Yes, a man." Careful not to pinch her fingers, Josie put the shirt in the wringer and cranked the wooden handle. It came out the other side as flat as a pancake.

"Was he handsome, this man of yours?" Sarah was inquisitive.

"Handsome, yes." The doctor's smiling face flashed before her eyes. "But he's not mine. To tell the truth, I hardly even know him." Josie sighed, remembering their kiss despite her efforts to the contrary. That kiss had been pleasant, there was no use denying it. Just the thought made her body come alive with a sexual tension that increased the longer the doctor was on her mind.

For God's sake, I'm lusting over him. She had to recognize that deep, yearnful stirring for what it was. Not love certainly, but some fool-headed passion that was aroused by a man she had no business dallying with. Clint Tanner's friend and thereby an enemy, she determined as she marched briskly over to the drying rack. Well, she would force herself to put him out of her mind.

That was a vow Josie nearly kept as she washed, dried, and ironed the stack of clothes that had been assigned to her. Indeed, she might have pushed the doctor from her thoughts eventually had she not heard his voice coming from the entryway.

"I've got three shirts, two pairs of pants, five

pairs of socks, an undershirt, longjohns, and two pairs of undershorts," he was saying. "I'd just as soon pay in advance."

"Then that will be a dollar and five cents," Nora Harper answered, no doubt calculating the amount on the abacus she kept on the desk. "Just give your garments to one of the girls."

One of the girls turned out to be Josie. "Well, well, well."

Thoroughly disgruntled, Josie took his clothing, stuffing them into her laundry basket. "Well, well, yourself." With a toss of her head she flung her long hair over her shoulder.

"So, you got a job here." His tone was sympathetic.

"Yes, here." She could have stood his anger, but his compassion peeved her. "Hard but honest work."

"Ohh, Josie." He looked down at her hands, red and covered by a rash, then at the perspiration dotting her brow. The desperation of her circumstances hit him full force. She had been reduced to this and all because of his high-handed scheme. So much for clever plans. "Josie I— "

"Don't. Don't you dare feel sorry for me!" she snapped. That would be an indignity she just couldn't bear.

"I don't." Oh, but he did. Despite her cockiness at times, he hated to see her humbled.

Josie hefted the clothes basket on her hip. "Are you in a hurry for these?" she asked, nodding to the stack of garments she already had in her tub.

"Tomorrow would be fine." He thought of a way

to rectify the situation. "Josie." He put his hand on her arm. "I didn't mean to offend you."

She glared at him. "No offense taken."

"Good." Reaching into his pocket, he withdrew an amount of money comparable to what he had "borrowed" from her, then thrust it into her hand.

She stared down at it. "You're supposed to pay Nora at the desk, not me," she exclaimed, pushing it back at him.

"That's for you." His gaze softened. "Think of it as a loan, Josie."

"A loan be damned. It's charity." She threw the money at his feet. "I wouldn't take money from you if I had to sleep out in the street." Oh, but he had some nerve! Some nerve indeed.

Bending down, Rafe picked it up, offering it once again. "I'm going to tell you one more time. Take the stagecoach. Go home, Josie, before something terrible happens." That said, he stuck the money in her basket, then stalked out.

"Go home, go home, go home," she mocked. Well, she would show him. Changing her work plans, Josie gave her full attention to doing the doctor's laundry, grinning impishly as she deliberately put starch in his undergarments.

"So, tell me, dearie. It wouldn't be the doctor you were thinking about earlier, would it?" Sarah's voice held a tone of laughter.

"It would." There was no use in denying it.

Touching her index finger to her tongue, then to the flatiron, Sarah tested the heat. "Something tells me it's an interesting story." She winked, then started ironing a shirt. "Need an ear? If so, me and the other girls are very good listeners."

At the moment "listeners" seemed to be just what Josie needed. That was why as she and the others worked she told of her confrontations with the doctor and of his lectures on the evils of gun-fighting.

"As if he has a right to practice," Sarah was indignant.

"Yeah," piped in another of the young women. "Seeing as how he ain't without sin himself on that score."

"Without sin?" Now it was Josie who was curious. Was it possible that the doctor wasn't as perfect as he pretended to be? "Just what do you mean by that statement, Emily?"

Sarah and Emily answered simultaneously. To Josie's stunned surprise, she learned that the doctor had quite a past, a past that included gun-fighting. Before taking up medicine, Rafe Gardner had stalked down the boardwalks many times, his hands poised at his guns. In fact, according to the women in the laundry, he had once had quite a reputation for being unbeatable. So much for Dr. Rafe Gardner's advice that "gunfighting was a nasty business."

Nine

The discordant notes of a honkytonk piano drew Rafe toward the only place a man could find peace and camaraderie, the saloon. The Mule's Ear, by name. A cool place where he could relax and forget all about a certain female with wheat-colored hair who refused to use good sense.

"Judas priest!" Pushing through the brown swinging doors, he determined to keep his nose where it belonged from now on. What happened from here on in was Josie Smith's business.

"Afternoon, doc." The cheery voice of the bartender greeted him through the foglike smoke that filled the large room.

"Afternoon."

The clatter of bottles mingled with the hum of voices. The saloon was crowded. Some men stood at the bar, others sat at the small round tables scattered through the room, playing poker or keno. Others played at billiards. All were drinking.

Taking off his tan Stetson, Rafe hung it on the rack, then walked over to the long mahogany bar that ran along the west wall. It was pitted and scarred by smoldering cigarette butts, matches, and fingernails, and stained here and there by spilled whiskey and beer, so it well suited the rest of the surroundings, which were not at all what anyone would call elegant. Comfortable was a more apt description.

The Mule's Ear was a plain saloon without artifacts or chandeliers. Here a man could relax when he wanted male companionship. On two walls was a collection of hunting trophies— deer and elk antlers, mounted snakeskins, and the stuffed head of a mountain lion. On the other wall were colored beer and whiskey advertisements that lent a festive touch to the drab walls. Behind the bar was a huge mirror, not just ornamental but a means of protecting customers from being shot in the back. Beneath the mirror were shelves of spirits, alcoholic beverages in bottles of various shapes, hues, and sizes.

"Give me a beer." Rafe rested one foot on the copper footrail and leaned against the bar.

"A beer it is." The bartender filled a large mug and pushed it toward Rafe, then handed him a twelve-and-a-half cent token as change. "Use it for a free lunch. It's sliced roast beef on Swedish hardtack bread today. With plenty of mustard."

"You know my habits well, Charlie," Rafe said as he handed him some money. Two beers were twenty-five cents, but he never drank more than one. His limit nowadays. The same could not be said for Clint, who waved at Rafe from the corner table.

"Howdy, Rafe ol' buddy."

It was useless to ignore him, thus Rafe waved back. "Afternoon, Clint."

"He's drunk as a skunk again, but so far not too obnoxious," confided the bartender, casting Tanner a wary glance. No doubt he was remembering the time that Clint had ridden a horse into the barroom, not an unusual escapade. It had been done before. What hadn't been done, however, was expecting the horse to be served. Demanding that the horse be given a beer, Tanner had collapsed in a tide of drunken giggles, setting the whole saloon into fits of laughter.

"At least for the time being." Rafe shook his head, wondering how many times during their friendship he had looked after Clint. Twenty or thirty, no doubt. Clint had a habit of getting into trouble.

"Rafe. Rafe, come over and join us." Not liking to be ignored, Clint waved his arms.

"Oh, all right." Rafe was in a less-than-cordial mood. Still, picking up his mug, he ambled over, hoping the subject of Josie wouldn't come up today. He just wasn't in the mood to talk about her.

But the subject did come up. Suffering under the jibes of an old man with whiskers who was sitting next to him, Clint was less than jovial. "Listen here, Zeke, if you think I'm going to let you make me the butt of your humor, you have another thought coming," he was saying, slurring his words. "That silly girl in men's clothes picked a fight, and I gave her one. That's the end of it."

"No, it ain't." Zeke banged the table with his fist and guffawed. "She's still in town and spoiling for a fight, so they say."

"Then I'll give her one. Woman or not, I'll shoot

her down the next time we meet." With a snort he whipped out his pistol, then took a gulp of his whiskey. "And shoot to kill."

"Shoot to kill?" Rafe could only hope that Clint was just talking. Still, he felt as if a cold, icy tide swept over him. "You can't mean it." He cast an anxious glance at his friend's expression.

Clint seemed determined. Or was it just that he was eager to impress the men sitting at his table. "I do. The little bitch is asking for it," he announced coldly.

"Damn!" Rafe slammed down his mug so hard that the table swayed. His lips tightened angrily. "I've got two hotheads on my hands."

"A hothead? Me?" Clint bolted to his feet, of a mind to pick a fight.

Rafe faced him down. "When you act like this, that's exactly what you are, Clint."

Brushing his fingers up and down his holster, Clint said threateningly, "I won't take that, even from you, Gardner!"

Rafe didn't flinch. "Oh, don't be a fool, Clint!" In disgust he turned his back, starting back toward the bar.

"Rafe!" The sound of a revolver being cocked warned of danger.

Stopping in his tracks, Rafe stood stock-still. "My job now is preserving and saving lives, Clint, not proving myself to be a man by harming someone else." He took three steps. "Put it down. Unless you're willing to shoot me in the back."

"Aw, Rafe."

Slowly Rafe turned around. "Put the gun away," he ordered.

Hanging his head and looking down at the ground Tanner returned his Smith & Wesson to his holster. "You know I wouldn't really shoot you."

In actuality Rafe hadn't been certain this time. Drink did things to a man. He ought to know. "I'm glad of that. It would be a hell of a way to end a friendship."

"It would. I agree." Grinning like a naughty child, Clint held out his hand. "Friends? Through thick and thin."

"Friends." Instead of shaking Clint's hand, however, Rafe quickly disarmed him, then grabbed him by the shirt. "Which is why I'm going to do this."

Before Clint had time to react, Rafe dragged him through the double doors and out to the street. Purposefully he pushed Tanner in the horse trough.

"There. That will cool you off." Actually he'd been waiting for a long time to do that, and despite the seriousness of the moment found himself laughing as the thought of doing the very same thing to Josie Smith crossed his mind.

Something had to be done to make the silly little fool see reason. She was making it hard for herself. Why couldn't she realize that? Why didn't she just give up her thirst for vengeance? She was a pretty girl with so many years of happiness ahead of her if only she would stop being so hell-bent on making trouble for Clint Tanner.

"Damn!"

Suddenly Rafe paused in his mental tirade. Just why was he making it his business anyway? Clint could take care of himself, and from the looks of it, so could Josie.

"Back off, Gardner. Let the woman live her own life." It wasn't his duty to be her protector. In fact, the more involved with her he was, the more complicated his own life was becoming. Oh, yes, she had certainly turned his whole life upside down from the moment she had looked up at him with those wide green eyes.

Rafe was in fact totally confused about his feelings. There were times when he was so angry at her he wanted to take her over his knee, and then again, there were times when he wanted nothing more than to just hold her, take care of her, and never let her go. He wanted to touch her, look into those fiery eyes, and kiss her mouth, her neck and—

"Blast it all!" Even now he found himself headed toward the laundry, knowing full well that it was quitting time. Why? To watch over her? To set himself up for another confrontation? Whatever the reason, he cursed himself for a fool and quickly acted nonchalant when he saw her appear in the doorway.

She looks so tired. Even from a distance he could see the way her shoulders were stooped, the way she hung her head. A feeling of tenderness swept over him— until he noted that she was not alone.

Who the devil? Rafe was quick to note that the young man, whoever he was, had put his hand on

Josie's shoulder. He moved closer, hearing the faint murmur of their voices. The cheerfulness. The laughter. There was a familiarity about their conversation, a camaraderie that she did not share with him. Against his will Rafe felt an unwelcome surge of jealousy until the visitor turned around and he caught sight of his face.

"Parish Harper." A young puppy if ever there was one, and Mrs. Harper's youngest son. Rafe satisfied himself that whatever the reason for the visit it had to be business. Even so, it was disconcerting when he realized that his presence had been discovered and that Josie was openly staring at him. Trying to act indifferent about the whole matter, he called out, "I came to get my laundry. Is it done?"

He could see her stiffen. "I thought you were going to come back for your things tomorrow."

"Ah, yes, tomorrow." Reaching up, he tugged at his hat, pulling it down lower on his forehead. For just a moment he was tempted to warn her about Tanner's outburst, to tell her about the episode at the saloon, but in the end he changed his mind, adhering to the advice he had given himself. Let Josie Smith take care of herself. What happened just wasn't any of his business.

Ten

It was the first time in her life that Josie had ever overslept. It was seven o'clock, and she had just enough time to dress in a shirt, trousers, and boots, comb her hair, brush her teeth, and get to the Harper laundry before sunup. That being if she ran all the way.

"Damn!" The only thing she could use as an excuse was that she had tossed and turned for several hours the night before just imagining the doctor toting a gun. That, coupled with the exhaustion of working in the laundry, was the cause of the morning's tardiness.

A gunfighter, imagine that! As she buckled her belt and slipped on her laundry apron, Josie saw the image of Dr. Rafe Gardner flash once again before her eyes. Arrogant. Proud. Strong. And surprised, when he went to put on his starched underwear. Those drawers of his could practically stand up on their own. She laughed at the thought, hoping that he would be a good sport about it or too embarrassed to report the incident to Mrs. Harper. Josie couldn't afford to lose her job.

"Well, what is done is done." Leaving her room, taking the stairs two at a time, Josie made her way to the laundry as fast as she could. Pushing through the laundry room door, she was surprised to see that the doctor was there ahead of her, pacing up and down.

Damnation! His impatience irritated her, though she refused to show it. Instead, she said lightly, "Here to get your longjohns, doc?"

"Those and my other garments," he answered, finding himself captivated by the way she smiled. Strange, how she could look so cherublike with those dimples of hers. "Are they done? If not, I can come back."

"They're done." Leading him to the front desk, Josie retrieved the bundle from the shelf and handed him the items.

"Thanks." Rafe tipped his hat, lingering in hope of conversation. He just didn't want to leave somehow.

"My pleasure." Putting her hands behind her back, Josie couldn't help but wonder how long it would take before the good doctor found out about the starch she'd used so mischievously.

"Oh?" Her pleasure. My, but she seemed congenial today, Rafe thought, liking the change in her. "You aren't still angry about the advice I gave you yesterday," he said. "I'm glad. I was only seeing to your best interests."

"Of course." She thought about the best way to approach the matter of the doctor's past and decided to be direct. "And, after all, you of all people should know the dangers of gunfighting. Firsthand, I might say."

Rafe eyed her quizzically, wondering just what

she meant. "My being a doctor and patching up bullet holes, you mean?"

There was a moment of silence, then Josie blurted it out. "No. Your being a gunfighter." There, it was out.

Taken aback by her bluntness, Rafe was silent for a long-drawn-out moment as all kinds of thoughts flitted through his mind. Thoughts and memories he had tried hard to forget. He wondered how she had found out.

She read his expression. "The truth travels quickly in a small town," she answered.

"The truth?" He was troubled by her discovery, wondering just how much she knew. The whole story or just bits and pieces.

"That you were one of the fastest guns around. Even faster than Clint Tanner." Taking a step closer, she came right to the point. "I want you to teach me." Without thinking, she clutched his shoulder. "Please."

Rafe pulled away. "Teach you to be a killer?"

"You were one once!" Knowing what she knew now, Josie wasn't going to abide his holier-than-thou attitude.

"I was a fool once," he answered hotly. "Until a tragedy sobered my egotistical thinking." He felt sick at heart as he remembered the young man his bullet had struck down, a young man just in the prime of his life. An innocent man. "Believe me, I regret the misery I caused more than you can ever know. That's why I took up doctoring. To try and make up in some way for the harm I had done."

Thinking about her brother, Josie was somber. "There is no way any man can make up for some things," she said.

"Exactly." He was glad she understood. "Where it comes to gunfighting, there are no winners. Only losers." With all sincerity he vowed, "Josie, I don't want you to be one of the losers." Clint's threat rang in his ears that next time he would shoot to kill. "I don't want you to die in some silly shoot-out."

"Neither do I," she said glibly. "That's why I want you to give me lessons." Putting her fingers to his lips, Josie silenced any protestations he might have made, saying, "Just think about it."

Hearing Nora Harper calling out her name from the laundry room, Josie hastily hurried back to work. Well, at least she had tried. Not that she was going to hold her breath waiting for Dr. Rafe Gardner to agree, however. He had said no with his eyes all the time his gaze had also said something else. Like it or not, he was attracted to her. Perhaps if she put her mind to it, she could think of a way to make use of that attraction.

"Daydreaming, Josie?" Emily's voice held just a hint of envy. "Well, why not. The doctor *is* handsome and unattached."

Filling her washtub first with cold water, then with hot water from one of the kettles, Josie was reflective. "So, there are no women in the good doctor's life?" she asked softly, wondering why she even cared.

"No rumors of anyone." Emily turned to Sarah.

"Have you heard any ladies brag of capturing Rafe Gardner's heart?"

Sarah rolled her eyes. "None who have succeeded, though just about every eligible woman in town has tried." Pausing in her task of ironing, Sarah sighed. "I suppose I might be interested too if I hadn't a husband at home."

"Having a husband doesn't stop anyone from looking." Emily giggled. "I might be wed, but I'm certainly not blind."

"Oh, I see!" Josie wouldn't have admitted it, but the way the two women were mooning over the doctor annoyed her. Withdrawing from their gossipy conversation, she "immersed" herself in work, doing double the normal load, and pausing only to eat half a sandwich. By the end of the day she could take pride in her accomplishment and basked in the warmth of Nora Harper's praise.

"Parish was right when he said I should hire you," Nora exclaimed, "but, girl, don't work yourself to death." Taking over Josie's washtub, Mrs. Harper insisted she leave an hour early. "Go have a sarsaparilla at the drugstore before it closes," she insisted, dropping a nickel in Josie's apron pocket. "On me."

A sarsaparilla sounded good. Too good to pass up. With a cheery thanks, Josie took off her apron, slung it over her shoulder, and marched good-naturedly out the door.

Strange, how dark it was, she thought. Even though she was leaving work early, the dark rain clouds blocked enough of the sun to make it look dreary. Dismal. Threatening.

"I better hurry and get that sarsaparilla and get back to the boardinghouse before it rains," she said to herself, heading toward the drugstore by way of the alley.

A sudden noise behind her caused Josie to pause in midstride and whirl around. "What . . . ?" Seeing that it was just a gray cat, she soon regained her bravado. Crouching down, she tapped her fingers against the ground. "Here, kitty. Kitty, kitty, kitty . . ."

There was another noise, louder this time. Before Josie could react, she found herself held captive by strong arms. She opened her mouth to scream, but before she could make a sound, a hand clamped over her mouth.

"Mmmm." Struggling in the grasp of her captor, Josie was furious. Of all the low-down, underhanded things!

"You're a lively one."

Tanner's voice. So, it was that skunk. "Hold still. Don't fight me. I'm just going to put you in a wagon. A wagon going west of here. A nice little town far away from me."

Put her in a wagon? In a pig's eye, he would. Using an old trick, Josie pretended to faint, going limp in Clint Tanner's arms. Then, when his guard was down, when his hold on her had loosened, she aimed at the part of him that would do him the most harm.

"Ouch!" Clutching his crotch, Clint Tanner was too busy with his own misery to give much attention to her.

"Nice to see you again, Tanner," Josie said with

mock sweetness, watching as he doubled over in agony. He did in fact look most miserable. Not so sure of himself anymore. He looked helpless, in fact, at least for the moment. But not so helpless that she wanted to stand around and stare. With a sarcastic "see you around," Josie ran down the alleyway, heading for Schwab's and a cold sarsaparilla.

Eleven

Resting her elbows on the counter, Josie generously applied the lotion she had just bought to her chapped hands, recalling her encounter with Tanner in the alleyway. So, things were beginning to steam up. She would have to look over her shoulder from time to time just so she wouldn't be caught unaware.

"Can I help you?"

The clerk seemed to come out of nowhere, startling Josie for an instant. Perhaps she was more addled by her encounter with Tanner than she had first thought.

"A sarsaparilla."

"Make that two."

Turning, Josie looked wide-eyed as Parish Harper took the seat next to her. Coincidence his being here? Remembering his mother's suggestion to visit the drugstore, she doubted it. Nora Harper had made no secret of intending to play cupid for her curly-haired son.

"Hello, Parish." With a friendly smile she welcomed his company. Somehow with him the chip on her shoulder seemed to disappear.

"Imagine meeting you here."

"Imagine, indeed." Taking note of the *Farmer's Almanac* in his hand, she asked, "Interesting reading?"

"So far all I've looked at is the weather report. It predicts rain for a couple of days. We can sure use it." He took off his hat and plopped it on the table. "And I've read my horoscope. It says I'm going to fall in love with an interesting lady." His eyes sparkled.

"Oh." Josie glossed over his comment, not of a mind to flirt. She wasn't interested in Parish that way, so there was no point in leading him on. All she wanted was his friendship.

"When is your birthday, Josie?"

"January eighteenth," she said, taking the glass from the clerk's hand. A time that had been happy in the past but which had been miserable this year. Charlie hadn't been there to cheer her.

"You're a Capricorn." Quickly thumbing through the almanac, he paused. "It says to beware of a tall, dark stranger." Parish's brows furrowed with worry as he took a drink of his sarsaparilla.

"It does?" Immediately Tanner's face flashed before her eyes. "Well, if it's talking about Clint Tanner, the warning comes a bit late." Briefly she told Parish about her meeting with the gunfighter in the alleyway. "But he didn't get the best of me. I kneed him in the groin; that took care of him."

"Oh, I see." There was a moment of silence, then Parish asked, "But *you* are all right?"

"Me?" She hurried to assure him. "I'm just fine."

Josie sipped the sweetened carbonated beverage

flavored with sassafras. But Tanner was light of complexion and hair. Maybe the horoscope was warning her of someone else. Rafe Gardner?

"Parish, what do you know about the doctor?"

"Dr. Gardner?" He stiffened, looking down at his hands to hide what by his expression seemed to be jealousy. "I know that all the women in town are crazy about him. Are you interested in him too, Josie?"

"Of course not," she said much too snippily, trying to camouflage the truth.

Parish looked up. "Then what exactly do you want to know?"

Now it was Josie who looked away. "Well, I heard he used to be a gunfighter. Did . . . did he kill very many men?"

"A few, so they say. He was said to he a cool, brave man with good manners unless you met him in a fight." Parish drained his glass dry, wiping his mouth with the back of his hand. "What would you think of a man who kept company with the likes of Dead-Eye Dick; Cold, Hard Johnnie; and Three-fingered Pete? Some things follow a man."

"*And* Clint Tanner," Josie scoffed. Above all, she now knew that Dr. Rafe was a hypocrite. "And he has the nerve to hang out a shingle. Ha!"

"But I don't always believe everything I hear," Parish was quick to admit, trying to amend his hasty words. "There are some people who say that those men were more Clint's friends than Gardner's."

"But a man is known by the company he keeps," she answered coldly. Coming right to the point, she inquired, "Do you know just what the good doctor's tie is to Clint Tanner anyway?"

"I don't know much. They grew up together in Kentucky. Their parents had neighboring farms. They both fought together in the Confederacy."

"Soldiers?"

Parish shrugged. "Most gunfighters were. I guess the chaos that followed the war spawned a breed of men who thought the gun answered everything. Anyway, from what I hear, Clint Tanner's temper got him into quite a lot of trouble. In all honesty, it's said that Rafe Gardner was the one with the level head."

"Level head?"

"Well, at least he seems to have tempered Tanner's recklessness a bit of late."

"And turned him into a model citizen." She laughed sarcastically. "A man beloved by the whole town despite the things that he has done. What I want to know is why?" She still couldn't understand it. What hold did Tanner have on Showlow?

"Because he's the town's watchdog, that's why, Josie." Reaching out, Parish took her hand. "No matter how angry you are at Tanner, you have to accept that."

"Watchdog?"

"It can be wicked out here. There are those men who think a Western community is just a place to get gloriously drunk, to shoot up the town, to bed immoral women, and to win at gambling. Tanner's reputation keeps the worst troublemakers away, at least that's what the townspeople believe."

"And because I called Tanner out, they view me as a threat."

"Exactly." Parish tightened his hold on Josie's hand. "Whenever anyone from outside arrives, the townspeople are uncomfortable. That you took up the gun and walked down the street made them afraid."

"Of me? I failed." A fact that still bothered her.

"Of what you might bring about. Gunfighters. Danger. First you and then another, and another and another. That thought sets off tremors of pure stark terror."

"I see." It was now all very clear in her mind. "So they don't care that Clint Tanner murdered— " Charlie's face flashed in her mind. "All they care about is that nothing happens to disrupt their carefully organized little community."

Josie pulled her hand away and stood up. "Then, like I've always known, I'm on my own in this town. Alone."

"Not alone, Josie." Picking up his hat, Parish followed her as she walked toward the door. "You can always count on me."

Josie couldn't doubt his sincerity. "And I appreciate that, Parish. Thank you for that friendship." For the first time in a long while she felt calm and untroubled as he walked her home.

Rafe couldn't have said that it had been an ideal day by any means. To the contrary, Josie's having learned of his "prior profession," made him ex-

tremely uneasy, so much so that he found himself
pacing. Back and forth. Up and down.

"There is no way any man can make up for some
things," she had said. Words that haunted him
now.

"No, there is no way . . ." No way to push away
the dreams that haunted Rafe many a night. Memories of the surprised look in some men's eyes when
a bullet cut them down.

Tiring of being on his feet, Rafe plopped down
in his black leather chair and reflected on things
he would rather have forgotten. All this time he
had been running away from the past, being foolishly stubborn. He had appointed himself a healer,
God's right-hand man in the fight against injury
and disease, but once he had not been so noble.

"Ah, Josie."

Closing his eyes, he imagined her walking toward him, her blond hair billowing around her
shoulders. She was smiling at him just the way she
had earlier that day, like a cherub. She was calling
out his name, telling him that what he had done
didn't matter. Then she was in his arms, holding
him close in the kind of passionate embrace that
was every man's dream.

"Josie. . . ."

"If you think that's who I am, then you have
been working too hard." Pushing his way into the
room, Clint Tanner was obviously drunk and in a
foul mood.

"It's late, Clint." Rafe was embarrassed and dis-
tressed that his privacy had been invaded.

"Yep, it's late all right. Too late for some things,"

he grumbled, throwing down a rumpled newspaper from a neighboring town.

"What's this?" Without waiting for Clint's explanation, Rafe read the front-page story so that he could find out for himself. It was an account of the gunfight between Josie and Tanner, an amusing retelling of what had happened. Far from being biased in Tanner's favor, however, it cast Josie in the role of a heroine, bravely fighting to avenge a wrong she had suffered at a bully's hands.

"See there. See there. Makes me sound like a real horse's ass, for God's sake."

Rafe raised his eyebrows, biting his tongue to keep from saying that sometimes Clint could be just that. "The reporter has a right to his opinion, Clint. There's nothing you can do."

"There is!" His face flushed. "I can ride into town and smash that paper's printing press."

"And then what? Silence everyone who goes against you?" Rafe shook his head. Clearly it was going to take more than a dunk in a horse trough to change Tanner's thinking.

"Yeah, starting with that brazen little trouble-maker."

Rafe felt a sudden fierce protectiveness toward Josie and disgust toward his friend. "Let it alone, Clint. Leave Josie alone."

"Leave her alone? Leave her alone, you say?" He guffawed. "Tell her to stay away from me." He puffed out his chest. "Or she will be going up against the whole town." He smiled, reminding Rafe of his prominence in the community. "They wouldn't dare go against me, especially for any woman." He grabbed the newspaper from Rafe's hand. "No matter what that stupid writer said, I'm the one who's in the right. No matter what I have to do, I'll win. You can tell Josie what's-her-name that the next time you see her." Wadding the newspaper up in his fist, Tanner threw it to the floor.

Twelve

The events of the next few days unfolded like a giant chess game, pitting Josie against a determined Clint Tanner, who was hell-bent on persuading the people of the town to be on his side. If his methods varied from diplomatic cajoling to out-and-out bribery, it didn't seem to matter.

"He's running scared," Sarah confided, reaching for a bar of soap and a knife. Taking out her anger on the hapless bar, she whittled it into flakes, adding it to the hot water. That newspaper article has gotten a few people around here to wondering."

"Yeah," Emily exclaimed. "Some of the women of this town, particularly those whose menfolk have tangled with Tanner, are saying that it's time the women in Showlow took a stand against his shenanigans."

"He hasn't fooled everyone around here, Josie. There are some who know he can be a real bully, particularly when he doesn't get his way." Sarah winced as she put her hands into the tub, sloshing a shirt up and down.

"Let's just say that Tanner's past isn't exactly a secret," Emily added.

"Besides, now that you have been here awhile,

had contact with some of our customers, the opinion about you is changing."

"Do you think so?" Josie had noticed that she wasn't being as ostracized as before. There were even a few ladies who actually talked to her when they came to get their laundry.

"I know so." Emily paused in her ironing to pat Josie on the arm. "Just give it time."

"Time?" That was something Josie was running short of. That and patience.

"You see, when Tanner first came to Showlow, it just wasn't much of a town. A few shacks, a couple of stores." For just a moment Sarah closed her eyes, remembering. "But as small as it was, it was wild. There were robberies, fistfights. Gambling."

"There were even drunks who used the stars for target practice. It got so a body didn't even want to be out on the streets after noon.

"Don't tell me," Josie chided. "Clint Tanner single-handedly fixed the problem to bring law and order to the town. Amen."

Emily nodded. "That's exactly what he did."

"He's a guardian angel."

"The epitome of justice." Emily snickered.

"A saint." Though usually Josie didn't have much of a sense of humor on this subject, she laughed. "Well, maybe he'll be wearing a pair of wings when I get through with him." And yet, for all her tough talk, Josie had to admit to herself that her hunger for an eye for an eye was waning. Perhaps because when she left the laundry and went home to bed she was so exhausted. She had too little energy for thoughts of a vendetta. Indeed, the only gun-toting she did these days was in her dreams. What happened that night after she left the laundry, however, changed all that.

Josie could hear the thud of her heels against the boardwalk, echoed by another sound, the heavy trod of boots, the jingle of spurs. *I'm being followed.* But by whom? She had a pretty good idea. Tanner.

Stopping in her tracks, Josie whirled around. Though her eyes touched slowly on everything that moved, she didn't see anyone. Her imagination, then? A crisp explosion of a shot changed her mind.

"Whoa!" Josie threw herself to the ground just as another shot was spit from a gun. The bullet struck the boardwalk just inches from her, leaving a permanent indentation. Another shot sent a splatter of dust in her face. Then there was only silence. Laughter.

More than the fact that being ambushed was a low-down thing, it was the laughter that moved Josie to action. Standing up, she took to her heels, running as fast as she could. Searching the streets and the alleyways, she soon cornered the culprit.

"Out for a stroll, Tanner?" Reaching for the revolver she had hidden beneath her apron, Josie took aim. Firing, she hit her target. Clint Tanner's hat. Her bullet sent it flying.

"What the hell?" Tanner started to reach for his gun but thought better of it.

"Don't even think of it. Just throw your gun down." Josie's expression clearly revealed that she was serious.

"What are you going to do?"

"Do?" She thought about it for a while. Of

course she couldn't just shoot him down, no matter the ill will between them. What, then? "Why, I think I'll persuade you to make apologies to me for your little ambush earlier."

"Ambush?"

Josie nodded. "Ambush. A sneaky kind of attack that had your name written all over it." She closed her ears to his protestations of innocence. It had been him, all right. The fact was, she couldn't think of anyone else who might have done it.

"I didn't shoot at you."

Josie was tired and grouchy. "I recognized the sound of your spurs, so don't give me any of that." Squeezing the handle of the gun, she stared him down. "Get down on your knees."

"What?"

"I said, get down on your knees. Apologize!" When he didn't move, she took a step forward.

"Okay. Okay." Glowering all the while, Clint Tanner hunkered down. Though he didn't actually say the words, Josie was satisfied in just seeing him humbled. It was a good lesson. "Now, go on your way."

"On my way." Bending over, Clint Tanner picked up his hat. "Just like that?"

"Just like that." As she spoke, their eyes met and Josie was chilled to the very bone at what she saw. If a man's heart could be read in the eyes, then his was as cold as stone.

"I'll get you for this. If it takes me forever, I will get you!"

* * *

Looking out the window at the crowd that was beginning to form at the Golden Cactus Saloon, Rafe knew in an instant that trouble was brewing. So Clint hadn't been joshing when he had said that he was going to hold a meeting that night that would instigate Josie Smith's being run out of town. And not too gently, if Tanner had his way.

She's dangerous," Clint had insisted, paying Rafe a call just before suppertime. Clint had been in a heated fury as he had related the incident in the alleyway. Rafe suspected the story was from a prejudiced point of view, of course, but from the way Clint had told it, he had been set upon with no provocation. A story he no doubt had repeated over and over again.

"I just don't believe it." Josie Smith could be stubborn and willful, spirited too, but from what he had seen of her, she wasn't so foolish as to attack someone twice her size. To Rafe's mind, the story just didn't hold up. Certainly something had happened, however. Just what, he didn't know. Still, he just didn't like to see anyone, particularly a woman, at the mercy of a crowd's anger.

Putting his tan Stetson atop his dark-haired head, he slammed the door shut with the heel of his boot and hurried down the staircase from his sleeping quarters to his office below. He had been summoned with the others to be on hand at the meeting, and so he would go, but for a different reason. Rafe intended to see for himself just what was brewing. Hurrying across the street, he paused at the double doors, listening for just a moment.

"Come on in, you silly bastard. Come on in."

The saloon owner's parrot in a cage by the front door greeted with vocalized profanity all who entered and blocked out any hope Rafe had of overhearing shreds of conversation.

"Okay. Okay. I'm coming in." The odor of tobacco, whiskey, and beer wafted throughout the saloon. The blue glass in the chandelier twinkled. Smoke rose up like a huge cloud. The brass spittoons by the bar were getting plenty of use.

As he entered the saloon, Rafe saw Tanner reflected in the huge mirror behind the bar. Standing on a chair, he was running the show in his usual engaging manner. Setting up drinks for everyone, he was playing up to the men's egos in order to get them to follow his lead.

"Rufus, how's the new bride? As lusty as she looks, you lucky devil? Sam, I heard you had a winning hand at poker, have an extra drink on me. Good evening, John. How's the new baby?" Rafe heard Tanner say. "He's beginning to look more like you every day."

He knew just what to say to flatter each man in the crowd.

"Damn." What charisma he had, Rafe thought with disgust. He didn't mean a damn thing he was saying. Clint never did. Just the other day he had told John's wife, Ethel, that the baby looked just like her. As to Rufus's bride, Clint had laughingly spoken of her as having the morals of an alley cat."

"Rafe! Come here, old buddy." He motioned with his hand, spilling his mug of beer as he did. The saloon owner's dog licked it up. "Drink it up,

Max," he said to the German shepherd, "it's on the house." He hiccuped loudly, then insisted Rafe have a beer.

"I'm on the wagon tonight, Clint." Rafe was going to keep a clear head.

"Aw, Rafe."

Clucking his tongue, he chided him, then quickly turned his attention elsewhere. Before long, the subject of his chatter turned from cordial greetings to the purpose of the gathering— Josie Smith. Detailing her attack on him, Tanner played the crowd. Jumping on top of the bar, he raised his arms in the air. The room became silent.

"And I tell you there isn't a man, woman, or child who is safe from the crazy little fool." He pointed to a skinny man standing in front of him. "You, Bradford. What would you do if someday she grabs you from behind like she did me? Or your wife? Or little daughter? Or worse yet, points her gun straight at your heart?" He nodded toward another man. "Or you, Horace. What if you anger the little minx and she calls you out? Why, hell, just her very presence in Showlow opens the whole town up to trouble. We'll be the target for every gunfighter in the West when they hear she's hanging around. Remember last year when that gunfighter from Kansas blew in, bringing all his friends? Johnny Ringo."

The men in the crowd remembered. A loud gasp swept through the room at the mention of his name.

"Ah-ha." Tanner thrust out his chest. "He might have driven Wyatt Earp out of Arizona Territory, but I faced him down. And chased him and his rowdy gang out of Showlow."

Rafe frowned in disgust. The real truth was that Johnny Ringo and his cohorts had been bored in Showlow and had soon passed right on through, though Clint had taken credit for their going. "Gawd!" He couldn't believe these men could be so gullible. But they were. Stationing himself where he could watch the others, Rafe was disturbed as the night wore on. The son of a bitch was working the mob into a frenzy. Everyone in the room was watching Clint in wide-eyed amazement and listening to his every word as he portrayed Josie Smith as a villainess out to ruin the town.

"Friends, we must see that this trouble-causing woman is run out of our community. Nobody invited her to come here. We all know that this place has already cleaned up much of the violence and the killings."

"Thanks to you, Clint," a voice called out.

"Her being here is causing a resurgence of the very things we do not need. Already it's begun to divide us."

"But, Clint, how can we run out a woman?" called out another voice, not as ready to be one of the sheep.

"Just because we found out that what we supposed to be a he turned out to be a she has nothing to do with the trouble the shooting incident has caused, or the outcome. She wanted to be mistaken for a man, we'll treat her like one."

"But our wives? They'll have a fit. Like her or not, they have definite ideas on how to treat members of their sex, even those who tote a gun," a man in the crowd exclaimed.

Clint shrugged. "I suspect that most of our women will be sympathetic with her at first. We can't help that. But after all, we're men, not mice. I leave it up to you to show your women who is master of your house, or soon we will be at one another's throats even in our own homes."

Rafe showed no surprise at what was being said. Words always slipped from Clint's lips as easily as acorns falling from an oak tree. He remembered that even as a boy Clint had seemed to enjoy trouble. And after all, he'd gotten Rafe to join the Confederate Army, hadn't he? Talk about convincing.

"So, how about it, men? Are you going to be cowardly, or are you going to show some guts?" Jumping down, Tanner reached behind the bar and, bringing forth a torch, lit it with a match. "Well?" He insinuated that anyone who didn't follow him was a coward.

"We're with you, Clint."

"We'll show her."

"Just lead us on."

Three strategically placed comrades of Tanner's each did their part to get the crowd moving. Soon with an angry murmuring they were surging toward the door.

"So, Clint strikes again." Rafe shook his head sadly. He had to get Josie to safety, at least until the crowd calmed down. He couldn't stay neutral in this argument now. Something had to be done before a tragedy ensued. Despite her spunk, Josie was no match for Tanner and this crowd. So thinking, he quickly and silently slipped out the side door.

Thirteen

Josie didn't usually have trouble falling asleep after a long and weary day, but she was having trouble tonight. Stretched out flat on her back, she stared up at the ceiling, her mind jumbled with so many thoughts that it was giving her a headache.

Because you are headstrong, Josephine, her father had always said when she had complained that her temples were pounding. *Someday it's going to get you into trouble.* After what happened tonight with Tanner, she was inclined to agree.

What else could I have done? What was I supposed to do, just ignore his nasty prank? He shot at me, could have winged me with a bullet. Experience had taught her that any show of weakness could be dangerous, particularly when dealing with a man who used intimidation so skillfully. But could there have been another way of handling the matter?

No! The only way to deal with a man like Clint Tanner was to stand up to him. She had wanted to remind him not to trifle with her. Even so, this time she couldn't help wondering if she had gone just a bit too far.

"Well, it's too late now. The deed is done." A deed that would no doubt come back to haunt her in some way or another. Undoubtedly the good doctor would hasten to give her a good tongue-lashing at the first available opportunity.

Ha, the good doctor. Who was once a gunfighter. A killer. Just the man to be giving other people advice, she scoffed. But that was in the past. A man could change. He was a doctor. Doctors saved lives. But was that reason enough to be forgiven for the misery he had brought upon others? Misery like Clint Tanner had brought to her and her family.

As usual, her opinion of the good doctor swung this way and that, like a pendulum. Just which was he, sinner or saint? For every man that he had killed, how many men, women, and children had Rafe Gardner, the doctor, saved? Enough to retrieve his soul out of hell when he died? And what about her? Was he right in his lecturing that her thirst for vengeance would bring about her downfall?

"Oh, I don't know anymore!"

Turning over onto her stomach, burying her face in the pillow, she tried to still the questions plaguing her mind. It had all seemed so simple when she had first come to Showlow. Tanner had killed her brother and had escaped punishment, therefore it had seemed only right that she take the law into her own hands. A life for a life. Now she just wasn't so sure.

"Josie. . . ." The soft calling-out of her name nearly went unnoticed, but the knocking didn't.

Bolting up in bed, Josie looked toward the door, remembering Tanner's aggressive action in the alley. He wouldn't dare come here. Or would he? Her heart hammered loudly at the thought. Perhaps when all was said and done, Tanner would dare anything to get back at her for having wounded his male pride.

"It's me. Dr. Gardner," whispered a low male voice. "Let me in."

Curling up in a ball under the covers, Josie chose to ignore him. Whatever he wanted would just have to wait. She was too tired to endure a social call or a lecture. Surely if she didn't answer, he would leave.

He didn't. The banging on the door was soft but relentless.

"Josie, I know you must be in there."

"Go away." Even if she hadn't been in her nightshirt, Josie would have answered the same. Though she might have been reckless in some things, she hadn't been raised to be careless about her morals. The women of the town thought ill enough of her without it being whispered that she had a man in her room past a reasonable hour. No doubt if there was even a hint of a scandal, Mrs. Howard, the owner of the boardinghouse, would throw her out on her ear. Josie couldn't afford that.

"Open up." His voice was insistent.

"For God's sake, it's the middle of the night," she rasped.

"I don't care." The doctor's voice was insistent. "Open up, Josie! I don't want to have to wake up the whole boardinghouse."

"You wouldn't."

"I would."

A reasonable and cautious woman would have

continued to say no, but Josie knew that neither adjective had ever applied to her. Scrambling out of the bedclothes, she called out, "All right. All right." Without even bothering to put on a robe, she opened the door, her eyes meeting his steadily. "What is it, doctor?"

"There's trouble," he said, shutting the door behind him.

"Trouble?"

"About twenty-five men are down at the Golden Cactus Saloon being brainwashed by Clint Tanner. He's turning them into a mob. They're coming after you."

"A mob?" At first she didn't believe it, but the sound of voices outside convinced her.

"Tanner did a great job of stirring them up."

"I'm sure!" Josie had never counted on this. So, Tanner *was* angry about her having made him apologize. But so angry as to stir up the whole town? She had known he was a bastard, but she was just beginning to see what a demon he really could be.

"From what I heard, they're planning an unwelcome, unfriendly visit to you here at the boarding-house, torches and all."

She was visibly shaken by the news. "Ohhh." A knot squeezed in the pit of her stomach. Facing Tanner was one thing, going against a mob another. She tried not to sound frightened, however. "Well, I guess what happens happens. She waved her hand nonchalantly. "Come on in and sit down and tell me what's going on."

He was hesitant just for a moment. "While you

pack up your things." Choosing a chair right by
the door, he sat down, took off his hat, and
stretched out his legs.

"While I pack." For just a moment she stood as
still as a stone. So that was it. Rafe Gardner was
going to take advantage of the situation just to get
his own way. It was unforgivable. "So you think
I'm going to run. Jump on the nearest stagecoach
like a hound with my tail between my legs?"

Rafe just didn't know what to think anymore,
but he didn't think that. "As a matter of fact, I
don't."

Josie combed her hair from her eyes with her
fingers. "Then just what did you think?" She was
not a coward, still, if she panicked, they would succeed in running her out. Suddenly she felt a burst
of rage. Anger that she took out on Rafe. "Oh,
why did you even come here? To say I told you
so, most likely."

"Which I did," he retorted coldly. He took a
step forward. "Oh, Josie." Strange, how quickly his
own anger died whenever he was near her. "I came
to warn you, to help."

"Why?" she inquired bluntly, folding her arms
across her chest defiantly.

Despite himself, Rafe stuttered. "Well . . .
well . . . I—I . . . guess you've just . . . just
touched me in some way."

"Touched you?" The way he said it made her
sound like a charity case. "You feel sorry for me.
Is that it?"

"Sorry?" He shook his head no, wondering just

how he could ever explain his feelings. "I— I care about you, Josie. Very deeply."

"Care?" Except for Charlie and her mother, she wondered if anybody had ever really cared about her. Was it any wonder, then, that she was suspect?

Rafe stood up. "You're special to me, dammit!"

Despite his swearing, there was something in his eyes that was like a caress. That look took her breath away and despite the situation made her smile. "Oh . . ."

Rafe took her by the hand. "Josie, you're going to get hurt, and I can't bear that." The words that came out of his mouth weren't in any way planned. They came from his heart. "Josie, I want to take you with me."

For just a moment her anger softened. Her voice sounded like a little girl's. "Take me with you where?"

"Home with me."

"With you?"

They stared at each other, two silhouettes against the window shade. Two shadows that moved closer to each other. Josie forgot her near-nakedness as he reached out and took her by the shoulder, his fingers melting through her nightshirt to touch her flesh with liquid fire.

"And just what . . . what made you think I would go?" she stammered, watching as his head lowered slowly to hers. He was going to kiss her. The thought brought a dizzying breathlessness.

"Just a feeling . . ." His eyes were tender and sincere, not angry or mocking as usual, but the kiss didn't come. Instead, the gentle roar of voices outside spurred him to action. Without another word Rafe pulled away from her and tugged at her arm. Still, the brief moment of closeness couldn't be forgotten.

"I know. Get packed." It took only a few moments for Josie to pull her carpetbag from beneath the bed and put a few clothes and other possessions into it. She was eager to get away from there if that was how they felt. But she would come back. Tanner had even more to answer for than before.

"Collect whatever items you really need and get dressed," Rafe ordered. "We've got to leave right this minute before they come marching over here to run you out forcibly."

They were too late. Like an angry swarm of bees and fireflies, some of Tanner's henchmen hovered right outside the boardinghouse's windows, some calling out Josie's name while others were already climbing up the stairs.

"We're trapped!" The thought made her both angry and frightened.

"No, we're not!" Rafe was familiar enough with the boardinghouse to know a back way, though it would be a long jump. "Come!"

"Okay." She had to trust him, following in her nightshirt as he tugged her out the door and down the hallway. He banged on a door, brazenly pushing inside when it was answered.

"What the . . . ?" An astonished woman in a lace nightcap protested the intrusion, but he ignored her. Opening the window, he put one leg through.

"I'll go first. That way you'll have something

soft to land on." Without a sound, he jumped. Leaning out the window, Josie was relieved to see that he had landed safely on his feet. Holding out his arms, he promised to catch her.

"Why not!" Hoping she wouldn't break an arm or a leg, Josie took a deep breath, then dropped downward.

"Whoa!"

Stretching out his arms, Rafe caught her, but the force of her jump sent them both tumbling to the ground in a tangle of arms and legs. Josie could feel the muscles of his body through the thin linen of her nightshirt as he held her close against him. For a moment her full, firm breasts were crushed against his hard chest. Josie's body seemed to melt into his as every inch of their bodies met intimately.

"Josie." Rafe caressed her face with fingers that were infinitely gentle, then he kissed her throat just behind her ear.

"Mmm." She closed her eyes.

"Oh, boy!" Clutching her to him, he was filled with a desperate desire to possess her. If only . . . Reason intruded on the insanity of the moment. Standing up, Rafe brought Josie with him. "Come on, sweetheart."

He took the lead, going down the alleyway, turning the corner. He wanted to be sure that the coast was clear. Leaning forward, he peered around the corner, moving stealthfully, cautiously. Spotting a single figure smoking a cigarette while leaning against the stable wall, he turned to her and shook his head. "We will have to wait a spell. There's someone there. We can't afford to take any chances. It's too dark to tell who he is."

Her hand began to tremble slightly. She pulled her nightshirt tightly around her body, feeling vulnerable for the first time in a long while. It was a very warm night, but nervousness had caused her to feel cold. Her knees grew weak as they stood waiting, but she calmed somewhat as the minutes passed.

"The coast is clear." His fingers squeezed around her hand.

Josie took a deep breath, expelling it as she said his name. "Rafe."

"Yes."

For a moment the words nearly died in her throat, then she whispered, "I'm . . . I'm glad you're with me."

"So am I." But they couldn't take time for words. Not now. The soft rumble of voices warned of that. With a sigh of regret Rafe put his arm around her waist as they headed down the dark street, taking refuge from time to time in the shadows.

Fourteen

The office was dark as Rafe and Josie stepped inside. Striking a match, Rafe lit a lamp by the staircase. "You'll be safe tonight. No one will think of looking for you here." He studied her face, his gaze lingering on her green eyes that so fascinated him, reading in them the strength of her determination tempered with a softness he had never seen before.

"I'll never know how to thank you, Rafe." Her voice was low, seductive.

The way she spoke his name made his heart pound, made him remember their embrace. Never had he wanted anything quite as much as he wanted her at that moment. He wanted to touch her hair, to let the dark blond strands slide slowly through his fingers. Like silken threads.

"I had to . . . wanted to— " He leaned his head forward, kissing her on the forehead, but as his lips touched her skin, Josie stood up on tiptoe, moving her mouth to meet his.

His kiss was fierce. Potent. A burning possession that stole her breath away. Through the flimsy cloth of her nightshirt she could feel his muscles tense, then his fingers tangled in her hair. His other hand slid over the curve of her hip, making her shiver as he touched her. Was it the danger they had faced acting as an aphrodisiac, or something else? She didn't know. All she knew was that it was as if she had stepped into another world, a place where there was no anger, no hate, only passionate feelings.

"Josie. Oh, Josie." Lifting his mouth from hers, he held her close. Dear God, what she did to him. Did she even realize?

She felt his breath ruffle her hair and experienced the sensation down the whole length of her spine. She felt as if she were flying, as if her feet didn't even touch the ground. Her heart was beating so loudly that it seemed to shake her body. The world seemed to be only his touch, the haven of his arms.

"Kiss me again." Her arms slid up to encircle his neck.

He swallowed hard, trying to get control of himself. "You'd better go up to bed," he murmured, but his arms tightened around her even as he spoke.

"What about you?" she whispered.

He took a deep breath and stepped away. "Don't worry. I'll just stretch out on my black leather chair."

Josie felt as if she were poised on the edge of a precipice, in peril of plummeting endlessly. Still, she said softly, "I don't want to push you out of your own bed."

"Don't worry about it." Slowly, languorously, his thumb traced the contours of her face. She was playing havoc with his senses. He wanted to make love to her so much that it hurt.

"But . . ." A chill touched her, and she longed for the warmth of his arms. She shivered.

With gentlemanly concern Rafe took off his shirt and draped it over her shoulders. "If you get cold tonight, there are blankets in the chest at the foot of the bed."

"I don't want blankets." The words were out before she even realized she'd said them. "I want you."

He didn't touch her. She was vulnerable just then. Shaken. He wouldn't take advantage of the moment. "Shhhh. Don't say any more." Silently he led her up the stairs. Opening the door, he motioned toward the bed. He didn't kiss her. He didn't even say good night.

"Rafe?" Her eyes touched on the soft white pillows. So inviting but at the same time so lonely.

The room was filled with tension. Rafe's breathing was deep and ragged. With each moment it was harder to turn away, but somehow he did. Seeing to her carpetbag, he put it on a chair by the bed.

Josie felt her stomach flutter as he moved to the door. "Rafe, don't go. Please." Sitting down on the bed, she patted the place beside her. "Can't we . . . talk for a while."

"Talk?" He moved toward her, then with a shrug sat down.

"I needed help tonight and you were there." Though it sounded like just gratitude her feelings went much deeper.

"I'm glad that I was." Angry mobs could often do more harm than they intended. He doubted that Josie could have come out unscathed.

"So am I." Aching with desire, Josie eagerly parted her lips, hoping. She wanted him to kiss her again, but he didn't. Still, he was so close. What would he do if she reached out to him? Would he think her much too bold. Did she really care?

Rafe felt her presence beside him without looking at her. His desire was a deep pain that gnawed at him, tempted him. No other woman made him feel like this. With the townswomen he always maintained his control. Now that control was slowly slipping away.

Josie noted the furrow to his brow and voiced her question aloud. "What are you thinking?"

"What am I thinking?" Her question took him by surprise. He turned, allowing his eyes to roam over her body. It left no doubt in her mind that his thoughts, his longings, were the same as hers.

"I was just wondering— " He leaned toward her. His mouth, hard and demanding, fastened on hers, exploding into a sensuous, passionate tool that triggered a burning response deep inside her, then he was pushing her down to lie beside him. "I want you, Josie. Right from the first I have," he murmured. "You're enough to drive any man out of his mind."

"I am?" She took it as a compliment, hoping that was the way it was intended. Wrapping one arm around him, she cuddled up against him.

"You *are*."

She had never thought much about desire before, but at that moment she knew it was what she felt. But did she want to act upon it? Or should she push him away before it was too late? Her body answered for her. Moving down to take his hand, she entwined her fingers with his, leading his hand up to touch her breast.

"Josie!" He started to pull away, but her fingers tightened, drawing his hand to the taut peak.

"Do you know what you're doing?" He didn't want this spark that had burst into a flame to be the source of her regret come morning.

"I know."

He groaned, closing his arms around her as he pulled her into the curve of his body. His touch made her forget that there had been anything else in the world between them except this.

This time his mouth was gentle. He kissed her in a careful, loving fashion, his tongue exploring her lips, then probing in between. Her mouth answered with a sweetness that turned to passion as his hands ran up and down the length of her body.

His breath came faster and faster. Josie wondered if she was even breathing at all. She didn't try to understand all that was happening to her. She knew only that Rafe was the only man she had met who could ever arouse such an urgent glowing need in her. Doctor or gunfighter, she yearned for him deep within her body and her soul. The danger tonight had merely intensified that yearning.

"You belong in my embrace."

"Mmm-hmmm."

No other woman had captivated him the way this young woman did. The powerful tug of her beauty set him ablaze. She reminded him of a desert wild-flower, loveliness tempered with strength. And determination.

Their lips touched and clung, enjoying a potent sweetness. Lying together in the darkness, their hands moved over each other, touching, exploring. Rafe's fingers parted the neck of her nightshirt, unbuttoning it so that he could reach inside to feel the soft flesh. He stroked and teased until she moaned low, whispering his name, yielding to his hands.

Have you . . . have you ever . . . ?" He had to know.

"Been with a man?" Josie shook her head. "No."

Rafe pulled back his hand. "Then . . . then we shouldn't. Help me to stop." But she was too tempting, too warm, too loving and responsive in his arms. He was a hungry man, driven by his desires. Even so, he was gentle. The thought that Josie had never known a man's lovemaking filled him with a passionate tenderness. He wanted to make everything that passed between them beautiful for her.

Stroking and caressing, Rafe removed her nightshirt and was aided by her own hands. He in turn moved away from her for just a moment as he slipped out of his boots, shirt, pants, and underdrawers. Seeking her out in the darkness, he leaned over her, drawing her smooth, naked body against him in a manner that wrenched a groan from his lips. Her skin was like velvet, caressing him like a thousand fingers.

"Josie, sweet but fiery Josie," he whispered,

pressing his face into the hollow of her neck. "I could never let Clint Tanner hurt you. You have to know that now."

"I do." She sighed as his mouth moved slowly downward from her throat to the skin of her bare shoulder. She tingled with an arousing awareness of her body. It was like discovering herself through Rafe. Her body was intensely sensitive. The lightest touch of his hands or mouth sent a shudder of pure sensation rippling deep within her.

Rafe's mouth flamed a path over her body. "I want to kiss you here." He kissed her breast. "And here." His lips moved to her abdomen. Josie's stomach tightened. A hot ache of desire coiled within her. She reached up to tangle her fingers in the dark hair of his head. No matter what happened, she would have this moment to remember, she thought. This special moment with Rafe. Even if Tanner shot her and she . . .

She refused to even think about it. Tonight was made for love, not for thoughts of violence or vengeance. So thinking, she moved her hands over him, marveling in his muscles and the warmth of his flesh.

"Josie, Josie, Josie." He moaned his approval, then pushed her down beneath him on the mattress. Like a fire, his lips burned over the soft mounds of her breasts, savoring the peaks with his mouth and tongue like the most cherished of treasures. "Your skin is so soft," he whispered against her flesh, outlining the small circles until the peaks puckered into succulent buds.

"Except for my hands," she whispered.

"I like their slight roughness. They feel so good. Touch me again."

She did, running her hands over the firm flesh of his chest, then, very tentatively, lower.

His body is beautiful, she thought. There was a grace about his lithe, strong body. His shoulders were so wide, his belly so flat. The part of him that made him a man was the most interesting of all, however. Without shyness she touched him.

"Ah . . ." Pleasure mingled with pain jolted through him as the pressure in his groin threatened to explode. He felt a rush of emotion, a driving tide of need.

His intake of breath, the way he gathered her deeper into his embrace, told her he enjoyed her explorations, thus she continued. Watching his face, she could see his pleasure. Then suddenly Rafe covered her fingers with his own, drawing her hand away.

"It's not too late to stop. I will if you— "

"No." It was too late for that. Driven by emotions she could no longer control nor even wanted to, she wound her arms tightly against him.

He rolled her over, pressing her beneath him. His stroking hands excited her, enticed her, fired her body with a burning dampness that made her press wantonly against him. She felt alive and soaring as he explored the center of her being. She opened up to him.

"Raise your hips. Guide me."

She did as he said, and for a moment their bodies met in the most intimate of embraces. The intimacy made her moan with pleasure, a sound that was smothered by his kiss.

Rafe paused, letting her grow accustomed to his invasion. Infinitely gentle, he took absolute care of her as he pushed through the obstruction of her virginity. He moved slowly, allowing her to learn the feel of him buried deep inside her. Like the warmth of the sun, her body drew his, joining them together.

Josie was consumed by his warmth, his hardness. Tightening her legs around his waist, she arched up to him, wanting him to move within her. When he did, she was astounded by the pulsating explosion of her body, the pleasure she felt as they moved together.

How could she have ever dreamed that it would be like this? It was as if she had been starving all her life but had only just then discovered her appetite. It was as if in giving she had received the ultimate gift. She had been so lonely, as if a piece of her were missing, but being with him made her realize the shattering wonder of being whole. Alive.

Rafe called out her name again and again, breathless from the jolt of his own emotions. He felt deeply fulfilled, but not just physically. A tenderness for Josie tugged at his heart. This was different from anything he'd ever known before, and for a moment that reality was frightening, causing him to frown as he surged one last time inside her. Then, as she cradled close in his arms, his reservations melted away. Fondling her gently, he pulled her tightly against him.

It was a long while before either of them moved

or said a word, but at last Josie voiced her feelings. "I've never felt like that before. As if we floated up and touched the sun together." But what would happen when they come tumbling back down? She would have to face tomorrow. Reality. The reality that was Tanner. Closing her eyes, she refused to think about it.

"It was like that for me too, Josie." He gently stroked her hair as they lay together. He couldn't get enough of her. Far from quenching his desire, what passed between them had only made him realize how much he really did care for her. Perhaps with Josie he could forget his past, forget the torment. Maybe together they could heal their wounds. Was it possible?

"Oh, Rafe." She whispered his name like a caress, snuggling up against the warmth of his chest. She didn't want to sleep, not now, but his fingers moving so slowly, tenderly, were like a soothing balm to her soul. With a sigh Josie closed her eyes and drifted off, happy in the shelter of his arms.

Fifteen

As the sun came up, Josie watched through the window, wondering how she would feel when Rafe, who was sleeping soundly, awakened. What would she say to him? What would he say to her? How would they feel about each other now? Certainly their relationship had changed. She couldn't imagine calling him "doctor." Not now.

Are we lovers? Or was last night just something that happened? Feelings that had to be explored. Desires that had to be quenched.

Rafe's arm lay heavy across her stomach, the heat of his body warming hers as she lay entangled with his legs and arms. It gave her a deep sense of peace and intimacy to be with him like this, but somehow it also made her feel a strange sense of fear. A person was always vulnerable when she let someone invade her heart.

Easing herself onto her elbow, she stared into his sleeping face, trying to sort out her emotions. For so long now the only feelings she had had were anger and vengeance. The emotions he inspired in her were so different. It was almost like the metamorphosis of her soul. She could almost imagine that all could be well, that the pain in her heart might be able to heal. Was it possible?

"I don't know!" she breathed, reaching out to brush at a lock of his dark hair. He was pleasing to the eye, handsome in a very manly way. Virile. Strong. Courageous. Intelligent. Certainly last night Rafe had been all she could have wanted him to be. Kind, gentle, understanding, a passionate lover. The question was, however, where did they fit in each other's lives? Where were they going from here?

It was a disturbing thought. Rafe was the town's doctor, someone everyone depended upon, she a woman they wanted to run out of town. It didn't appear there was any kind of future together. What then?

"Oh, Rafe." As her eyes touched upon his finely chiseled mouth, she felt the urge to kiss him, but though she longed to have him love her again, she contented herself with watching him sleep. His chest moved the covers up and down as he breathed, and as she looked upon him Josie remembered the feel of that chest against her naked breasts.

As if he sensed her thoughts, Rafe's dark lashes rose, revealing his sparkling blue eyes, eyes that were looking at her. "Good morning." He flashed her a lazy smile. "I hope that you slept well."

"Well enough," she answered, stiffening slightly as a bit of embarrassment swept over her momentarily. It wasn't every day she woke in a man's bed.

"I slept like the dead." He raised his eyebrows. "I hope I didn't snore."

Now she smiled. "You didn't. Or at least if you did, I didn't hear."

Rafe appeared to be calm and self-assured, but the truth of the matter was that he was far from that. He could not deny the poignant and heated passion that had been unleashed the previous night, but it troubled him. His intention had been to help her in time of peril, to be a shoulder to lean on. He had not meant for their kisses to lead to the ecstasy they had shared. He had not meant for his attraction to her to get out of hand. He had not meant for them to become lovers. Now that they had, it complicated things.

For so long now Rafe had avoided getting involved with any of the women in town. He valued his freedom. He had wanted to be able to do as he pleased. To succumb to his emotions without having to explain. Last night had changed that, at least in his mind.

"Josie, I . . ." He wanted to talk with her about his feelings, but as she looked at him with those huge green eyes, the words died in his throat. Though she could be all bristling and swearing, he sensed her loneliness. She was independent, feisty, and strong willed yet she needed someone to care. *To care, Rafe Gardner, not to totally lose one's head.* Which was exactly what he had done. She had attracted him like a moth to a flame. She was pretty. Full of spice. Full of life. In the deep recesses of his mind he had fantasized about making love to her. Now he had. A situation that couldn't be rectified. Not easily. Last night couldn't be undone.

Nor her maidenhead restored. God, he felt like a cad.

Something in his eyes made Josie feel uneasy. She was almost afraid to listen to anything he said. Was he going to give her an "I'm sorry" speech, tell her that sometimes things just happened, or was he going to play it noble?

Well, what did you expect? Frantic whispers that he loves you? Did you expect him to get down on one knee? Or to grab you in a passionate embrace and repeat last night's encounter? And what of me? What was he expecting me to do, or to think, or to feel? Sitting up in bed, she pulled the covers up to her chin, deciding to broach the subject. "Rafe, we need to talk."

She took him by surprise; still, he nodded. "Indeed, we do."

Although last night had been very special to him, he felt a burden of guilt. The moment he had learned that Josie was innocent of a man's touch, he should have pulled back, gone downstairs, and slept in that damned black leather chair. But he hadn't.

"Ummm, I . . . I just wanted to tell you thanks for saving me from Tanner and . . . and— " She felt a sudden urgency to save face. "And to tell you good-bye."

"Good-bye?" He was stunned. She had been so stubborn about leaving, so determined to get back at Tanner that he had suspected something quite different. Perhaps he had expected her to wait out the storm of angry feelings in Showlow, to hide out for a time, then bounce back undaunted. But she intended to leave. The idea of never seeing her again made him feel empty.

"Yes, good-bye. I can't stay here with you forever." She looked him squarely in the eye, a part of her wishing that it could be that way. She liked being with him. "I'm not your responsibility, Rafe."

Then why did he suddenly feel that she was? He didn't love her, did he? Damn, but he wasn't sure just how he felt. All he knew was that after last night he somehow couldn't just let her walk out of his life. "Yes, you are, Josie."

His words made her feel a warm glow. So he did care about her, then. Leaning toward him, she smiled, searching for just the right words. She wanted him to touch her again, to love her. "Rafe."

"Last night changed things, Josie." It changed everything. "Neither of us was really thinking." Certainly he wasn't. He should have thought of the consequences of lovemaking. Babies. He hadn't been careful. "You're pretty and desirable and evidently I have little willpower. But I promise to set the matter to right."

"Set the matter to right?" He sounded so cold, so professional. As if he were diagnosing an illness. "Well, tell me, doctor. Just how do you intend to do that? Just what do you intend to prescribe?"

"Marriage," he blurted out. After all, it would be a way of protecting her from Tanner and the town, a way that she could stay. And after all, he had taken her virtue, so he owed it to her.

"Marriage." A chill touched her as she searched his face. A proposal not out of love but out of guilt and nobility for what had happened between them. But he had not taken anything she had not wanted to give. "Well, I'll be damned. So that's the way you're going to handle it. I'd wondered."

He could see in an instant that he had somehow offended her, and he hurried to make it all right. "I've never met a woman like you, Josie. Right from the first I—"

"You wanted to sweep me off my feet. Carry me off to your vine-covered cottage." She felt her eyes burn with unshed tears.

"No, but I wanted to protect you." It was the truth.

"Protect me?" She was horrified. Insulted. "Well, forget it, mister. I can take care of myself." Bolting from the bed, she snatched up the blanket and wrapped it around her. Stalking about, she searched for her clothes. "And . . . and I wouldn't marry you if you were the last man on earth!"

"Josie!" His pride was bruised and battered. He had never imagined that she would say no. Or that she would get angry, for that matter. What had he done wrong? Certainly he had offered her what just about every single woman in Showlow would have welcomed. Women! No wonder he had made it a habit to slake his passions at the bordello and not let his emotions get out of hand.

Outraged, feeling humiliated to have let him have his way so easily, then treat her like some "mistake" that had to be corrected, she verbally lashed out. "Just think of last night as payment, doctor."

"Payment?" He winced. "For what?"

"For teaching me how to shoot." Her voice was icy. "Which I assume that you will do, seeing as how you have already been compensated."

"What!" His anger threatened to explode. "So that was all it was, a ploy, a way to get me in the palm of your hand." Climbing out of bed stark naked, he pulled on his pants. "Well, you know just what that makes you, lady!"

She knew what he was insinuating. That she was a whore. Picking up a vase, she aimed it at his head. "Yes, I do. Stupid." Bitterness washed over her.

"If you thought I'd put on a holster again for anyone, then that's just what you were. I'm a healer now, not a killer or an accomplice to such an act."

"Well then, let me just tell you that I don't need you. I'll find someone else to teach me how to be the fastest on the draw, and then both you and that damned Tanner had better beware."

Rafe picked up the shattered vase, once his favorite. "Oh, yes?"

She stared him down. "Yes." She was breathing heavily as she shrugged into her shirt, then her trousers. She felt the sudden need for a bath, to wash her body of last night's shame. Oh, damn the man! He had ruined everything! Worst of all he had made her cry. A weakness in women she had always abhorred.

Turning his head, Rafe took note of the moisture on her cheeks and his anger quickly cooled. He'd hurt her, and for that he felt like a heel. His expression was regretful, sad. "Josie . . ."

Tugging on her boots, she picked up her carpet-bag and headed for the door. She had a little money saved from her job at the laundry. She'd make do somehow. She always had. She didn't need the doctor, or anyone else for that matter.

"Josie, don't go."

For just a moment his words held her back.

"Oh, all right." He couldn't just let her go like this. She might get herself killed, she might fall on hard times, she might . . . "You win!"

"I win?" She eyed him skeptically. "Win what?"

He couldn't let her be at the mercy of Clint and his crowd. If she was so determined, at least she might be able to give Tanner a run for his money. At least he could do that for her. "I'll teach you."

By now she was emotionally drained; still, she felt a small twinge of elation. It had taken her a long time, but he had at last said yes. "Agreed." She held out her hand as if they were business partners. "Shake on it."

The touch of her hand stirred his feelings, and he wanted to make love to her all over again. But that was impossible now. He had spoiled every-thing, thus all he could say was "Then let the les-sons begin."

Part Two

The Lady Gunfighter
Cochise County, Arizona Territory

Sweet is revenge— especially to women.

— Lord Byron, *Don Juan*,
Canto 1, Stanza 22

Sixteen

The dark sky glistened with thousands of stars. The desert was alive with sounds, nightbirds, insects, and creatures that slithered and crawled. Josie listened to every noise, cautious lest she be captured by bandidos or Indians. Hearing a soft thud behind her, she tightened her hold on the horse's reins and reached for her gun.

"Josie, don't shoot. It's me." Rafe's voice.

"It's about time," she answered, not bothering to hide her sigh of relief.

Rafe and Josie had left during the cover of night, their destination Rafe's ranch house near Willcox in Cochise County. Putting his patients in the care of Dr. Jefferson Colby, a retired doctor in his sixties, and putting out the word that he had prescribed for himself a restful vacation, Rafe had ridden out of Showlow ahead of Josie. Artfully avoiding detection, she followed his trail to catch up with him at this appointed meeting place, a deserted adobe hut in the desert outside Showlow.

"How far now, doc?" She was eager to get where they were going so that she could get out of the saddle.

"If we ride all night without stopping we should be there by early daybreak," he answered, taking quick note of how she sat in her saddle as easily as any man. In the shadows he could see that the faded blue cotton shirt and tight-fitting denims she wore graced her soft curves and the slender lines of her legs. In the dark her long hair tumbled over her shoulders, looking like dark burnished gold. She made an enchanting silhouette.

"Then let's get going." Josie intended to keep her promise to match Rafe Gardner's horsemanship. Feeling pride in herself, she managed quite well as their horses galloped along, despite the fact that he had set for them a grueling pace.

"Do you want to rest?" he called out several times, turning in his saddle.

"Rest? No." Her answer was always the same, although that her backside ached and every muscle in her body soon throbbed. But admit it? Not on your life. She'd show him, she vowed, and show him she did. In the end it was Rafe who stopped, supposedly to check the constellations to determine their position.

The pause was all too brief. Soon returning to their hectic pace, Josie was certain that her bones had been shaken out of their sockets and that she would never again be able to sit down. As the sun came up, however, she thought to herself that it was worth it. From the hill the red-tiled rooftops of Willcox proclaimed they had arrived.

As if Josie couldn't see that for herself, Rafe proclaimed, "We're here!"

At last, she thought but didn't say. Instead, she reined her mount to a halt, stretched wearily in the saddle, and took off her hat as she took a look around. Although the ranches in the hills and valleys near Willcox were said to be notorious as refuges for fugitive gunslingers, the town itself seemed quiet.

Combing her fingers through her hair and wiping the smudges from her face, she at last allowed herself to relax. But not for long. Nudging her horse down the slope, Josie felt compelled to issue a challenge. "Last one into town is a sour apple!" she called over her shoulder, heading toward the first of the adobe buildings.

"You're on."

Horses' hooves clopping over the hard-packed dirt street, saddles creaking, they rode. To Rafe's dismay, it was he who came in last. Easing his horse up beside her, he couldn't help but notice the subtle hint of mischief in her eyes and the corners of her upturned mouth. Well, at least she was smiling. The first such expression he had seen since he'd angered her.

Alas, it was the last smile he was to see for a while. As they rode through the wide, dirt-packed streets lined with adobe buildings and cactus, she remained tight-lipped and silent. Rafe wondered if she would ever forgive him for what he had done.

"My ranch is just west of town. You can settle down to a hot bath and some breakfast once we reach it."

A bath! Food. As they made their way through

the streets, pausing only long enough for Rafe to get food and supplies from the general store, that was all Josie had on her mind. It was hard to ignore the gnawing in her stomach or the aching that went to her very bones. As a matter of fact, she was even too exhausted to be peeved at Rafe. She would wait until after breakfast to rekindle that annoyance.

"We're almost there, Josie," Rafe assured her, troubled by her lack of conversation. "I swear it."

Following a rough dirt road out of town, passing under the poles and crossbar that marked the entrance to the Lazy Z Ranch, Rafe proved that he was true to his word. Squinting against the sun, Josie could see a plastered adobe house marked at each end with a chimney. Small but charming, it had carved doors, iron grillwork, and a balconied walkway around the second-story gallery.

"Just tie your horse to one of those trees over there," Rafe suggested, heading toward the only two cottonwoods they'd seen for quite a while. "I don't have a stable." He laughed. "Or a barn, or cattle, or much of anything, I'm afraid. I'm just too busy to do any work around here. But my dream is to one day hang up my shingle and stay right here."

That Rafe had neglected the place was apparent the moment Josie stepped inside. Not only was the ranch house's furniture covered with a powdery red dust, but the rooms smelled musty.

"I told you I didn't spend much time here," Rafe apologized, coming up behind her. Taking off his bandanna, he hastily dusted off the furniture in their path as they walked through the rooms. He nodded toward the stairs. "The guest room is to the left at the head of the steps. Why don't you go and freshen up while I brew us some coffee and fry some bacon and eggs."

"I will," Josie said softly, adding over her shoulder, "thank you."

Trudging tiredly up the steps, Josie pushed open the door, pleased the moment she saw the little room. There was a patchwork quilt on the brass bed, a dresser, a padded brown leather chair, and a window that overlooked the small town. Taking off her hat and throwing it on the bed, tossing her carpetbag on the chair, she was certain she would be comfortable here. There was even an oval-shaped mirror that revealed her appearance from head to toe.

"Ohh, I look horrible." Worse yet, she smelled of horses.

Making herself at home, Josie wandered down the stairs and out the back door, searching for the bathhouse. Finding it, she hastily built a fire in the stove so she could heat some water, then searched about for the tub. She found it resting in the corner, a huge brass one.

"And the soap." Having learned a trick from the laundry, Josie picked up a sharp rock, powdering some of the soap. Once she added the warm water, it made an enticing bubble bath. Quickly stripping off her clothes, Josie eased herself down into the depths, sighing as her aching body was submerged. Picking up the soap, she scrubbed her body and lathered her hair, washing off the grime, then she leaned back. Closing her eyes, she didn't mean to fall asleep, but as the soothing womb of wetness enfolded her, she just couldn't help herself.

Searching all around for her, it was in the tub that Rafe found her, snoring so softly, it sounded like a sigh. "Oh, Josie." His eyes were gentle as they touched upon her. Asleep she looked almost as innocent as a child. And beautiful. But hardly childlike as he came closer and let his eyes roam over her womanly curves and long legs that seemed to go on forever. Curves he had felt beneath his hand in the dark of night but which were lovely beyond compare in the daylight.

A tremor ran through him as he let his eyes feast on her ivory skin, lingering on the perfectly formed breasts that peeked through the bubbles. He wanted to reach out to her, let his hands mold the round fullness, massage the dark-tipped peaks.

Rafe could hear his own rasping breath as he bent down. He wanted to touch her, to know every intimate part of her, to slide his fingers inside her as he had while they were making love. Instead, he simply reached into the water, picked her up in his arms, and pulled her from the tub, cradling her wet body against his shirt.

"Mmm." With a sigh she leaned her head against him, her arms encircling his neck of their own volition.

For an endless moment Rafe gloried in the closeness of their bodies, feeling somehow that it was in his arms that she belonged. He clamped her to him, fighting against his desperate hunger, breathing hard into her hair. Then with resolve he kicked open the door and headed back toward the house.

her full image in the dresser-stand mirror, my so-... her hard lips, her ruffled hair... *she* with a voice she sucked open the door and darted back toward the ...

Seventeen

Josie stirred in her sleep, dreaming that she lay naked beneath a tall cottonwood tree whose cool leaves were floating down around her. Leaves that felt so good against her skin. Leaves that were covering her now.

"Ahhh."

Stretching, she moved, glorying in the feeling of floating down with the leaves. Floating. Falling. Whirling dizzily back to earth. Back to Rafe.

Rafe!

Josie snapped awake instantly, turning her head. Out of habit she expected the window to be to the right; instead, it was to the left. "Where . . ." Startled, she sat up, watching as a breeze ruffled the curtains. She was puzzled and confused for a moment, but then she remembered. She was at Rafe's ranch. In his guest room. But how? The last thing she remembered was falling asleep.

"Naked in the tub!" But she wasn't naked now. Her nightshirt covered her slender figure. Had Rafe put it on? Or had she walked upstairs in her sleep? Oh, what did it matter? Certainly she could hardly pretend to be virtuous or shy after what had happened between them.

Trying to put it out of her mind, Josie luxuri-ated in the cool feel of sheets, the softness of the mattress. After all those hours sitting in the saddle, it felt good to relax. But what time was it? A clock chiming away the hour answered her question. It was four.

"I've slept away the day." But after having rid-den all night, she couldn't really fault herself.

"Josie."

Slowly she sat up, looking toward the door where Rafe stood.

"Good, you're up."

He said her name again, his eyes taking in her pert prettiness, remembering how he had carried her upstairs, tugged the nightshirt over her head, then buttoned every button. Placing her softly on the bed, he had wanted so to lie down beside her. But he hadn't. And he wouldn't.

"I guess I must have been tired." Somehow it seemed like an admission of weakness, thus she frowned.

"I was too. I slept until about fifteen minutes ago." He stepped inside the room but purposefully stayed away from the bed. "You missed breakfast, but there's dinner. Stew."

"I'm famished." She cocked her head, suddenly asking, "Are you a good cook?"

"Passable. Usual bachelor fare."

"Oh." The way he said it sounded so lonely that for a moment she felt sympathetic, until she re-membered the way the women in the laundry had chattered. If Dr. Rafe Gardner wasn't married, it surely must be his own fault. Particularly if he proposed to anyone else the way he had proposed to her. Even now the memory bothered her.

Rafe recognized her expression. Trying to distract her from her thoughts, he took two apples from a basket on the dresser. "Here, catch!"

Though taken by surprise, Josie caught each one. Rubbing the ripest on her shirt, she started to take a bite, thinking of it as an appetizer.

"No."

"No?"

Rafe laughed. "Those aren't for eating but for practice."

"For practice." She looked at him as if he'd lost his mind. "I said I wanted to be a gunfighter, not a juggler."

"Gunfighters have to have strong fingers." Picking up an apple, he clutched at it, then relaxed his fingers, then clutched the apple again. "Go ahead. Do it."

Josie did, soon finding it monotonous. "There," she said, "that ought to be enough."

"Enough?" He shook his head. "I want you to do that fifty times."

"Fifty times a day?"

"Fifty times every waking hour. That is if you are serious about wanting to be a dead shot with a gun." Opening the dresser drawer, he brought forth a piece of paper and a pencil, hastily scribbling. When he was finished he handed it to her. "Read it."

She did.

1. Always shoot first and never miss.
2. Squeeze trigger, don't pull it.

3. Never try to run a bluff—a six-shooter is made to kill.

4. Try to hit your man first where his belt buckle would be—that's the broadest target from head to heel.

5. Never try to shoot the other man in the head.

6. If you point at something, don't raise your finger to a level of the eye and sight along it. Simply point by instinct and your finger will always point straight.

7. Learn to point the barrel of a six-gun by instinct.

"Memorize everything I've written," Rafe exclaimed. "I won't even start you on your lessons until you do."

"Memorize it." Josie looked disgusted. "I feel as if I'm in some silly schoolroom."

Folding his arms across his chest, he looked every inch the stern schoolteacher. "You are. The only thing is that here there is much more at stake than just grades." His tone was harsh. "Your life."

"Okay. Okay. I get it." She put her chest to her knees, her voice singsongy. "When you shoot, pray; when they shoot, duck. Draw carefully and aim well. Fast is important, but not so much as a good, steady shot. How's that?"

"It's a beginning. But only that. You've got some hard work ahead of you, Josie. That is, if you were serious about wanting to be fast on the draw."

This time her attitude was one of seriousness. "I was." Just to prove to her how much she had to learn, Rafe drew her into a "friendly" competition with empty guns right after dinner, a competition that Josie promptly lost.

"So." Her pride was wounded. She had thought she was much better with a gun than she actually was. No wonder she had so easily lost to Tanner. "I guess you are right. I guess I do have some hard work ahead." It was a sobering confession.

"Considering the fact that were I Clint Tanner, you could be dead right now, I would say that was an understatement." Putting his Remington back in his holster, Rafe came to her side, touching her on the shoulder. A touch that passed like sparks between them. He pulled back. "Starting tomorrow, I want you to be up, dressed, and ready for our lessons at five o'clock."

"Five?" That was even earlier than she had had to be at the laundry. "That's even before the sun is up."

Rafe grinned. "Precisely."

The days that followed were busy, so filled with learning and remembering and trying to put into practice everything Rafe instructed that Josie was exhausted by the end of the day, both mentally and physically. Why, just practicing the many exercises he had set up to strengthen her legs, arms, hands, and fingers was strenuous work. In some ways more so.

"I'm going to have the strongest fingers in Arizona Territory," she quipped, squeezing, then releasing the rocks in her hands that had replaced the apples. "Or the sorest." She looked at Rafe, disappointed by his lack of reply to her remark. He was acting so strange, so cold, so unemotional. Like an army sergeant.

"I want you to use smaller and smaller rocks every day, until they are merely pebbles" was all he proclaimed.

Later that morning Rafe tied a lead weight to one end of a short, thin hemp rope and a big stick to the other, making it into a sort of pulley. Holding the stick one hand at each end, Josie was to slowly pull the weight upward by rolling the rope around the stick, then reverse the procedure by unrolling the rope. Easy, until she had done it time after time after time.

"You seem to have gotten the hang of it," Rafe said, noticing that she had improved but careful not to give her too much praise. "Now, how about some knee-bends and arm exercises?"

Josie's expression was sour. "When can I shoot?" She was growing impatient. As of yet, she hadn't even picked up a gun.

"If I've told you once, I've told you again and again," he said sternly, "not until you're ready!"

"Ready?" Dropping the lead weight on the ground, she bit back the words she wanted to say, but asked, "And just when will that be?"

"When you've learned all the rules, selected the right firearm, one that will be appropriate for your finger strength and the size of your hand, and when you have learned how to handle a gun safely."

"Safely?"

"Yes, safely. There is more to being a gunslinger

than just pointing the weapon and firing." He demonstrated, loading only five cartridges in the rotating chamber of the Remington he held in his hand.

"Why just five?" Josie was curious.

"To guard against shooting yourself in the foot," he explained, letting the hammer down on an empty chamber. He told her that the practice had begun after a gunfighter named Clay Allison had maimed himself that way while practicing his draw. "Take care in loading. Unless you are careful, Josie, you could injure yourself. Guns can misfire. A bullet can even set off a chain reaction of shells in the adjoining chamber."

"Oh." It irritated her that Rafe had somehow made her feel foolish.

"Now, once again, what are the rules?"

Feeling like a little girl in the schoolhouse, she repeated them. "Always shoot first and never miss. Squeeze the trigger, don't pull it. Never try to run a bluff— a six-shooter is made to kill. Try to hit your man first where his belt buckle would be— that's the broadest target from head to heel. Never try to shoot the other man in the head. If you point at something, don't raise your finger to a level of the eye and sight along it; simply point by instinct and your finger will always point straight. Learn to point the barrel of a six-gun by instinct."

Rafe added a new one. "Never pull the trigger unless you are aiming at *something*, Josie."

"Of course!" She couldn't help but be sarcastic. "In other words, don't shoot into the wind." She mumbled beneath her breath, "What do you take me for, a fool?" Oh, what silly nonsense. But nonsense or not, she had to humor him if she wanted to learn from him.

"I'm serious, Josie. Guns can kill the innocent as well as those you have judged to be guilty. All by accident." Taking note of her expression, he added, "Bullets can ricochet."

"Okay. Okay." Wiping her hands on her trousers, Josie set about doing the knee-bends Rafe had prescribed. He was right about one thing. If a person wanted to do anything really well, they had to be physically strong. "Up, down, up, down. One, two, one, two." Life really was the survival of the fittest.

Look at her, so determined. So stubborn. So all-fire sure she can do anything. Nonetheless, Rafe had to admire her resolve, her determination never to give up despite the fact that it had been his purpose to deflate her ego. There was just no humbling Josie. But then, he should have known that.

And yet how he wished that just once she would act more like a woman. Flirt a little, show a little softness. Though he had tried to put it out of his mind, Rafe couldn't forget about the night they had made love, nor the vision of seductiveness she was lying naked in the bathtub. He fantasized about her during the day and dreamed about her at night. His bed was lonely, more so knowing that she was right across the hall, her bedroom door only a few feet away.

Josie too remembered. It was one of the reasons she chose to work so hard. At least it got her through the day and left her too bone-weary at night to think about it. But not to dream. Dreams that left her feeling unfulfilled and empty.

All the while Rafe pushed her harder and harder, whether to discourage her and make her give up or to force her into perfection, she just wasn't certain. All that she did know was that it was rough going, hard work, discouraging more often than not. Still, she wouldn't give up. She tried to be patient. She learned. And all the while she waited, she secretly longed for the feel of his arms.

Eighteen

The sign on the door read JEREMIAH CARLETON, GUNSMITH. As Josie followed Rafe through the door, she was elated. At last. The time had come that she had been looking forward to. First to find the right gun, and then the fun would begin.

"Rafe!" The man behind the counter bounded over to him the minute they passed the threshold. "You old son of a gun!" The tall, thin, gray-haired and mustached man patted him on the shoulder. "Where have you been keeping yourself?"

"In Showlow mostly." Rafe's gaze was centered on the display case that had row after row of firearms.

"Oh, still a lot a trouble from gunfighters? I suppose you're busy just patching up bullet holes," the gunsmith said.

Thinking about why they were there, Josie cringed and absentmindedly rubbed her just-healed arm.

"No, things have settled down a lot since last we spoke. Except for an incident or two," Rafe looked straight at Josie. "The most excitement we've had has been the birth of Ellis Andrews's triplets."

"Oh, well, things have heated up here. Smuggler's Trail isn't too far away, as you know. And then there's Tombstone."

"Ah, yes. The town too tough to die."

"We get a lot of floaters in town sometimes." Jeremiah Carleton shrugged. "But otherwise it's peaceful." He paused. "But, say, just what brings you into town?"

It was then that Rafe introduced Josie. "Jeremiah, meet Josie Smith. She's, uh . . . a friend of mine. A friend looking for a gun to protect her."

"Oh." Holding out his hand, taking hers in a firm handshake, the gunsmith looked her up and down, his smile saying that she met his approval.

"So, I was thinking about a short-barreled Peacemaker, point forty-five, scroll engraved. The one with the four-and-a-quarter-inch barrel."

"The Peacemaker, huh. I understand a lot of gunfighters prefer its easy handling, so I think it would be just right for the young lady." Going to the display case, he brought the requested gun. "Try this." He handed it to Josie. "It's the gun most likely to be whipped from holsters, waistbands, or coats."

Hefting the gun in her hand, Josie tried it out and was impressed. It was lighter than the other one she had, easier to handle. Was it any wonder, then, that she eagerly handed over her other gun, an old Starr double action, to Jeremiah Carleton to use in trade as a down payment?

"Wait, Josie." Rafe held up his hand. "I want you to be sure."

Jeremiah Carleton brought out a case of guns of

various shapes and sizes. Smith & Wessons, Colts, Remingtons, and a Winchester or two. There were pistols and revolvers galore. Some had wooden handles, some had pearl handles, some even had engraving. They were long-barreled, short-barreled, and some in between. Bending over the case, Josie slowly and carefully assessed each one, at last picking up a long-barreled Smith & Wesson Schofield.

"Ah-ha. That model was said to be Jesse James's choice," the gunsmith exclaimed. "That forty-five caliber lifts a man right off his feet." He smiled serenely. "But then, you being a lady and all wouldn't care much about that."

"Oh, yes, I would." Picking it up, Jesse toyed with the hammer. "If you're going to do something, you might as well do it right."

"Oh, a woman with spirit!" He winked at Rafe. "Maybe just the woman to match you."

"Maybe." Looking down, Rafe centered his attention on a Colt single action Army Target model, basically the same as the Peacemaker except for its seven-and-a-half-inch-long barrel. Oh, she was spirited all right. So much so, he doubted she could ever really be tamed. Perhaps that was why she so intrigued him, he thought.

"What about this?" Josie picked up a Remington Frontier .44. She liked the grip and the hammer, but Rafe shook his head, saying that its balance was judged to be inferior to the Peacemaker he had in mind.

Though Rafe put his hand on the short-barreled Peacemaker .45 that Josie had first favored, she stubbornly searched on. It was as if, in this way, she wanted to defy him, wanted to have a say in something. Up to this moment he had made all the decisions.

"How about this Peacemaker with a cutaway trigger guard?" Jeremiah explained that the cutaway modification saved the shooter a split second in reaching the trigger. "Or this Frontier double action forty-five."

"Let me see." Josie was interested, but again Rafe shook his head. "Why?"

"The double action means that squeezing the trigger performs the double duty of drawing back the hammer, then releasing it. But this makes it less accurate."

Josie almost told him that she wanted it anyway, but some gut feeling told her not to make that choice. Once again she picked up the short-barreled Peacemaker, fingering its pearl handle and intricate scroll engravings on the chamber and the barrel. It seemed to suit her somehow. "This."

"I'll get the ammunition while you settle with Jeremiah," Rafe said, strolling to the case containing cartridges.

Buying the gun, even with her other gun in exchange, cost Josie nearly every penny. Was it worth it? Thinking of Charlie, she quickly answered yes, although somehow it seemed some of the anger inside her had died. Now, why was that? Rafe? Or some other reason. She shrugged the question off, sticking her new purchase in her holster to make certain that it would fit. It did. Perfectly.

"Okay, next lesson." Coming up behind her,

Rafe's body brushed hers as he touched her shoulders, turning her sideways. "When someone is aiming at you, turn like this, not full-bodied. That way you aren't as big a target."

"As if anyone would want to shoot at anyone as pretty as her," Jeremiah Carleton complimented.

"Oh, you'd be surprised." Rafe stuffed the bullets he had purchased into his saddlebag, engaging in a little man talk with Jeremiah. Conversation about politics, who had won what at gambling, who had made a fortune in the mines, and whispers about the latest "girls" in Madame Annie's brothel. That last talk really got on Josie's nerves. Maybe that was why she walked to the window.

Out of the corner of her eye, she saw a shadow making a wild dash for the gunsmith's. "Rafe! Come here." A gut feeling told her something was wrong.

Then it all happened quickly. She saw the man go for his gun, knew instinctively that there was going to be trouble. When the man burst into the gunshop, his guns pointed at Rafe and Jeremiah, she knew she was right.

"Up against the wall!"

As he held Rafe and his friend at bay, Josie looked on in horror. The man appeared to be a desperado, out to steal guns and ammunition. The problem was the way he was acting seemed to insinuate that someone just might get seriously hurt in the meantime, that someone being Rafe.

"Say, don't I know you?" Something in his tone told her he recognized the doctor, but not from the point of view of a patient.

"I don't know."

"I do! The gunfighter. You're Bat Masterson's and Wyatt Earp's friend."

"Not anymore." Rafe's tone was stern. "I'm a doctor now."

"Doctor." The gunman guffawed. "Good ploy, but I don't believe you." His stance was threatening. "From what I remember, you have quite a reputation. I ought to make quite a little reputation for myself by shooting you."

Josie stifled her outburst with her hand. "Oh, no!" The man was strutting around, threatening to kill Rafe. Josie was determined to do what she could, which appeared to be fairly easy considering the fact that because she was a woman the man wasn't bothering to train his guns on her. He didn't even seem to notice that she was wearing a holster and a gun. A gun whose chambers were empty, however.

Never try to run a bluff. A six-shooter is made to kill, she remembered. It dissuaded her from whipping out her empty gun and training it on the man. But if she had bullets . . .

Slyly, stealthily, she slid her hand into the ammunition case while the man was occupied in badgering Rafe. Remembering which bullets Rafe had chosen, she grabbed a handful, stuffing them hastily in the gun's rotating chamber.

"You there. What are you doing?"

Josie's heart hammered as she coyly put her hand behind her back. "Nothing." *Always shoot first and never miss. Try to hit your man first where his belt buckle would be. Squeeze, don't pull the trigger.* Rafe's words haunted her. Then with a speed that amazed herself she pulled her gun forward.

"Josie. No!" Rafe's heart was in his throat as he looked on. The little fool was going to get killed! But she got off a shot before the man even had time to aim at her. A shot that punched him up against the wall. Slowly he slid down to the floor.

"Oh, my God!" Josie was stunned. "Is he dead?" Unthinking, she whispered, "Someone call a doctor."

Rushing forward, Rafe reminded her over his shoulder, "That's what *I* am." He kneeled down to examine the man. "No, he's not dead. You got him in the stomach, Josie, but I don't think you hit anything vital. I think he'll survive."

"You know who that is, Rafe?" Jeremiah Carleton, kneeling down beside the doctor, seemed stunned. "That's Sam Wade! He's wanted all the way from Arizona Territory to Kansas City. A mean kind of killer. Pure trouble." He looked at Josie in surprise. "And she nailed him."

"Which only goes to prove Miss Smith is far from shy and retiring," Rafe exclaimed. Then, worried that Josie might get a swelled head, he was quick to say, "She got off a lucky shot, that's all." He addressed his next comment to her. "I wouldn't want to try it again were I you. You still have a lot to learn."

"No doubt I do." Josie was peeved at his lack of appreciation. Undoubtedly she had just saved Rafe's life, but the damned fool wouldn't let his stubborn pride admit it. Far be it from him to say thank-you. Still, as they left Jeremiah's store, Rafe looked at her with newfound respect.

Nineteen

Strange, Josie thought, how quickly a person can settle into a routine: up before the sun, then breakfast, target practice at bottles, tin cans, and scarecrows, lessons, lunch, lessons, dinner, and more lessons. A routine that might have been monotonous and wearisome had it not been for the teacher. Far from being bored with it all, Josie had to admit that she found herself looking forward to her instruction.

Because I want be the best gunfighter around, she told herself, remembering the dangerous encounter with the man she had shot in the gunshop. But no, not entirely. It was being in Rafe's company. To put it simply, she liked being with him, despite the fact that he could often be stern, curt, and unyielding. Somehow, beneath it all, she realized it was just a cover-up for his true feelings. She had seen his eyes appraising her when he thought she wasn't looking, a slight smile upon his lips. No, he certainly was not indifferent to her. It was all an act. He seemed always to be watching her. She could never escape his eyes.

"Rafe's eyes tell me he hasn't forgotten."

For that matter, neither had she. During the

days they had been together at the ranch each of them had been on guard, watching what they said and how they looked at each other. Though they had talked, neither one had mentioned that passionate night, yet with each glance it was obvious to see that it had not been forgotten.

Rising from the bed, Josie tugged off her nightshirt, thinking about the situation as she slipped into her undergarments. There was a wall between them, a wall that she had helped to erect by her reaction to Rafe's proposal of marriage. Her pride had been stung by his gesture of obvious guilt and thus she had rightfully scorned him, yet perhaps she had scorned him too well. The truth was, she wanted him to admire her, to find her attractive, to make love to her again.

Padding on her bare feet to the dresser, she poured water into the basin, splashing it onto her face, then, picked up her hairbrush and ran it through her hair twenty times. Instead of putting her luxuriant waves into braids as usual, she decided to let her hair hang free today. And her clothes. Instead of her old blue shirt, she'd wear her green shirt today, the one Rafe had pointed out in the general store that day in Showlow. Laughing softly, she remembered that he had said the shirt matched her eyes, a rare compliment.

"Well, we'll see what he thinks today," she said to her image in the mirror as she buttoned up the shirt, then slipped into her tight-fitting denims. Tugging on her boots, she was in a particularly cheery mood as she hurried down the stairs to the kitchen.

"Good morning." Without turning around, Rafe poured coffee into two cups, then set them on the table. He reached for a bisquit on the plate, then, as he buttered it, said, "I think we'll have a mock shoot-out today."

"To see if I can get the drop on you?" Josie hefted a bisquit in her hand, thinking to herself that it was as hard as one of the rocks she used to exercise her fingers. Oh, well. She was hungry.

"Precisely." It was at that moment that he looked up, his eyes widening a bit as he saw her. He liked her hair hanging down her back that way, but it certainly made it impossible for him to forget she was a woman. And her eyes. What was it about them today that made him feel as if he could drown in their depths?

"Then I'll do my best."

Though Rafe didn't utter one word of flattery, Josie knew that her efforts this morning hadn't been all in vain. That thought made her feel a warm glow deep inside as she watched him finish his breakfast. She, likewise, assessed him. The red and black plaid shirt looked good with his dark hair. His blue denims clung to his long, muscular legs. He looked virile. More like a cowboy or ranch hand than a doctor.

"That . . . that man I shot. What happened to him? Has he recovered yet? Have you heard?"

Rafe felt the thud of his heart against his throat as he remembered the incident. Foolishly brave girl, she could have been killed. The very thought nudged him with a strong urge to protect her, to watch over her, to hold her in his arms. Instead, all he said was "The doctor in Willcox patched him up, then turned him over to the law."

"Oh." Without even bothering to sit down, Josie dipped her bisquit into her cup of black coffee to soften it, then hurried to finish eating. Today was the day she had waited for. She and Rafe were finally going to get down to real gunplay, not just tomfoolery. And, oh, how she wanted just once to hear him give her praise. "Well, let's get on with it."

The "gunfight" took place in the field behind the bathhouse. It was a level piece of ground that was rockless, grassless, and treeless. A perfect place, Rafe had said. There would be nothing to distract her. Nothing to look at but her "quarry." And *his* shadow.

"Look there, Josie," Rafe said, pointing it out, "and remember not to look at a man's shadow again. Shadows are a false picture of the target. Look at the *man.*" He explained that most experienced gunfighters preferred a shoot-out at noon, when there was no shadow. On the other hand, at sunset a man's shadow was the longest and most distracting.

"Got it. Don't look at the shadow." Clenching and unclenching her hand, Josie was eager to get on with it, eager to show him just how good she could be.

"Right!" He offered another reminder. "Draw for accuracy first, then for speed. It doesn't matter that you get your gun out first if you miss."

"Yeah. Yeah." Josie felt her hands sweat. Edgy, and a bit ill at ease now that the moment was here;

she wiped her hands on her pants. A gnawing desire to succeed made her suddenly self-conscious.

"Okay, get ready." Rafe took note of the gleam of anticipation in her eyes, her self-assured stance. And her softly rounded breasts that moved up and down beneath her shirt as she breathed. "On the count of three."

"The count of three." Josie took a deep breath, then licked her lips. Lips whose fullness Rafe couldn't help but notice, remembering how they had felt beneath his own. He shook his head, forcing such thoughts out of his head.

For a moment they both stood as if frozen. Then he began to count. "One, two."

Josie began to walk, her strut bringing her closer and closer. She stopped when Rafe waved his hands all around.

"Stop!"

"What?" her voice was shrill.

"For God's sake, Josie. Don't get so close. It's true it makes your opponent a bigger and easier target, but the same is true for you!" He demonstrated, moving slowly and deliberately in a measured tread, staying a careful distance away. "Do it like this."

"Like so?" She mimicked him, drawing his attention to her waist, legs, and hips.

"Yes." She was an eye-catching sight. Well-shaped bottom, long legs, a waist a man could span with his hands. Rafe found himself imagining how that gently curving body had looked undressed. "Try it again," he said curtly, only by sheer willpower detaching his mind from her appearance. "One, two, three."

It happened, and happened quickly. Josie went for her Peacemaker, but Rafe's Remington cleared its leather holster in an instant. "Bang!" He looked into her flashing eyes.

Josie realized she had lost. She had been an instant too late in her draw. Thrusting her gun back in its holster, she cursed. "Damn!"

"If I had been Tanner, you would have been dead."

Putting her hands over her ears, she said, "I know. I know. I know." She read his mind. "But I won't give up." She stayed in her rigid, challenging stance as he moved toward her, but he noted a glimmer of uncertainty in those pretty green eyes. "You can put that out of your head."

Rafe growled low in his throat. "I didn't suppose that you would."

He knew just where she had made her mistake. The gun had to be grasped by its handle with the wrist twisted downward while the finger reached down at a forty-five-degree angle for the trigger. At the same time the thumb cocked the hammer. In that way a man could draw, cock, and fire all in one smooth, lightning-quick movement.

"Come let me show you something."

Her walk was slower as she came toward him. Rafe noted that some of her poise and self-confidence had left her. But not for long. Within moments she had bounced back.

"Okay, show me."

There was no way around it. Rafe had to put

his arm around her as he demonstrated, his fingers brushing hers. "See." As he drew in his breath, he inhaled the fresh, sweet scent of soap on her skin and hair. A fragrance that was more stirring than any perfume.

She felt the entire length of him pressing against her. "Umm-hmm." Her breath caught in her throat. It felt so good to have him touch her again, to feel his warm breath on the back of her neck.

"You draw in one smooth action." He drew her closer and closer, marveling in the lithe firmness of her body. He felt her tremble.

"Smooth action," she repeated. Liquid fire traveled through her. She felt a deep yearning, a need.

What would she do if I took her chin in my hand, raised her face to mine, and kissed her? He wanted to. Instead, he pulled back.

"I think you get the picture." His jaw tensed. His tone was impersonal.

"I do." She felt isolated, forsaken, without the nearness of him, but she didn't show it. Indeed, she acted as if the matter of their touching so intimately was merely business. "And I thank you for showing me."

"You're welcome." He looked down at his Remington, toying with the handle, yet even that distraction couldn't quench the hungry aching he felt just to be near her. That was why he announced abruptly. "That's all for today."

"That's all?" Josie had just begun. She couldn't hide her disappointment. "Why?"

"I have some things to do." He started off toward the ranch house.

"What about me?"

He unbuckled his gun belt and slung it over his shoulder. "Practice what I just showed you. And . . . shoot at some bottles."

"Bottles!" She was taken aback. "I've shot at bottles until I'm cross-eyed."

"Shoot at some more. I really don't care." All he wanted was to get away. Far away from her to a place where he could think.

Twenty

Rafe rode at a furious pace toward Willcox. As fast as if the devil were on his heels, he thought. Only this devil had long blond hair. He muttered beneath his breath, something about his stupidity. Why in hell had he ever agreed to this witless, senseless, muddle-headed, asinine agreement to teach Josie Smith how to be a gunfighter? What had possessed him?

I fell for a woman's wiles. A pair of green eyes. A smile. Dimples. A pair of perfectly formed breasts. Long legs, he chided himself mockingly. It had been lust, pure and simple. The most soul-stirring sex he'd had in a long, long while. An experience that must have made him totally lose his head. How else could he explain it? And from a virgin, no less. One who had played his sense of nobility for all it was worth.

Oh, yes, Josie Smith had gotten exactly what she was after. She had demanded, asked, and pleaded. By her own admission, when that hadn't worked, she'd thought of another plan. And he, fool that he was, had fallen right into the trap. But had he learned? No. Just that morning he'd been so hot for her that he hadn't even been able to keep his hands to himself. So much for his self-control.

Taking the long way into town in the hope of coming to terms with his frustration, Rafe did a lot of thinking. Though he wanted to place all the blame for what had happened on Josie, he knew that part of it rested on his own shoulders. Oh, yes. The moment she had tried to shoot Tanner he had known she could be trouble. Even so, he had allowed himself to become more and more involved with her, more tangled in her life, more personally involved than he should have been. He had even taken her to his quarters over his office, for God's sake. Was it any wonder the inevitable had happened? And it would happen again.

Oh, no, it wouldn't. Why? Because he recognized the feelings he had for Josie for what they were. Bodily hunger, that was all. He had worked too hard, kept himself too isolated, pushed away from his sexual appetites too often. When she had come upon the scene he had been without a woman too long. Well, he wouldn't make that mistake again.

When a man is hungry, he eats, he mused; when he's thirsty, he quenches his thirst, and when a man wants a woman, there are always women more than ready to comply. Women who would not bring with them a tangle of problems. Women with whom spending a night wouldn't get complicated.

"Yes, indeed." By the time he had reached Willcox, tethered his horse, and was walking toward the Red Rider Saloon, it had all become very simple.

"Help you?" The mustached man behind the bar greeted him like a friend.

"A whiskey." He relished the bite to his tongue and the blessed oblivion the drink brought to his head as he swallowed glass after glass.

"Careful, buddy." Withholding the bottle, the bartender wasn't so friendly anymore. "You don't want to end up in the bull pen."

"The bull pen?" It was a high-board fence adjacent to the rear exit of the saloon, where overly rowdy customers were sometimes put until they sobered up. "Naw." He shook his head. "I'm fine. Just fine. Just need a woman, that's all." The trouble was, it was *that* woman. Somehow the heat she had ignited could not be denied.

"A woman!" A pretty, tall, red-haired saloon girl dressed all in emerald green was more than willing to answer his request. Taking his arm, she led Rafe upstairs. "Just what do you like?"

Taking off his shirt, he grinned evilly. "The works!" He reached into his pocket and started to put a gold piece in her hand just to insure that it was the best. He dropped it.

"Sure. Sure." Bending over, she offered him a view of her ample décolletage. "Just lie down on the bed."

Rafe did, eyeing her up and down all the while. Her skin was smooth, the color of dark cream, her body curved in all the right places. The legs covered by black lace stockings were long. She was plump and pretty, the kind of companion who could make any man forget for a while.

"Come on over. Let's get acquainted," he said, slurring his words. When she did, he noticed her long, dark lashes, the mouth covered with pink.

The strong scent of lilacs emanated from her skin. A harsh contrast to Josie's natural loveliness.

"So, hello!" Sitting on the bed, she boldly ran her hands over the smooth skin of his neck, moved down the muscles of his chest, tugging at his belt buckle.

"Damn!" All Rafe thought of all the while was the way Josie's fingers had felt on his skin. Soft. Cool.

"Relax. Just relax. Why, a lady just might think this was your first time," the red-haired woman cooed.

"Hardly," Rafe countered. Closing his eyes, he thought maybe that would block all thoughts of Josie out of his head. Instead, her face swam before his eyes. Laughing. Taunting. The little minx. That image of her played havoc with him, chilling any desires he might have had for another woman. As the evening progressed, it was proven so. The truth was, he couldn't feign desire. He didn't even want to try.

"Honey . . ." She cocked her head, a knowing look on her face. "A woman. You've got it real bad."

"Yeah." He turned over on his stomach. "Real bad." And nothing like it had ever happened to him before. Not such a strong longing. An ache that no other woman could fulfill.

"Well, she's lucky, whoever she is. You're a right handsome man." Reaching down at the foot of the bed, she grabbed a blanket and covered him over. "Hope she knows that."

"I don't think that she does," Rafe mumbled.

"Oh, I don't know. Women have a funny way of being stubborn sometimes. " She ruffled his hair. "And so do men." She laughed. "Sleep it off, sweetheart. Sleep it off. You might feel different in the morning." Without another word, she left Rafe all alone.

Twenty-one

Rafe didn't come back that night, an unusual occurrence that was cause for Josie's concern. Worse yet, he had ridden off without saying where he was going. Pacing her bedroom, looking out the door from time to time in the hope that he might have returned, Josie was surprised at how lonely it felt in the house without him. Utterly lonely, and miserable.

"Where is he? Why hasn't he come? What if something has happened?" He could have fallen off his horse, could have met with foul play in town. What if another gunfighter recognized him and went for his gun and she wasn't there to protect him? What if he were lying in an alley somewhere in Willcox?

Oh, listen to me, she thought. As if Dr. Rafe Gardner couldn't take care of himself. He was a strong, intelligent, and very capable man, not the kind of man who needed a keeper. It was just that she couldn't bear the idea of his being hurt. Or, worse yet, of not seeing him again. There was something about him that drew her, something that went beyond his good looks.

Oh, my God. He's becoming important to me! More

important than she wanted to admit. More important than she wanted to allow. She was starting to care about him. Really care. And that could be disastrous. It just wasn't the right moment for love. She had too many conflicting emotions in the way. Too many things yet to be done. Too much bitterness in her heart. Too much anger.

"I have Charlie's death still to avenge." As if to force herself to remember that vow, she moved toward the bedpost, running her hands along the holster and gun slung over it.

It has to be done. I have to keep up my courage and determination. Otherwise how can poor Charlie rest easily in his grave? And to avenge Charlie she needed Rafe Gardner. That was all it was. He knew all the ins and outs of guns, and she needed that knowledge.

Or was there something more? Her mind said no, but her heart, the very core of her being, said yes.

"Oh, bother!" she said aloud. Right from the first moment, Rafe had captured her imagination, her fascination. Why was it that life could be so complicated? She didn't want to give Rafe her heart, yet there were times when she sensed she was perilously close to doing just that.

Wrapping a blanket around her shoulders, she made her way down the stairs. She couldn't sleep anyway. Why not fix herself a cup of coffee? Strong. Black. Just the way Rafe always fixed it.

"Rafe." He was like a song whose refrain echoed over and over in her mind. She liked being with him. Admired him. Desired him. His very presence beside her did things to her body. Made it come alive. She was learning how powerful desire could be, and how frustrating. Her willpower seemed to slip when Rafe was near. But what about her emotions? How were they tied up with him?

I don't know. I just don't know.

Putting the coffeepot on the cast-iron stove, she watched as it it sputtered and bubbled. *And what about Rafe? How does he feel about me?* In some ways he was like her. Afraid of an emotional tie, afraid of the commitment that went with the heart's involvement. Yet surely he, like she, could see how perfectly their bodies were in tune.

The room was totally silent except for the rhythmic tick, tick, tick of the grandfather clock. Pouring herself a cup of fresh coffee, she looked into the dark depths as if into a crystal ball, wishing she could see into his heart, his mind.

Josie thought of the previous morning, remembering his nearness, and once again her emotions were turbulent. Coiled in her stomach was the familiar sweet ache she felt whenever she was with him. Closing her eyes, she tried to quench the stirring in her blood at the memory of his long-fingered hands touching hers, but the thought tormented her with yearning. For just a moment he had acted as if she were precious to him. . . .

Then something had gone wrong. Rafe had acted so strangely. One moment he was so near, the next moment he had pulled away. She searched her memory, trying to remember what could have triggered the change in him. Something she had said? Something she had done?

Oh, what did it matter? He was gone, and from the looks of it he wouldn't be back that night. Undoubtedly while he was in town he had been called upon to doctor somebody. Perhaps at this moment he was watching over his patient, or sleeping soundly beside him in a chair.

She yawned at the thought. It was past the time when she would be getting up to ready herself for her shooting lessons. It was nearly daylight. Nearly morning. Looking toward the window, she watched as pink shards of light disturbed the darkened sky, and it was at that moment that she saw his silhouette moving toward the door.

He's back! She met him at the door. "I was worried."

"You shouldn't have been." Rafe couldn't meet her eye. He felt somehow guilty, though he knew she had no hold on him.

"You rode off so fast, I thought someone had set a match to your horse's tail," she quipped, then, seeing that he didn't even smile, asked, "Where have you been?"

"Where?" Remembering the futility of his outing, he scowled and refused to answer her. A man had to keep some things to himself.

That he smelled like perfume, that his hair was messed up, that his clothing was wrinkled, seemed to answer her question. The good doctor had been bedding some woman. "Ohhh." And here she had worried about the bastard!

"Is there any coffee?" He raked his fingers through his hair, yawning.

"It's on the stove." She watched as he poured a

cup and cautiously sipped the steaming brew, then set it down.

Josie waited for his explanation of where he had been, but none was forthcoming, and this irritated her. She wondered what he would do if she decided to just come and go as she pleased instead of following his "rules' concerning the strict times for their lessons.

"Josie. . . ." Slowly he turned his head, looking at her, remembering the hot sweetness of her mouth, the glory of her breasts. He wanted to carry her upstairs, make love to her with wild abandon; instead, he said softly, "I think we should go back to Showlow."

"Go back?" It was the last thing she expected to hear. "Go back! Just like that?" She snapped her fingers.

"Yes, just like that." Before he did something he wanted to do but shouldn't. Being alone with her in this damned ranch house was inviting trouble.

"What's a matter, doc? Running away from an irate husband?" she asked, referring to his escapade of the evening.

He flushed but kept his poise. "Not at all. It's just that I think yesterday morning should have shown you that you just aren't ready for gunfighting. I got the draw on you. So would Tanner. Admit it and give up."

"Admit it?" She was so angry she nearly choked. "Never." She clenched her fists. "So that's it."

"That's what?" For just a moment he feared she could read his mind.

"I came closer to beating you at the draw this morning than you will admit. It stung your ego." Standing on tiptoe, she met him eye to eye. "You're afraid I'm going to be just as good as you. That's why you left this morning. You chickened out!"

"Chickened out?" The accusation was galling. "Hardly." Taking her by the shoulders, he started to tell her what he really thought, but suddenly it was the last thing on his mind. He thought of her lying naked in his arms, and once again desire engulfed him. His eyes darkened with passion as he lowered his mouth.

"Rafe. . . ." The touch of his mouth smothered any protest she might have made, then suddenly his lips were everywhere— her cheeks, her neck, her mouth, his tongue plunging deeply, insistently. Then he was sweeping her up in his arms and carrying her toward the stairs.

Sunlight streamed through the open curtains, casting shadows on the wall as Rafe made his way up the stairs with his struggling bundle. Kicking open his bedroom door, he made his way to the bed with Josie in his arms.

"What are you going to do?" A foolish question. She knew it the moment it was out of her mouth.

His eyes bored into hers as he laid her on the bed. "If you insist on continuing your foolishness, let's just say I'm calling in another 'payment.' "

"Oh!" She could have denied him had she wanted to, or said some cutting remark, but Josie merely closed her eyes.

Rafe's mouth was hungry as it took hers, plundering, moving urgently as he explored her mouth's sweetness. The pressure of the kiss should have hurt her, but it didn't. Instead, it drained her very soul, poured it back again, filling her to overflowing. Despite his anger, that kiss proved to her that he cared. It was not lust alone that fueled him, no matter how he might act to the contrary.

So thinking, she returned his kiss, her defenses devastatingly demolished by the cravings of her own body. There was nothing in the world for her but his mouth. She surrendered to him completely without even a token resistance, wishing the kiss could go on forever. If he wanted to dissuade her from her "foolishness" as he called it, he'd chosen the wrong penalty. Twining her hands around his neck, she clutched him to her, pressing her body eagerly against his chest. She could feel the heat and strength and growing desire of him with every breath.

Rafe pulled his mouth away, looking deep into her eyes. "Is there any medicine that can get you out of my system?"

"I don't think so. Nor do I think there is any to get you out of mine."

"Then just what are we to do?" His hands gently traced the curve of her neck and shoulders, moving downward.

"You're the doctor," she whispered, reaching out to touch his face. "What would you prescribe?"

"This," he said, molding his hand to her breast. "And this." Lifting up the hem of her nightshirt, he began a searching exploration, his fingers little more than a tickle on her taut abdomen. She felt the warmth of his fingers as they touched and caressed.

"Rafe. . . ." As his hands outlined the swell of her breasts, she sank into the softness of the feather mattress. The velvet coverlet beneath her was warm and soft, and she remembered that it was green, her favorite color. She remembered something else as well. "Last night. That perfume . . ."

"Upon my word, I did not make love to another woman, Josie. My thoughts were on you. . . ." His head was bent low, his tongue curling around the tip of her breast, sucking gently. She gave a breathless murmur of surprise and her body flamed with desire. She ached to be naked against him. Did that make her a wanton? Then so be it.

Rafe breathed deeply, savoring the scent of her hair. The enticing fragrance invaded his flaring nostrils, engulfing him. Damn. What had she done to him? The moment he had walked through that door he had been swept away by something stronger than mere lust, deeper by far than just desire.

"Josie. . . ." She seemed to be the answer to his loneliness, and yet she was also his torment. "I want you. . . ."

Raising himself up on his elbow, he looked down at her and at that moment he knew he'd put his heart and soul in pawn. Removing his shirt, he pressed their naked chests together, shivering at the sensation. The sensation was vibrantly arousing, sending a flash of quicksilver through his veins.

"I want you too. . . ." she moaned, and her body twisted beneath him.

His fingers lingered as they wandered down her stomach to explore the texture of her skin. Like velvet. He sought the indentation of her navel, then moved lower to tangle his fingers in the soft wisps of hair. Moving back, he let his eyes enjoy what his hands had set free.

"Do you have any idea how much I want you? Do you?" he breathed. Then he laughed. "Of course you do. Well, you've won. I'm putty in your hands." Swearing softly, he took her hand and pressed it to the firm flesh of his arousal. She felt the throbbing strength of him as her eyes gazed into his. Then he bent to kiss her, his mouth keeping hers a willing captive for a long, long time.

The warmth and heat of his lips, her fingers touching that private part of him, sent a sweet ache flaring through Josie's whole body. Growing bold, she allowed her hands to explore, reacquainting herself with the firm flesh that covered his ribs, the broad shoulders, the muscles of his arms, the lean length of his back. He was so perfectly formed. Beautiful for a man. With a soft sigh her fingers curled in the thick, springy hair that covered his chest.

Feeling encumbered by his clothes, Rafe pulled them off and flung them aside. Their bodies touched in an intimate embrace, and yet he took his time, lost in this world of sensual delight. She was in his arms and in his bed. It was where she belonged. She was his, he would never let her go. Not now.

"Josie! Josie!"

They lay together kissing, touching, rolling over

and over on the soft bed. His hands were doing wondrous things to her, making her writhe and groan. Every inch of her body caught fire as passion exploded between them with a wild oblivion. He moved against her, sending waves of pleasure exploding along every nerve in her body. The swollen length of him brushed across her thighs. Then he was covering her, his manhood probing at the entrance of her secret core. She was so warm, so tight around him that he closed his eyes with agonized pleasure as he slid within her.

Burying his length deeply within her, he moved with infinite care, not wanting to hurt her, instead initiating her fully into the depths of passion. And love. Yes, love, for that was what he felt at that moment. Love or something very akin to it.

Tightening her thighs around his waist, Josie arched up to him with sensual urgency. She was melting inside, merging with him into one being. His lovemaking was better than before, if that was possible, filling her, flooding her. Clinging to him, she called out his name.

Rafe groaned as he felt the exquisite sensation of her warm flesh sheathing the long length of him. He possessed her again and again. He didn't want it to end, didn't want the violence of their world to intrude into this warm, wonderful haven they had all too briefly created.

Rafe filled her with his love, leaving her breathless. It was like falling and never quite hitting the ground. Her arms locked around him as she arched to meet his body in a sensuous dance. A sensation burst through her, a warm explosion.

Even when the magic was over they clung to each other, unwilling to have the moment end. Smiling, she lay curled in the crook of Rafe's arm, and he, his passion spent, lay close against her, his body pressing hers. They were together. It was all she had for now. For the moment it had to be enough.

"Sleep now," he whispered, still holding her close. With a sigh she snuggled up against him, burying her face in the warmth of his chest, breathing in his manly scent. She didn't want to sleep, not now. She wanted to savor this moment of being together, but as he caressed her back, tracing his fingers along her spine, she drifted off.

Twenty-two

The linen sheets felt cool against her skin, the mattress was as soft as a cloud, and the body that touched against hers full-length was strong and warm.

"Any regrets?" Josie heard Rafe whisper in her ear.

The sound of his voice was deep and comforting, "Only one." Instinctively she cuddled up against him. "That we haven't awakened together like this every morning we've been down here." She felt safe and loved, and happy for the first time in a long while. *I've been only half alive until this moment,* she thought.

"Mmm-hmm. It would have been nice." Running his fingers through her hair, he gently tugged at several strands and tickled her nose. "But it's not too late to make up for lost time by waking up beside each other from now on."

"No, it's not."

For a moment she didn't move. Instead, she just wanted to savor everything about being so close to Rafe. The feel of his muscles against her skin, the sound of his heart, the masculine smell of him.

How could she have ever thought that anything in the world was more important than this?

"Josie. . . ."

Seeing a glimmer of quiet concern in his eyes, she silenced him with her fingers. "Hush. No apologies, no promises." That was what had ruined everything last time. "Let's just appreciate what we have now."

"Now. . . ." One of Rafe's hands brushed across her hip, his fingertips caressing a warm trail over her soft skin. A few moments later they were making love again. More passionate, more heated than before. It was a feast of sensual awakenings that made Josie discover appetites she hadn't even known she possessed. A hunger Rafe fulfilled with a skill that left her breathless.

Afterward she lay still, feeling calm and serene but curious about this man who had just taken her to the sun and back. She knew so little. Now she wanted to know everything. "Rafe, tell me . . . please."

"All about myself?" For just a moment his expression was guarded, then the mask came down. He laughed, undisturbed by the request he realized was important to a woman. "I was born in a little town north of Perryville. In Kentucky."

Josie remembered Parish telling her that. "And spent your childhood Sundays fishing and swimming in the old swimming hole. Am I right?"

"Exactly!" He gathered her into his arms. "How did you know?"

"Because that's just what I did. Me and Charlie, my brother." Happy memories.

"You went fishing?" He should have known. "No stiff, starched petticoats, long stockings, and sitting with hands in your lap for my girl, huh?"

"Nope!" He'd called her "my girl" and she treasured his possessiveness. "I never touched a doll in my life or played house. I guess you would call me a bona fide, dyed-in-the-wool tomboy."

"And just where did this take place?"

"Youngstown, Ohio." For just a moment she was homesick for the gently rolling hills and the many rivers. "On a farm."

"A farm!" He reached out and touched her chin, then nuzzled it with his mouth. "I grew up on a farm as well. Small world, isn't it?" They had more in common than he might have believed. "But I will bet that you didn't leave that farm to march off to war." The way he said "war" held a hint of bitterness.

"No, but you did."

He nodded. "On the South's side. An experience I will never forget." Rolling over on his back, he crossed his arms across his chest. "I fought in the battles at Mill Springs and Perryville. Sorry battles of plunder and death." He didn't want to bore her with the details, but he did tell her about how the Rebs had gone barefooted and hungry in the last years of the war, himself included.

Closing her eyes, she tried to imagine it. "I heard it was a sorry sight."

"A sight I will never forget. It hardened my heart for a time, I'm afraid, Josie. And perhaps that explains—"

"How you became a gunfighter."

"I felt a lot of anger at the injustice dealt out after the war toward those who had fought on the losing side. We were punished, made to feel weak, dealt with unfairly. My parents lost their farm partly because of me and the side I had chosen." His tone was emotionless but his eyes revealed his inner anger. "Wielding a gun made me feel strong and gave me a way to seek vengeance on those who had wronged me and mine."

Josie had already heard that much. "But something made you put up your gun. What, Rafe?"

He shuddered at the memory. He didn't want to talk about it. Even so, he found himself saying, "I would give everything I possess to undo what was done. Everything, Josie."

His face wore such an agonized expression that her heart went out to him. Something terrible had happened to Rafe Gardner, a troubled secret. He wanted to forget, to suffer his anguish alone, but she knew it would be better for him to talk about it, to share his memories with somebody.

"Tell me what happened, Rafe. Please."

"I shot someone by mistake. Someone who was unarmed." He was consumed by the memory as if it were happening all over again. A boy, Josie, he thought but didn't say. Or at least a young man who was little more than one. An act for which he had been paying every day of his life the last few years.

"Oh. Someone unarmed." It was more serious than she had supposed.

He grew silent. Sullen. It was as if the air once again rippled with gunfire, as if he could see the scene unfolding in slow motion. He and Clint walking down that damned street in Tombstone. The two men coming upon them with guns drawn and pointed. And then a third, a dark-garbed figure coming up behind. He remembered that a gun at his back had discharged, wounding him in the side and that he had instinctively turned and fired.

"Someone I . . . I thought was after me . . . but I was wrong. He didn't even have a gun. A costly mistake. For him." Suddenly he pulled her to him, pressing his face against her heart. "I took a vow at that moment to put up my gun. A vow I kept until you bewitched me."

"And coerced you to go against your principles." Her hand stroked his hair. "I'm sorry for that, Rafe. I can be so damned stubborn."

"It doesn't matter." His arms tightened around her.

"But it does." She had been so hardheaded, so consumed with hate.

"Now, listen here, Miss Josie Smith, I say that it doesn't." Rafe brushed his lips lightly across hers.

Josie Smith he had called her. A phony name. She had to set him straight. "Not Smith, Rafe." She flushed with embarrassment as she confided to him her true identity. "McLaury. My name is Josephine McLaury. I've traveled under a false identity for my own reasons."

"Josephine McLaury." He was stunned; it showed in his expression.

Uncomfortable with his surprise, Josie confided to him for the first time the story of her brother's death. "He was shot on the street in Tombstone. Poor, dear Charlie."

"Poor Charlie," he repeated, his face turning pale at the mention of the name. Dear God. It wasn't possible. Charlie McLaury. Full force Rafe's past came back to haunt him.

Twenty-three

Picking up his razor, Rafe stared long and hard at the image that looked back at him from the mirror above the washstand. Were this another man, just what would he think of him, he asked, his eyes assessing the thick, dark hair, strong jaw, straight nose, unsmiling mouth, mustache, and piercing blue eyes?

"Not a bad-looking fellow, but one I'm not certain I'd trust," he said to himself with biting sarcasm. "Something in the eyes. Shifty, ruthless, unrelenting, secretive. The eyes of a liar."

A liar? Well, not really. Not purposefully. And yet, were he to go on allowing Josie to believe that Clint Tanner killed her brother when he now knew it was *he*, that was exactly what he would be, Rafe thought self-critically.

And yet, how can I tell her? How can I destroy the heaven I've known in her arms the last few days? How can I throw myself out of paradise? How can I bear to see the same hatred in her eyes for me that I have seen for Tanner? How can I tell Josie that she has slept in the arms of her brother's killer?

The answer was that he could not. Though Rafe had always prided himself on telling the truth, he knew that this time the truth would put an abrupt end to the only happiness he had known in months. And yet, how could he live with himself if he buried it inside?

Hell! He was in a real quandary. Damned if he did, but just as damned if he did not. Eventually a lie catches up with a man.

Oh, sure, he could keep Josie McLaury in Willcox for a time on the pretense of showing her all that he knew with a gun. He could relish her company, hold her in his arms, even capture her heart for a time, but he couldn't keep her down here forever. Sooner or later when they returned to Showlow she could have to know.

I can't let Clint pay for what I have done, can't risk his dying to cover up my sin. More important, he couldn't take the chance of Josie being hurt. If there was any chance of that, he would have to tell her.

"Meanwhile," he whispered, wetting his face to soften his stubble, then covering it with foamy white lather, "I'll just grab happiness while I can and wait for that harrowing moment of truth." A truth he feared would come sooner than he wanted. Much sooner.

"Shaving?"

Rafe whirled around, nearly dropping the razor from his hand as he did so. He hadn't heard Josie come in. How long had she been sitting on the bed? How much of his verbalized introspection had she heard?

"Thought I'd scrape off some lather and see what my face is like under this five o'clock shadow," he answered, picking up the razor without even turning around. Somehow he just didn't want to look at her.

"Want me to help?" Her voice was seductive, teasing. His broad shoulders gleamed in the dancing sunlight, riveting her attention.

"No!"

Coming up behind him, she put her arms around his waist. "Then I'll just watch," she purred, pressing her check against his bare back. She melted against him, her hands running teasingly up and down his chest. "Unless you'd rather do something else." She knew she wanted him and hoped he wanted her.

He did. He had the urge to pull her into his arms, kiss her, hold her, bury his face in the softness of her hair. Instead, he took a long, shuddering breath and said, "Later."

"Okay." Loosening her arms from around him, she stood up on tiptoe and kissed him on the neck, then leaned against the washstand, watching him avidly. She was silent until he raised the razor to his upper lip. "No, don't shave it off!"

"Don't shave it?" He smiled, enjoying her attention. "Am I to infer that you like the way it tickles?"

"That, and I like the way it looks. It gives you an air of distinction."

"Of course. That was my intention." Boldly he winked at her.

Slowly, leisurely, Rafe went through the motions necessary when a man slices through his whiskers. He tilted back his head, lifting his chin as he shaved his neck, tightened his upper lip, carefully scraping around his mustache, then amused Josie with his facial contortions.

"You missed a spot." Reaching up, Josie flicked a dab of lather away.

"Thanks." Taking her hand in his, he raised it to his lips and kissed the palm where the lifelines crossed, a gesture that made her sigh.

Suddenly she wanted nothing more than to be with him, to care about him, to shut out the world and live in this dream they were creating. But that wasn't possible.

"Rafe. . . ."

Finishing his shaving, he wet a towel and dabbed it over his face. "Yes, lovely lady?"

"When do we have to go back to Showlow?"

Her question wrenched at his heart. "Do you want to go back so soon?"

"Yes and . . . and no." Nervously she toyed with a button on her sleeve. "It's just that I know you have your practice and we can't stay here forever."

"Are you eager to be chased out of town by a mob again?" He growled out the question.

"No . . . no." In the face of his inquiry her confidence faltered. Perhaps she wasn't ready to face Tanner just yet.

Seeing the look on her face, Rafe regretted his surly attitude. They had been holed up in the ranch house for days upon end. The only time they'd been in town together was when they went shopping for her gun and they had met with that gunman. Maybe they both needed some socializing.

"There's a dance in town every Saturday night. Would you like to go, Josie?"

"Dance?" She started to answer no, remembering that she seemed to have two left feet. Then she thought again. "It might be fun, but— "

"But what?"

"I don't have a dress."

Coming up behind her, he feverishly ran his hands up and down her body. "I'm sure you can think of something— " Then for the moment all thoughts of the dance were the furthest things from their minds as they succumbed to their desires.

A long lime later Josie remembered the dance, and decided to improvise with her attire. Ripping open the leg seams on a pair of her denim trousers, combining that with several colorful neckerchiefs to make panels down the front, back, and sides, she had soon fashioned a very attractive skirt for herself. The skirt, plus a red shirt and her boots, made a very fetching outfit.

Artfully braiding her hair with ribbons that matched the neckerchiefs, coiling those braids atop her head in a most complementary style, she slowly made her way down stairs.

Taking in the vision she made, Rafe whistled. "Well, Josie my dear, you seem to have invented quite a nice-looking garment for yourself. I'll have the prettiest girl at my side. I hope the other men won't be too envious." Taking her arm, he accompanied her out the door and to the stables. In a gesture of gallantry he helped her onto her horse, then climbed onto his own.

"Damn, I'll have to ride sidesaddle," Josie complained, swinging one leg over the saddle horn. "We'll have to go slow. I've never had to ride this way before." Flicking the reins, she sent her horse into a trot down the hill, easing the animal into a slow gallop as she gained confidence. Soon it was all Rafe could do to keep up with her.

Music greeted them as they arrived in Willcox. The party was being held right in the middle of the blocked-off main street. Tables had been set up on the boardwalk in front of the general store, tables loaded down with food. A small band composed of a fiddle, a washtub bass, a washboard played by moving thimble-covered fingers up and down, a banjo, an accordion, and a guitar played rousing music. It was impossible to keep one's foot from tapping in time to the rhythm, especially when everyone began to clap their hands. With laughter Josie joined in.

"May I have this dance?" Without waiting for an answer, Rafe pulled her out onto the gravel dance floor, whirling her around until she was breathless.

"Swing your partner, now do-si-do your corner lady and promenade her home," sang out the caller as he put them through their paces. As the music played on, the dancing moved faster and faster as the caller spoke faster and faster. Then with a frustrated laugh the entire square fell to the floor in an exhausted, laughing heap.

When the band started up again, a balding man claimed Josie as his partner for a dance known as the circle of fire. Next Rafe took her back for the

Virginia reel. When the caller announced another square dance, Josie felt a tap on her shoulder.

"May I?"

Turning, Josie was astonished to see someone she knew. "Parish!" She was delighted to see him, though Rafe scowled at the prospect of giving her up yet again.

"Josie!" Instead of dancing, he led her toward the punch bowl. "Mom and I have been frantic," he said, ladling some of the whiskey-laced brew into a cup and handing it to her. "We heard Tanner was planning to chase you right out of town."

"He was." With false bravado she explained the situation. "But, hell, it was nothing." She drank the punch down in three gulps. "I hid out overnight, then came down here for a spell. Until things cooled off." She raised her brows. "Have they?"

"Yeah, but Tanner is taking the credit for having frightened you off!"

"What?" Josie's temper exploded. "Why, that lying bastard! I'm not scared of him at all."

Parish grinned, trying to lighten her mood. "Then just what are you doing down here, Josie?" he teased.

Looking toward Rafe, trying hard not to give her feelings away, she felt secretive. "I'm here on . . . on a private matter," she answered, not wanting to give her intentions away lest Tanner hear of it before she was ready.

"Private?"

From across the street Rafe was feverishly waving at her, trying to coerce her back to his side.

Parish's face flushed as he looked first at Josie, then at Rafe, then back to Josie again, as if guessing just what that matter might be. "I see." He jumped to his own conclusions. "The doctor. So that's where he up and disappeared to."

"Parish. . . ." Josie laid her hand on his arm, but he shrugged it off.

"I'll just bet it was no coincidence, his vanishing at the same time as you." His face grimaced with unsuppressed jealousy. "Don't you think he's a bit old for you?"

"Old?" She really hadn't given age much thought. Looking toward Rafe, she judged him to be in his late thirties, while she had just turned twenty. "No, I don't think so at all."

"Well, I do. Too old and too experienced." The wishful expression in his eyes seemed to say that he, to the contrary, was just the right age.

"Dr. Rafe Gardner is hardly Methuselah, Parish." Her cup clanked as she set it down on the table.

"You're just no match for him, Josie."

"Oh, is that so?" Delight at meeting a friend turned to irritation.

He decided to be blunt. "Doctor or not, to put it simply, he's not the marrying kind."

Josie stiffened. "Well, to put it simply, it's just none of your business." Turning her back, she stalked off, returning to Rafe's side. But the evening was ruined.

Twenty-four

The midmorning sun cast a shadow on horse and rider as Rafe guided his stallion down the dirt-packed street. It was Sunday, a day of churchgoing, thus the streets were empty of people. Those towns-people who weren't in church were undoubtedly sleeping off the effects of the previous night's gaiety. There had been not only dancing, but drinking and fistfights galore. Even that morning there was some evidence of the doings. Discarded whiskey bottles flung haphazardly in horse troughs, along the boardwalk, and beneath bushes were awaiting cleanup; dogs were busily wolfing up scraps of discarded food. As he tethered his horse to the hitching post, he saw two of the hounds fighting over a turkey bone nearby.

"Easy, boys, easy," he said as they growled. "I've already eaten this morning. I don't have room for even a morsel."

Indeed, in a rare gesture of helpfulness Josie had been the one to fix breakfast that morning—coffee, eggs, bacon, bisquits, and fried potatoes.

"In gratitude for your taking me to the square dance," she had said, though her smile somehow hadn't really touched her eyes. "But don't plan on my doing this every day."

"No?" He had teased, whirling her around as he had while they were dancing. He had thought to himself how much he enjoyed being with her and having her there. With her his life wouldn't be boring. She added spice to it. Too bad it wouldn't last. Not when Josie learned his secret.

The planks of the boardwalk creaked in rhythm to Rafe's stride as he walked toward Jeremiah Carleton's gun shop. His excuse for the visit was that the rotation chamber on his Remington had jammed, though in truth his mind was on an entirely different matter. Josie. Finding out that she was the sister of Charlie McLaury had come so unexpectedly, so traumatically, he still hadn't fully recovered from the shock or the guilt. Worse yet, his feelings for the girl complicated the matter irrevocably. It troubled him during his waking hours and haunted him at night. He desperately needed someone to talk to about the matter, someone who knew what had really happened, a person who was wise and one that he could trust. In a word, that was Jeremiah. Pushing through the door of the gun shop, he sought him out.

"Well, morning, Rafe." Not succumbing to the rule about working on Sundays, Jeremiah Carleton was sitting behind the counter, cleaning a rifle. "Saw you dancing last night. Thought you'd be sleeping late this morning." He winked. "So I wasn't wrong after all, supposing that you had more on your mind concerning that pretty girl than teaching her how to shoot."

"No, you weren't wrong." Rafe set the Remington down on the counter.

Jeremiah raised his thick gray brows. "Soooooo. Any danger of wedding bells ringing out soon?"

Rafe shook his head. "Not hardly. A funeral toll might be more possible."

"What?" Setting down the rifle, Jeremiah stood up, picking up the Remington and hefting it in his hand. "Don't mean you're returning to gunfighting, do you?"

"Not voluntarily," Rafe said beneath his breath, then quickly changed the subject. "Something's wrong with my gun. Thought you might be able to fix it this morning."

"Hmmm," putting on his spectacles, Jeremiah took a look, distracted for the moment. "Looks like something's stuck." He examined it, trying to turn the revolving chamber with one hand as he poked at it with a thin metal rod with the other.

"Anything serious?" The Remington was his favorite gun. As familiar to him as his own hand.

"Old age." Jeremiah chuckled. "Just like people, guns wear out in time."

"Can it be fixed?"

"I suppose so." He poked around with the gun some more, then said, "Would you consider trading it in for a new one? I think that's the better option. I have a fine Remington revolver right here that I know you will like. That would give me time to fix the old one up for resale later." Jeremiah went to the cabinet and brought back a beauty of a revolver that Rafe couldn't resist. Not fancy. There was no pearl-carved handle, but it was just the right size and weight and he could tell that it was well made. A good, sturdy revolver.

As Rafe looked the gun over, his eyes glistened with admiration. He hefted it and it felt just right in his hand. "You've got yourself a deal," he remarked. "Now, how much more do I owe you?"

"Tell you what I will do," Jeremiah said. "I'll knock two dollars off the price if you will explain to me just what is bothering you."

"Bothering me . . . ?" Why was he surprised? Jeremiah had always been able to read him like a book.

"Yep. Ever since you walked into the shop this morning I knew there was something terribly important on your mind. Something besides that old gun of yours."

Rafe took a deep breath. "What would you do if I told you that Josie's name isn't really Smith."

Jeremiah shrugged. "What's in a name? Josie Jones, Josie Brown, Josie McGilicutty. Unless . . ." He leaned over the counter. "She isn't wanted, is she?"

"No." Without preliminaries Rafe blurted it out. "Her name is Josie McLaury. *McLaury.* You know what that means."

Jeremiah was silent for a moment, tapping his fingers on the counter as he sorted out that information. "You don't mean—"

"I do!"

"That . . . that boy's relative of some kind."

"His sister."

"Ohhh." He looked at Rafe over the top of his

spectacles. "That's what you meant about the funeral bells."

Rafe put the new Remington in his holster. "That's exactly what I mean. I'm teaching her to shoot so that she can go after the man who killed her brother."

"What?"

"She came into Showlow gunning for Clint Tanner. She lost. I doctored her up. Tried to give her advice." He shook his head. "It's a long story."

Sitting back in his chair, Jeremiah proclaimed, "I got plenty of time."

Pacing back and forth in front of the counter, Rafe related the entire story, even going so far as to confide in Jeremiah that he was sleeping with the lady in question. "I swear to you, Jeremy, that I didn't know. I had no idea she wasn't Josie Smith, as she proclaimed herself to be. Had I known, I would have reacted far differently."

"How?" A pointed question.

"Well, I wouldn't have made love to her, I can tell you that." A shadow passed across Rafe's eyes. "As it is, I'm doomed. I've finally found a woman I could love, do love, and yet it's only a matter of time until I know she will hate me."

"Because you're going to be a damned fool and confess?" It was obvious Jeremiah would not have been so noble.

Rafe banged his hand against the counter. "What else can I do? Be a bystander as she goes up against Clint Tanner again?" He shook his head. "You and I both know Clint can be a pigheaded idiot at times, quick to anger, fast on the trigger. But he didn't kill Charlie McLaury."

"It was an accident. You didn't mean to kill that boy. You thought he was armed. It was one of those things."

"It was murder. He didn't have a gun. Clint covered for me." Rafe began his pacing again. "To put it bluntly, he lied. Tried to keep me out of hot water by telling the story that the boy had come gunning for him. That it was self-defense. But you and I and he know the truth. And so does Josie McLaury."

"How?" Jeremiah's laugh was scoffing. "She wasn't even there."

Rafe laughed. "Believe me, she knows." He tapped at his heart. "In here. She knew her brother's habits. Knew he wasn't a gunman."

"Maybe she won't go after Tanner." Jeremiah leaned forward in his chair. "Maybe she'll realize she just isn't cut out to kill anybody. Even to fulfill the biblical passage of an eye for an eye."

"She'll go after him." Rafe closed his eyes. "If you knew Josie the way I do, you'd realize that she just won't rest until she's avenged her brother. She thinks that Charlie won't rest peacefully in his grave until she does."

There was a glow of compassion in Jeremiah's eyes. "So what do you plan to do?"

"I plan to make a gunfighter out of her. One so good that she won't have to be afraid to go up against anyone. Even me."

Twenty-five

Josie felt perspiration run down the back of her neck, matting her blond hair to the skin of her neck. Shrugging off her denim jacket, dressed in a white shirt that revealed her firm, full breasts, and denim trousers that hugged tight to her long, shapely legs, she stood like a lovely, lithe statue. Her black Stetson was cocked at an angle that spoke of her bravado and at the same time shielded her face from the sun. Still, the rays jabbed at her eyes as she waited, her right hand poised above the Peacemaker's handle. It was time for another shoot-out, and she was resolute this time that she would get the draw on Rafe.

"Parish said that damned Tanner has told the whole fool town that I ran. That he chased me. That I was scared."

"And weren't you?" Rafe asked, his lips curving upward.

"Well . . . yes. But he'll be eating humble pie when I ride in and call him, out, eh, Rafe?" she asked, thinking all the while how strange it was that Rafe had so drastically changed his opinion on the matter. Once he had been so all-fired ready to condemn her for wanting to get revenge on her brother's killer. She had sensed that though he was making a great show of teaching her his "art," he was holding something back. Now he seemed just as desirous that she would be skilled and ready to meet her opponent when the time came.

"We'll see, Josie," Rafe answered, feeling desperately sick at heart. He was teaching her to get the draw on the man who shot her brother, all right. The only problem was, that man was he, though she didn't know it yet. "Just remember everything I've taught you."

"I have everything you've taught me permanently embedded in my mind." She tapped at her hat. And she should. The days following the square dance, Rafe Gardner had been a relentless taskmaster, so much so that Josie had joked with him that he seemed driven in his efforts to assure her perfection. *Now, why do you suppose that was?* She shrugged off the question as she spread her legs apart, affecting the gunfighter's stance.

"Or at least you think you have." Dressed in jeans, a collarless white cotton shirt and brown leather vest, low-heeled brown boots, and a dark brown Stetson, he looked just as determined as Josie felt.

"Just as you have said, we'll see."

They both froze in pulsating silence. Flies buzzed. Birds chirped. Boots crunched over gravel. With long, swift strides, Josie moved toward Rafe Gardner, determination glittering in her eyes.

"One."

Though there were blanks in the gun, Josie felt her heart pounding.

"Two . . ."

Nervously wiggling her fingers, she took a deep breath.

"Three . . ."

The pistols were drawn in the blink of an eye. A shot rang out. Josie, for all her bluster, was surprised that it came from her gun. "Well, I'll be . . ."

In a salute, Rafe touched the brim of his Stetson with the barrel of his Remington. "You did it, Josie." Rafe was torn between his pride in her and his anxiety about his own well-being. He had just taught this young woman he deeply cared about how to kill him.

Strangely enough, Josie was quiet and subdued in the face of her victory. Her voice was soft as she suggested, "It might have just been a fool's luck. Shall we try again, Rafe?"

"As you wish, quick-draw." Though his tone was teasing, there wasn't a hint of a smile upon his face. As a matter of fact, Josie thought that his expression was vaguely undefinable.

"Two out of three!"

"You're on." He shouted out the countdown again, this time winning.

"But only by a hair," Josie exclaimed. Taking a deep breath, glowering in savage determination and concentration, she prepared to do it all over again.

"No countdown this time. In a square-off with your opponent you won't have that luxury. Just watch me closely, and when I go for my gun, go for yours."

"Okay."

A split second later, Josie's Peacemaker cracked out a sound that would have been a murderous shot had the bullet had gunpowder.

"Two out of three . . ."

Forgetting herself, she ran full speed at him, wrapping her arms around his neck as he lifted her up and twirled her around.

"So, Josie, my duty is done." The ill-fated day was drawing near, a truth that made Rafe's stomach tighten. All too soon now he would have to tell her the secret that was haunting him, the terrible truth that was standing in the way of their happiness.

"Mmm." She touched her mouth to his neck, stifling her reply. She remembered how good it had felt to have his arms clamped around her body that morning, how heavenly it felt to wake up beside him every sunrise.

"We'll get ready to go back." And the moment they arrived back in Showlow, he would have to talk to her.

"Go back?" She hugged him closer, wanting to feel his lips on hers, not hear talk of their departure. Not now.

"Tomorrow morning." Why draw it out? All he could hope was that she would somehow find it in her heart to understand.

"That soon."

"Oh, Josie. What am I going to do?" Her hat had come off and her hair streamed down her

face, soft and sweet-smelling. Burying his face in
her hair, he relished the moment, fearing what the
future had in store.

That night Rafe came to Josie, enfolding her,
kissing her, making love to her with a tenderness,
an urgency, that was more intense than ever before.
Touching her, caressing her, he made her appreciate fully the joy of being alive! Being loved!

Josie was lost to his passion. It was as if he were
draining her very soul, drawing it out to merge with
his own, yet at the same time filling her with feelings so infinitely precious that she was lost to anything else but the wonder. Her heart pounded so
fiercely that it shook her entire body. She couldn't
think, couldn't breathe, couldn't move. His hands,
his mouth, were the only reality, his arms her only
world.

"Oh, Josie." Rafe held her against him with a
feeling of sadness. What if they were making love
for the very last time?

No, he wouldn't ruin this moment with such
thoughts. He would simply hold this moment in
his heart, savor everything about this night, love
her as she would never, *could* never, be loved again.

Josie was quickly becoming addicted to the taste
of his lips, the gentle pressure of his hands. She
felt his warmth and power, felt her emotions spinning out of control. A shiver danced up and down
her spine. She leaned against his hands, giving in
to the stirring sensations.

Always before when they had made love, Josie

had been just a bit shy, holding a small piece of herself back from her pleasure. Now she held nothing back. Reaching out, she boldly explored Rafe's body as he had done to hers—his hard-muscled chest and arms, his stomach. His flesh was warm to her touch, pulsating with the strength of his maleness. As her fingers closed around him, Rafe groaned.

"Josie!" Fire raged like an inferno, pounding hotly in his veins. His whole body throbbed with the fierce compulsion to plunge himself into her sweet softness, and yet he held himself back, caressing her once more, teasing the petals of her womanhood until he could tell that she was fully prepared for his entry. Her skin felt hot against his as he entwined his legs with hers.

"I wish—" Rafe whispered, regretting so many things.

"Wish what?"

For a moment he didn't answer, then he said simply, "I wish we had forever."

Forever. That one word deeply touched her, but though she wanted to tell him that they did have eternity together, she couldn't make that promise. Not yet. Not until this matter with Tanner was settled.

"Oh, Rafe—" Her words broke off as he buried his face against her neck, nuzzling her ear, whispering.

Love for her washed over him, bittersweet and painful. With her he was contented, felt complete, happy. So gloriously happy. Slowly, gently making love to her, he tried to show her the depth of those feelings.

Sweet, hot desire fused their bodies together, yet there was an aching sweetness mingling with the fury and the fire. Josie responded to Rafe's love with all the potency of the feelings she had kept pent up for so long. With their hearts and hands and bodies, in the final outpouring of their love, they spoke words they had never uttered before.

Twenty-six

A dark pink glow lit the sky as Josie gathered her belongings, grabbed a quick cup of coffee, then headed outside toward the horses. Sliding her foot into the stirrup, she swung herself up in the saddle. Casting a long, regretful farewell look over her shoulder, she said good-bye to the place where she had known so much happiness.

"Ready, Josie?"

As Josie was looking at the ranch house, Rafe was looking at her. Dressed in trousers that clung tightly to her hips, her wheat-colored hair stuffed underneath a brown Stetson hat, perched atop her horse she looked a lot like she had that first day in Showlow when everyone including Tanner had mistaken her for a young man. But Rafe knew beneath the britches she was very much a woman. A woman he wished with all his heart could be his woman.

"I'm ready." Josie nodded, admiring her traveling companion just as he had been admiring her. Dressed in a white shirt, a gray Stetson, black boots, and denims, he reminded her of a dime-novel hero.

"Then let's head out."

The horses moved at a slow trot as Rafe and Josie moved away from the ranch house side by side, but as they headed toward the road, the trot turned into a gallop. It was flat land there, easy on the horses. A good spot to get in as much distance as possible before they ran into rocky ground.

So, I'm on my way to Showlow. Now that the moment was at hand, Josie had second thoughts about it all, though she knew she couldn't back down. Still, it seemed her gun belt, slanting from her waist down over her right hip, was heavier than before, her Peacemaker more cumbersome. The gun pressed against her hipbone, making itself known even through the thick denim pants she wore. An instrument of death, Rafe had once called it. Now, as they traveled, Josie couldn't help but wonder what it felt like to kill a man. Or if the worst happened, what it would feel like to die.

"Rafe?" For just a moment she was tempted to turn back, to forget about it all. Maybe Rafe could set up his practice in Willcox. Maybe they never had to set eyes on Showlow again.

"You look troubled, Josie." He pulled his mount up beside her as both their horses slowed. "What is it?"

Carefully avoiding his eyes, she started to tell him her true feelings, then said simply, "Nothing." The unspoken answer hung in the air. *And everything,* she thought, once again contemplating what it might be like to die. She couldn't. She wouldn't. She had so very much to live for. Being with Rafe had emphasized that.

"Nothing," Rafe repeated. He doubted that. The

way she said *nothing* sounded like just the opposite. Turning in the saddle, he studied her. What was ticking inside that pretty head of hers? What was she up to? What was she thinking? He watched as she turned her head, wishing he could delve into her thoughts. Was she frightened at all? Regretful? Or was she as all-fired sure of herself as she always pretended?

Why shouldn't she be sure of herself? She got the draw on me two out of three times. A fact Rafe couldn't ignore. Even if he was using a gun that was new to him, that wasn't a good enough excuse to brush off Josie's newfound skill. She was good. Good enough to be the death of him, were that what she decided.

"Josie, what would be your reaction were you to find out that Tanner didn't really kill your brother, that someone else was the guilty one?"

"What would I do?" She thought a moment. "I'd call whoever it was out, gunfighter or not."

"Then the punishment would be the same for anyone."

"That's right. Though I'd be disappointed if it wasn't that puffed-up bullfrog Tanner." She eyed him with curiosity. "Why? You know something you're not telling me?"

It was his chance to bring the subject of his guilt up, to tell her the truth, but in the face of her big green eyes, Rafe lost all nerve. He'd wait until they got to Showlow. "No. Just making conversation, that's all."

"Conversation?" Josie's eyes narrowed. She jerked her mount to a stop. "Well, if you're thinking to sing that same old song about how wrong gunfighting is, forget it, Rafe. I've busted my tail for this moment. I won't be cheated." That said, she urged her horse into a furious gallop, riding like the wind.

Riding after her for mile after mile, Rafe stayed a horse's length behind, at last calling out teasingly, "Well, has your temper cooled yet?"

The flanks of Josie's horse heaved in rhythm to the hoofbeats, and she felt each pulsation. Fearing that she might overly tire the horse, she slowed down. "Temper? What temper?" she called out over her shoulder. "I was merely scouting out the terrain."

"And did you like the view?" Rafe grinned. "I know I do." The hard ride had jostled her clothing and popped two buttons off Josie's shirt. The neck was open just far enough to give a tantalizing glimpse of the valley between her breasts, a sight he relished.

"Not particularly," she answered. She hadn't expected to see anything of interest while riding across this stretch of land, so she wasn't disappointed. "There are red rocks, rocks, and more rocks and lots of sand." She reined in her horse. "And a small stream. Look there, Rafe."

They both dismounted and let their horses drink, but after tasting the green-tinted water, Rafe told Josie not to drink it. "There's copper in it. Makes a person break out in copper boils." He reached out and touched her cheek. "Wouldn't want you to spoil that lovely skin of yours." He pointed in a northeasterly direction. "Besides, Showlow is right over there. We can wait."

"Right over there?" Once again Josie was troubled. They were coming into Showlow much too soon. She wasn't certain she was ready for a confrontation with the townsmen and Tanner just yet.

"About another half hour's ride." He sensed her apprehension but didn't embarrass her by mentioning it. Instead, he said simply, "That is, unless you want to take the long way around. The way that is more appealing to the eyes."

Josie looked at him with gratitude, knowing he was trying to spare her pride as well as salve her uncertainty. "I do want to take more time."

Moving closer together, their eyes met and locked in an intimate moment of understanding and unspoken love.

Twenty-seven

Josie reached Showlow a few hours after sunup, a little ahead of Rafe, who was purposely lagging behind so as not to create too much gossip by arriving together. Pulling her mount to a halt at the edge of town, she brushed off her pants, straightened her shirt, checked the Peacemaker strapped to her hips, then steeled herself for the ride into town.

It was hot and dry. Josie's skin felt moist with perspiration. She swallowed hard, getting command of her emotions and the uneasiness that she felt. Taking off her hat, she half rose in the saddle, hesitating slightly. This time it would be different. She was well prepared for whatever happened. A smile curled the corners of her mouth.

Sitting tall and straight in the saddle, Josie knew that the impression she made riding in was of the utmost importance. She had to appear confident, fearless, and in complete control. Her appearance would not go unnoticed, therefore she wanted Clint Tanner to hear she was back and quake in fear.

"Okay." Nudging her horse, she moved down the bustling main street.

It was noisy. Hectic. A busy time of day. There were plenty of people to notice Josie's return, which is exactly what they did. Her arrival incited a great deal of excitement. All eyes automatically shifted toward her. Some stared silently, others gawked openly, while a few whispered to their neighbors.

"Isn't that . . ."

"Of course it is."

"Thought Tanner ran her out!"

"What is she doing back?"

"Hope there isn't gonna be trouble."

Though she was the talk of the town, Josie retained her composure. Expertly handling the reins of her mount, she bent forward in the saddle, saying to one of the bystanders, "Whether or not there is trouble depends on Tanner, ma'am."

Tanner. Just where was he? As she rode, Josie kept a sharp lookout for him, hoping he would make himself known. When he didn't, she put out the word to those she passed by that she was looking for him.

I might as well get this over with. Then and only then can Rafe and I get on with our lives. That is, if— But she wouldn't even think about that. Besides, if she were lucky, maybe Tanner would be the one to run. Far, far away.

He didn't. As Josie rode up to the rail in front of the Golden Cactus Saloon, she saw his ginger head bobbing up and down above the swinging door. He was laughing, joshing with a few of his companions.

"Well, he won't be laughing now." Tying the reins, Josie mounted the steps and crossed the boardwalk. Fuming, she walked briskly through the swinging doors.

"And just what have we here?" The man behind the bar pointed at their intruder. "Do you gents see what I see?"

All heads turned.

"Well, I'll be. If it isn't Miss Sureshot herself." Tanner's guffaw was forced.

"Hey, ladies aren't allowed in here."

"She ain't no lady."

"Think she must be lost," a balding patron said.

"Yeah. The dressmaker's shop is next door."

Tanner looked her up and down. "And it sure looks as though she needs a visit."

Josie cleared her throat. "And you look as if you need a tailor, Tanner, one who will make you a nice new suit." Her voice got louder. "To wear in your casket."

Tanner drew back in mock terror. "Oh, I'm so scared." It was obvious that when he was surrounded by his cronies, he felt the need to be obnoxious.

"Well, you should be," Josie replied, undaunted by all the scorn. She didn't feel the slightest tinge of humiliation. These men would soon eat their words when she proved her skill. "I'm not the greenhorn I was before. I know all the ins and outs of gunfighting now. I've been trained by an expert."

The tension was palpable. "Trained?" their upraised eyebrows asked the question. "By who?"

"By me!" Rafe's voice rang out behind her.

"By you?" Tanner was incredulous. "Rafe, you must be kidding."

Rafe's face never changed from its determined expression as he walked toward the door. "I'm deadly serious."

"You son of a bitch!" Tanner's voice cracked over Rafe like ice. "Why the hell would you do such a low-down thing? Particularly after what I did for you. Why, I—"

Rafe interrupted. "I trained Josie in gunfighting so that she could take revenge on her brother's killer." He passed between the tables to reach her side. "What she doesn't know is just who that someone is."

Josie cocked her head as she looked at him. He was so pale. So grim. Now, why was that? She wasn't prepared for the answer.

"I killed Charlie, Josie." He felt sick to his stomach. She was going to be devastated.

"You? Sure." She thought that he was joking. "Well, go ahead and play martyr if you want; it won't save your friend here." She tapped at the handle of her Peacemaker. "I'm going to make him cry uncle."

"Me?" Tanner nudged Rafe in the ribs. "Why, when he really was the one who did it? I just lied for him because he was such a dear old friend."

"It's true, Josie."

Something in his face told her that it was.

"No!" She wasn't prepared for this. She felt the room begin to spin and reached out to brace her weight against a chair. "You're lying!" Her voice was so loud that it was nearly a scream.

"It's the story I told you about, Josie." He revealed it once again, trying to say it in a way to soften the blow. "I thought your brother was armed. I shot—"

"You bastard!" Her hand flashed out and fastened to his shirt, clenching it so tightly that she tore it with her fingernails. Her head ached, her throat felt dry. "You knew. All the time that you . . . that you and I . . . were . . ." He had destroyed her. Coldly. Calculatingly. Heartlessly. He had made love to her knowing all the while that he had killed the dearest person to her.

"I didn't know at first. Not until we were . . . were lovers, Josie." He gently peeled her fingers from his shirt. "You called yourself Josie Smith. I thought that was who you were. Only later did I learn."

"Later?" Even so, she couldn't forgive him.

"I wanted to tell you, Josie. I didn't want you to learn it this way. But I . . ."

She was numb. "Oh, how I loathe you." She wished that were true, but it wasn't. Even now. "Oh, how I wish . . ." That he was dead? No.

"Josie . . ." Rafe reached for her hand, but it was too late. Completely shaken, Josie had run out into the street.

Part Three

The Showdown

Showlow, Arizona

Nothing in life is so exhilarating as to be shot at without result.

— Sir Winston Spenser Churchill,
The Malakand Field Force

Twenty-eight

Josie took her brother's photograph from its safe nesting-place in the bottom drawer of the chest in her room at the boardinghouse. Looking at it for the hundredth time that day, she reached out, touching the face that grinned at her from the picture.

"Oh, Charlie." Never had she felt so estranged from everyone, so alone.

Looking at the darkening image, she vividly remembered him as a little boy who had so trustingly put his hand in hers. "Take care of your little brother," her mother had always said, and she had.

"But I wasn't there to take care of you that day, Charlie." That day he had gotten in the way of a gunman's bullet. Now Charlie was dead.

Killed by my lover. A brutal reality that had completely shaken her. She couldn't eat, she couldn't sleep, tortured by the fact that Rafe had kept such a secret from her. *How could he have made love to me knowing that he killed my brother?* It was reprehensible. Unforgivable. All the while he had been holding her in his arms, touching her with his hands, he had known that those hands were stained with her brother's blood.

"Ohh." Tears glistened in her eyes as she reached out to touch the photograph again. She had watched Charlie grow from a little boy to a boy who thought he was a man. A gentle creature whose long-fingered hands had been able to create such marvelous pictures with paint and canvas. Now those hands would never again work magic. Because of Dr. Rafe Gardner.

Her thoughts flashed back to their first meeting and the things he had said. "All a gun brings is death! Killing a man in a gunfight is hardly justice, just murder." Well, he was right about that. It had been murder. Charlie's.

But he and Tanner acknowledged that it was an accident. Can you still hold him accountable for that? He thought Charlie was armed, thought that he was going to shoot him. Did that make a difference? "Oh, I don't know. I just don't know."

And what about Rafe? What was he thinking just now and feeling?

Josie remembered how diligently he had trained her, how patient he had had been even after he found out that he was the guilty party. He had taught her how to shoot so well knowing that he might be the target. Didn't he deserve some consideration for that? Wasn't that the act of a brave man?

Or was he a guilty one who knew he deserved just punishment, she thought, clenching her teeth in anger. But could she punish him?

For so long hatred had goaded her on, been her only motivation, her only emotion, it was nearly impossible to turn it off now. Yet how could she hate Rafe when she loved him so? Yes, loved.

There could be no denying that. And loved him still.

Clad in a white nightshirt, her hair loose about her shoulders, Josie sat huddled in a chair by the fire, her eyes fixed on the fading embers. How long she sat staring into the hearth she didn't know. Minutes? Hours? How many days had it been since she had learned? Two? Three? Four? And still she hadn't come to terms with it all. There was so much she needed to think about to drive out the agony that was tearing her in two.

Trembling, she glanced toward her turned-down bed, but her mind had been too active, too troubled, to permit sleep. Leaning her head back, she tried to quench the flame in her blood that the memory of Rafe evoked, but his hot, soft exploring mouth and husky voice tormented her with yearning. She imagined his strong arms holding her, caressing her, thoughts that sent tickling shivers up her spine. He'd held her so tenderly, as if she were precious to him.

Precious? Or was he just trying to salve his soul? Make up to her for what he had done? She just didn't know.

Seeking the safe haven of her bed, she pulled the covers up to her chin to bring warmth to her chilled body. Again she tried hard to push all thoughts of Rafe Gardner from her mind, but she could not, no matter how hard she tried. Her mind, her heart, the very core of her being, longed for him. Her body, lying warm and yearning for the touch of his lips, rebelled against her anger. Desire was all too primitive and powerful a feeling.

But so is hatred. That destructive feeling she had held for Clint Tanner in her heart. Could she hate Rafe now that she knew he had killed her brother?

Immersed in a cocoon of blankets where everything was soft and safe, Josie stared up at the ceiling of her bedroom. She couldn't sleep. How could she after what had happened? Beams of moonlight danced through the windows, casting figured shadows on the roof overhead. Two entwined silhouettes conjured up memories of the embraces they had shared. She lay awake for several long, tormented hours, but when at last her indomitable will won out over her fevered, longing body, she closed her eyes. Wrapping her arms around her knees, she curled up in a ball, envisioning again the face of the man who haunted her now. At last she gave in to the blissfulness of sleep and dreams.

She was at the square dance twirling and whirling. Moving her feet across the floor, Josie tried to join in, but the music was faster, louder. Colors blended into one another until the features on the faces were indistinguishable.

"Dance, Josie!" A chorus of voices cajoled her, but she couldn't remember the steps. It was as if she were on a treadmill, trying to join the others before they vanished, but falling short again and again. Waving her arms frantically, trying to keep her balance, she turned just as the floor dropped out from under her feet. She was falling downward into a great gaping hole.

"No!"

Hands reached out to grasp her. "Josie . . ." A voice whispering her name.

"Rafe?" She reached out to him as he steadied her. "Oh, Rafe!" She sought the safe shelter of his arms, but he turned away, moving through a cloud of translucent people. Running, she tried to catch up with him just as another figure beckoned.

"Shame, shame on you, Josie. How can you be in his arms after what he did to me?"

"Charlie!" Mists of fog enfolded her and she tried to push the clouds away. "Charlie!"

"Because of him I'm in my grave. He shot me. Here?" Opening his shirt, the phantom Charlie revealed a bloody, gaping wound, a sight that made Josie moan in her sleep. She tossed her head from side to side as visions swirled through her mind.

"There she is! Catch her. She shot Rafe Gardner!" Clint Tanner pointed his finger, leading a group of scowling men toward her, torches in their hands. She had to find a place to hide.

"Rafe!" He was up ahead of her, beckoning her to come to him. "Help me!"

"She's a murderer!" A chorus of voices gave warning. "Hang her!"

"Not now! Please. I didn't mean to . . . I didn't . . ."

"Hang her!"

Bright daylight played across her face, teasing her eyelids awake. Rubbing her sleep-filled eyes, Josie propped herself shakily up on one elbow and looked around her. "Dear God!" A dream. Just a silly dream after all. And yet . . .

Twenty-nine

He had lost her. Time after time Rafe dwelled upon that terrible thought, still hoping deep within his heart that it was not true. Yet he knew it must be. Feeling as she did about her brother, how could Josie find it in her heart to forgive him, now or ever?

"She can't." The words he spoke aloud slammed like a bullet into his heart.

Worse yet, he was worried about her. It was as if she were shunning everyone in town, blaming them in her way for what he had done. Since the morning she had ridden into town to confront Tanner in the saloon, she had holed up in that boardinghouse and hadn't poked her nose outside. Not once!

From the window of his office, Rafe's eyes kept wandering in that direction, watching and waiting.

"Just like I always said. Gunfighting is nasty business." Now Rafe knew he was going to have to pay for the biggest mistake of his life.

"Oh, Josie!" Her name was a soulful cry upon his lips. What might have happened between them if not for her brother's death? Perhaps they could have reached out and touched the very stars with the passion of their love. Instead, there was a wall between them now, a wall that threatened not only to destroy all that they had been to each other, but which might bring about an even greater tragedy.

"You moping about too?" Clint Tanner's words startled Rafe out of his reverie.

"Don't you ever knock?" Though he and Clint had been through some hard times together, Rafe treasured his privacy on this matter, a privacy Tanner didn't seem to respect.

"Door was unlocked, so I just barged in. Thought you might need some company." He made himself at home in one of Rafe's chairs.

"Not yours." Rafe couldn't forget or forgive that Clint had blurted out the truth before he'd had a chance to explain the story to Josie. Still, it wasn't his fault that things had taken the turn they had.

"You know, now that she isn't after my hide, I have to admit she really is quite pretty." Putting his feet up on the back of Rafe's desk, he leaned back. "And full of vinegar. I always liked them that way, though you always seemed to go for the more refined types."

"Doesn't seem to matter what I like now." Grumbling beneath his breath, Rafe kicked the chair out from under his boyhood friend. "Besides, I don't want to talk about it, Clint. Good day!"

Only managing to retain his balance by the quickest reflexes, Tanner escaped a tumble to the ground. "Now, hold on, Rafe. I don't want any hard feelings. Seeing as how she said you had taught her how to shoot, I thought you had betrayed me. In anger I guess I just sort of shot off my mouth."

Rafe wasn't placated. "You know me. Do you really think I would have let her shoot you, knowing the circumstances?"

Tanner walked toward Rafe's gun collection, taking a Colt .45 with an eagle-engraved handle off the wall. "Wasn't this the gun ol' McBain used?"

It was. "Yes." In anger he started tearing all the guns down, throwing them to the floor. "Don't even know why I kept these. As a gruesome reminder, I suppose. Fool. That was me!"

Tanner shrugged. "Oh, I don't know. You were pretty good in your day. Almost as good as me." He grinned, knowing well that Rafe had been much better. "But the question is, can you outdraw that little spitfire, or have you just put a notch in her gun? For you."

"I don't care!" At the moment he didn't. "She can shoot me if she wants to, if that will make her feel better." More than anything, he wanted to bring her peace of mind.

"Her? Or you?" It was a rare intuitive statement from Clint Tanner. "Do you want to be a martyr? Do you, Rafe?"

"I don't know." It had been said that time heals all wounds, but would time be any good in this instance? Would Josie ever forgive and forget? Could he put it out of his mind? "I just know that I want to do what is right."

Clint Tanner was quiet, a rare occurrence, then, as he looked at Rafe, he showed his astonishment. "You really love her!"

"Yes, I do. More than my life."

"Whoa!" Tanner grabbed Rafe by the shoulders. "Get the cobwebs out of your brain, friend. No woman is worth that."

Ignoring his friend, Rafe put his hands behind his back and stared into space. "Love is thinking about the other person above and beyond yourself. Caring about their welfare above your own. That's how I feel about her."

"Hmmmm. An interesting theory." Tanner had to think long and hard about that one. Walking to the window, he stared out. "A theory it looks as if you might have to prove sooner than you thought. He tugged at Rafe's suitcoat sleeve. "Look! Out on the street, old buddy. Damn!"

Rafe stared out the window, feeling a chill creep up his spine. Out on the boardwalk, holster hugging her hips, was Josie. "What time is it, Clint?"

"Noon."

"At least she remembered what I taught her." Taking blanks out of a bottom drawer of his desk, he filled his Remington. Then, whispering a prayer, Rafe walked out the door to meet his fate.

The moment was here. A moment that caused a lump in Josie's throat the size of a brick. She felt hot. Tingly. Apprehensive. A feeling of regret consumed her. That and a feeling of fear. Either she was going to kill Rafe or he was going to kill her.

"No. It doesn't have to be." Every instinct was screaming at her, telling her to get away before it was too late.

Running her fingers over the handle of the gun, she was indecisive. Sick at heart. Nothing really seemed to make sense anymore. Certainly not this. And yet like a sleepwalker she was going through the motions, walking down the boardwalk with her holster strapped around her waist.

A feeling of sadness overwhelmed her. Her emotions were in such turmoil that her stomach churned violently. She remembered all the times Rafe had held her in his arms, all the times he had kissed her. She thought about the way he looked in the mornings when his hair was tousled and his face was unshaven. She pictured in her mind the way he sipped his coffee. His smile. The way he walked.

"I'm going crazy!" Putting her hands to her throbbing temples, she tried to put her thoughts into some kind of coherency. He was the wrong-doer, not her, she told herself. He had shot her brother. Lied to her. Made her believe in love only to betray her in the worst of ways. Whatever happened to Dr. Rafe Gardner, he deserved it. So thinking, she drew her gun out of its resting place, clutched the handle, and put her finger on the trigger.

Josie's chest rose and fell. Her breath came out in a heavy sigh through parted lips. For an ago-nizing moment all she could do was stand perfectly still and stare. It was too late to change her mind. Too late for so many things.

Thirty

A stillness hung over the street, a quiet so complete that the dull sound of Rafe's boots could be heard loud and clear as he strode the boardwalk on his way to meet Josie. Strange, he thought, watching as she walked toward him, that the last time they faced each other it was a mock gunfight, only for play. Now what passed between them was deadly serious.

"So, there you are," he heard Josie shout out.

"Yes, here I am." Rafe looked at Josie's dark green eyes, eyes burning with bitter anger. Dressed all in black, from her hat to her boots, her hair hanging down her back in wild disarray, she looked like a grim avenging angel.

"Already dressed in your suit. Good," she called out, tauntingly, sounding far more hateful than she felt. "That will be convenient for the undertaker." Her stomach was churning. Now that she was actually facing him, she found herself regretting this impulsive action. But what was done was done.

"Josie, why are you doing this?" It wasn't the time for accusations or anger, but for good, solid reasoning.

"You know very well why." She had tried and

tried to find it in her heart to forgive him, but the truth was she couldn't. No matter how she felt about Rafe, her brother had to be avenged.

"Killing me can't bring back Charlie. What was done was done and I'm sorry as hell." So sorry that he had been tormented the past few days. Surely Rafe's conscience and his regret were a far worse punishment than Josie could deal out. "But one death can't be vindicated by another."

"I think it can." For so long her anger had goaded her into seeking out and killing Charlie's murderer that she was driven beyond all self-control, and yet the thought of shooting Rafe, of watching him die, made her feel numb inside. Breathing deeply, she tried to dispel the sick, queasy feeling in her stomach.

Neither of them seemed to be aware of the eyes watching them from behind closed doors, peeking around buildings, from underneath overturned wagons or even from beneath a haystack where Parish watched in silence, waiting for the deadly shots to ring out. Neither Rafe nor Josie noticed. Neither of them cared. They were too concerned with each other.

"Well then, if you are deadly serious about this, Josie, and there is nothing I can do to change your mind, let's get on with it."

"Yes, let's get on with it." Keeping her stare fixed on his gold belt buckle, her jaw was set with grim determination.

"May the quickest draw win." A chilling proclamation.

It was a tension-filled moment as he and Josie

stared each other down. Josie took a step; Rafe did likewise. She took another step and he did too. All the while each was hoping that the other would back down and throw a gun to the ground.

Oh, Rafe. Josie's hand hovered only inches from her Peacemaker. She did not touch it. However, it seemed to burn her hand like a live coal. Her heart ached as she regarded his mouth, remembering how his lips had felt on her own. Oh, if only she could put Charlie's death out of her mind. If only she could truly forgive Rafe. If only . . .

Standing straight and tall, Rafe was far more shaken than he appeared. His breathing was unsteady as he looked at Josie's Peacemaker. Would she do it? Would she shoot him? Could she really hate him that much?

"Josie!"

She ignored him, continuing to stare at him with a cold, impassive anger.

Rafe's heart hammered against his ribs. His hands were sweaty. He was nervous, but Josie looked poised and ready, that is, until he took a step closer. As he did, he could see that she was trembling. With fear? Did she really think that he could harm her? He knew full well that he had blanks in his gun. Should he tell her? Should he let her know that if she shot him, it would be murder?

"Josie," he said again, disappointed that she did not move from her rigid, challenging stance.

Oh, Rafe. Her poise was quickly deserting her. She was agonized by the turmoil of emotions inside her head. She wanted to answer him, wanted to call the whole thing off. Why, then, didn't she? Was her pride so fierce that she could not back down in front of the town? Or had her thirst for revenge destroyed her just as Rafe had said. Vengeance was a two-edged sword, harming he who seeks it most of all, he had told her. Was that a prophecy that was soon to be fulfilled?

"Josie, let's use reason." Reason. Was it possible for her to be reasonable now? Or was her hate for him so intent that she would go through with it?

"Reason." She looked at Rafe, and it was as if a knife had been thrust into her heart. *I love him. I always will, no matter what he has done.* She took a halting step forward, then another and another, her hand moving as if in slow motion toward her gun.

So the moment has come, Rafe thought, bracing himself. His only hope now was that she wouldn't prove to be too good a shot.

Instead of reaching for her gun, however, Josie reached for the buckle of her holster. "May Charlie forgive me," she whispered. Unfastening her holster, she threw it with stunning force at the ground. Looking Rafe full in the face, she said, "Damn you, Rafe Gardner. Damn you to hell!" Turning, she ran away as fast as her feet could carry her.

In stunned surprise, Rafe walked to where she had discarded her gun and holster. Bending over, he picked it up and draped it over his shoulder, watching as she scurried toward the boarding-house.

Thirty-one

The room was in a state of complete disarray. Boots, shirts, stockings, and trousers were strewn haphazardly on the floor and on top of the unmade bed. The drapes were drawn, shutting out the sunlight. The pitcher atop the washstand was tipped, dripping water on the floor. Sitting cross-legged on the floor, Josie hardly noticed. Staring at her carpetbag, she sat agonizing over her predicament. What was she going to do now? Where was she going to go?

"I sure as hell can't stay here!"

Not after having humiliated herself out on the street. She had heard the whispers. The townspeople had branded her a coward. They were laughing at her. And why not? She had arrogantly come into town like a whirlwind, obsessed with retaliation. She had made threats, she had boasted, she had pranced about like a fighting rooster. But in the end she had backed down. It had all been nothing but a bluff.

"I couldn't do it. I just couldn't shoot." She couldn't have killed Rafe under any circumstances or maybe anybody else for that matter. Then why had she made such a mess of things? Why had she blustered so? Why had she blundered?

Cradling her face in her hands, Josie was far beyond tears. She had kept everything bottled up for so long it was difficult to find a release now. And besides, even tears could not soothe her irretrievable loss— of Charlie and of the love she might have known with Rafe. All she could do now was find a way to survive.

"She had to find a way to rebuild her life." But on what foundation? For so long her need to avenge Charlie had completely dominated her life. Now Josie felt lost. Alone. Empty.

"I shouldn't have . . ." Done so many foolish things. But it was too late for regrets. Single-mindedly, doggedly, she forced herself to put it all out of her mind. Only then could she have any chance for happiness. She had to leave Showlow without a backward glance, had to get away.

Rising to her feet, Josie moved toward the bed. Folding up her clothing, she stuffed each garment into her carpetbag, pausing as she picked up first the green shirt, then the denim skirt she had made for the square dance. They brought back memories.

"I had better leave them behind." There was no time to dwell on the past. She had to forget and hope that this whole mess would be at least a lesson learned. A painful lesson. She would take the stagecoach out of town and never come back.

Never. A sad word. But somewhere out there was a future for her. A purpose. But what in the world was she going to do? She was alone, without money or friends.

"Knock, knock."

The sound of Parish's voice was the most welcome sound in the world.

"Umm, the door was open. Thought you might need some company. I . . . I . . ."

"Oh, Parish!" Impulsively she ran to his arms, hugging him tightly. "I feel so stupid. So foolish. I went out on the street intending to—"

"I know. I saw."

"You did?" Remembering herself, Josie pulled away. "Then you know that I threw down my gun."

"Thank God!" He put his hand on her shoulder.

"I couldn't shoot him, even if he did kill my brother. Even if he . . ." Her mind whirled, her heart poised on the brink of breaking into a hundred pieces. Slowly she moved about the room, gathering up her possessions.

This sadness will pass, she told herself. She wouldn't let what happened destroy her. She had fallen in love with a shadow, a dream, a man who didn't really exist. Her body had betrayed her. But it would be all right. She would get by.

"I thought you might be angry with me for what . . . what I said in Willcox." Parish looked down at his boots. "It really was none of my business." Picking up one of her shirts, he used great care in folding it.

"It was your business! I should have listened." Taking the shirt from his hand, she toyed with the button. "I was a fool, Parish, in more ways than just one. But I want to put that behind me."

"What . . . what are you going to do?"

"Take the stagecoach." Funny. Wasn't that what Rafe had always wanted her to do? Right from the very first that had been his staunch suggestion. If only she had . . .

"Go away?" Parish grabbed the carpetbag out of her hand. "No!"

"I have to." She tried to maintain her calm and her pride. She didn't want Parish to know how truly desperate she was. Short of ten dollars tucked in her shirt pocket, she was without funds. But she would survive somehow. She always had.

"No, you don't have to." His heart was in his eyes. "Come out to the ranch house, Josie. Live there with Mom and the family for a while."

"No!" Her tone was sharp. She had vowed never to trust a man again, or depend upon one. Besides, she just wouldn't abide charity.

"Why?" Still holding her carpetbag, he sat down upon the bed, as if intending to stay for a while.

"I have to go it alone, Parish. I don't want to impose my troubles on somebody else, or several somebodies."

"Impose?" He made a face. "Impossible. You know how much Mom likes you. She always has. She'd be as happy as a pea in a pod if you'd come, even for a little while. You see, I think she gets kind of lonely. That's one of the reasons she works at the laundry so hard when she could spend more time at home."

"Lonely?" Now that she thought about it, Josie

realized Nora Harper really was lonely. It had been there in her eyes.

"Your coming to stay would be a favor."

"And I could help around the ranch." There would be horses to break, outside chores to be done as well as housework.

"Yeah." Parish smiled. "And the ranch is far enough from town to keep you away from all the chatter but close enough so it will be convenient if there is anything you need."

Josie hesitated as the thought bounced around in her mind. Should she? Or should she just up and leave on the stage the way she had planned? A stab of hunger helped her make up her mind. There had been times when she had gone hungry. Did she want to go through that again?

"Please, Josie. Please say that you will come. You need friends."

Friends. At the moment perhaps that was her greatest need. People who cared, who would help her get her life settled again.

"Okay." She smiled. "But I'll stay for only a little while." That said, she finished packing, made the bed, straightened the pitcher, wiped up the spilled water, and hefted the key to her room in her hand.

"Follow me!" Parish was in a cheery mood as he led Josie down the stairs. She was likewise in a fairly decent mood, that is until she faced the dark-haired woman who owned the boardinghouse. That usually smiling matron was sullen and frowning as Josie handed her the key.

"So, you're going!" The way she said it seemed to say "at last." "Taking the stage?"

"Nope, she's going with me. She's going to be my family's houseguest for a while." Parish gave that bit of news out very proudly.

"Oh!" She eyed Josie up and down. "Well, you had best watch your step, or you might find yourself the target of a gun."

"I'm not worried."

"Maybe you should be." Reaching behind her desk, Gwen lifted up a leather object which she dangled in front of Josie's face. "I think this belongs to you." She dropped Josie's gun and holster on the counter. "The good doctor thought you might be needing it."

The good doctor. "Thank you." Picking it up, Josie fondled the gun, remembering the day they had bought it. Rafe had wanted her to pick out just the right one.

"Come on, Josie." Parish was eager to leave. Tipping his hat to Gwen, he gently pushed Josie toward the door.

"Wait!" Josie's heart lurched. For just a moment she was apprehensive about going through the door and facing the townspeople outside. No doubt they would be just as hostile as the woman behind her had been. Timidly she opened the door, her heart pounding. There were droves of people on the boardwalk. Proper citizens all. How would they react to her?

"Josie, just hold up your head." Good advice that she followed as people walked past her, bumped into her, and openly snubbed her. It seemed that if Tanner was well liked in town, Dr. Rafe Gardner was looked upon as an icon of respectability. Josie realized that her confrontation with Rafe had set her up once again in the townspeople's minds as a troublemaker. A troublemaker and a coward.

"Hey, girlie," a voice shouted behind her. "Want to have a gunfight?" There was guffawing in response to the jibe.

"Come on, strap on that gun. Or maybe peashooters at twenty paces is more in your line," said another voice. "That way you won't get hurt."

Parish's hand against the small of her back pushed Josie hard. "Now, Josie, don't be hurt."

Hurt? For just a moment Josie's temper threatened to burst. Whirling around, she faced the two grinning youths. Strapping on her holster, she slowly moved her hand up, then yelled out, "Boo!" Frightened, the two boys ran off.

"Well, that was the end of them!" Parish couldn't hold back his laughter. "I don't think they'll be offering any challenges for a while."

"No, I don't think so." She grinned, feeling better than she had in a long while. The incident had somehow given her back her spirit. She wouldn't let anyone or anything get her down. Not anymore.

"So, what do you say, shall we ride on out of here?" Parish nodded his head toward the stables.

"We ride," was Josie's reply.

The moon had set. The room was dark. It was the middle of the night, yet Rafe's eyes were blurred with sleeplessness, remembering that moment when Josie had conceded their fight. Why?

What thoughts had been swirling through her head the minute before she had laid down her gun? What were her feelings?

She didn't kill me. But she hadn't exactly said that she still loved him either. Even so, Rafe held a slim hope that maybe there still was a chance for them.

Josie needed time for her bruised emotions to heal, time to get her thoughts back into perspective. Maybe then she would realize how sorry he was for shooting her brother, how regretful he felt for causing her so much pain.

Maybe when all is said and done there will be something I can do to make it up to her. Like what? He couldn't bring her brother back to life. Couldn't wipe away the heartache of the last few years. But surely there was something he could do, some way he could show her how very much he loved her. "I have to make her see that life has to go on."

Pacing back and forth in his bedroom, it was all Rafe could do to keep himself from going to Josie. He wanted to hold her, stroke her hair, comfort her, tell her that she would always have his heart. But it was too soon. Instead, he just kept walking and walking until he was certain he had worn a hole in the rug. And all the while his eyes were riveted on the window, looking in the direction of the boardinghouse.

Thirty-two

The sun was a bright golden orb above the distant hills, the river reflecting its rays in the dirty water. Flocks of birds winged their way across the sky, sailing toward their source of fish. Two jackrabbits sprinted across the dirt pathway, casting wary glances at Parish and Josie as they rode along.

"Won't be too long now. The ranch is just a hop and a jump from here," Parish announced, pointing eastward.

"And you're sure that my staying will be all right? I feel strange about intruding."

"You won't be intruding at all. As I've said before, my mom likes you a lot and . . . and she knows how I feel about you, Josie." His blush was as bright as a sunburn.

"You have been a good friend, Parish. The best." Hastily Josie looked away, concentrating on the scenery, at last seeing the Harper ranch come into sight.

"See. There it is." Parish's voice rang with pride as they came upon a big adobe casa with red tiles on the roof. Around the ranch house was a wall and a forest of oak trees that huddled around like lookouts. Behind the trees were several acres of land that held the outbuildings and ranch animals.

"Impressive."

"For a woman who owns a laundry?" Parish laughed. "When my father ran off with a fancy woman from Tucson, Mom was left with the ranch and three young sons. She feared she'd lose everything, but— "

"But she knuckled down, and realizing that a town full of men would need somewhere to wash clothes, she made quite a profit with soap, washtub, and washboard."

"Right."

"A determined and resourceful woman. I admire that." Nora Harper was one of a kind.

The sound of laughter, neighing horses, barking dogs, rustling of cattle, the clatter of pots and pans from the cook shack, the grating boots on the hard ground, welcomed Parish and Josie upon their arrival at the Harper ranch.

"Quite a lively place."

"It will get livelier."

In a moment Josie knew just what he meant. From the corral two young men waved at them, then ran to their horses, swung up in their saddles, and galloped out to greet them.

"Ted and Ed," Parish announced.

Their shouts of glee let it be known that they were happy to see their young brother and the lady accompanying him.

"Who is your lady friend, little brother?" A man who looked a great deal like Parish only older and with a mustache rode up first.

"Just Josie," Parish called out, grinning as he recalled what she had said that first day they had met.

"Josie McLaury," Josie corrected him.

"Ted Harper." His eyes swept over her appreciatively. It was obvious that Parish was going to have some real competition for her affections.

"Ted is the ladies' man of the family," Parish said in warning. He turned to his other brother. "This is Ed. He's the daredevil of the Harper tribe."

Dark-haired, and shorter and stockier than the other two, Ed was the spitting image of his mother, even to the eyes and the smile. "Howdy." Taking off his hat, he swept Josie a bow.

"Josie is going to be staying here for a while." Parish looked at Josie and winked. "Until the furor dies down in town."

Parish and his brothers led Josie to the stables, where the horses were put into stalls. Then, taking her by the arm, Parish led her up the five curved stone steps to the house.

Through the open door to the rooms beyond, Josie could see the white stuccoed ceiling and walls and the wooden ranch-style furniture, two couches, four chairs, and a large rectangular table.

"I made the furniture," Parish said, leading her into the drawing room.

"It's homey." Red drapes were pulled aside to allow the rays of sun to stream in through the large window, adding a touch of warmth and light to the room. That light revealed a painting on the wall that caught Josie's eye. A lovely dark-haired woman with a smile like the Mona Lisa looked down at her as she walked by.

"Mother. She was quite a beauty in her day."

"She is now."

"Why, thank you, my dear." Dressed in a white lace dress, Nora Harper stood in the doorway, looking every inch the grande dame of a hacienda. "And welcome."

"Parish asked— "

"Because I told him that you would always be welcome here." Hurrying forward, she took Josie's hat, putting it on a peg near the door. "I heard what happened, Josie, and I'm sorry."

"So am I. More than I can say." Rafe's face flashed before her eyes.

"Well, for what it's worth, I think you were very brave. It took courage to back down."

"And stupidity to be out on that street in the first place," Josie replied quietly. In her heart she knew it would take a long, long time to forget all that had happened. Rafe was emblazoned in her heart and mind like a brand. Being surrounded by the Harpers, however, might be just what she needed.

Nora Harper ignored Josie's self-criticism, saying only, "Dinner is always at eight. Everyone is on their own for breakfast."

"I want to earn my keep." Josie was insistent on that.

"Good. I need help around the house. We can't afford a cook or a maid, so there will be plenty to do." Her laughter was melodic. "But as I recall, you were never a lounge-about."

"I'll keep this ranch house spotless." Josie didn't want to admit quite yet that she was a terrible cook. That was why Rafe had always done most of the cooking when they had been in Willcox. *Oh, Rafe.* Sad how often he came to her mind.

"And I'll help." Bounding up, Parish took her by the hand. "Come on, Josie. I'll show you to your room." He smiled sheepishly. "Mine."

"Yours?" For just a moment Josie was taken aback. Parish had sensed that there had been something between her and Rafe. Surely he wasn't suggesting . . . didn't think that she was . . .

"I'll sleep in the bunkhouse."

"Oh, no, you won't. I will!" Josie wasn't about to push Parish out of his own bed.

"We'll toss a coin." It was a toss that Josie won. Parish's room would be hers for her stay. A small room that was masculine from top to bottom. There were no ruffled curtains, no frills. Parish had furnished the bedroom with only the basic necessities. A single bed was covered in a serapelike bedspread, several Indian rugs were strewn on the wooden floor, the walls were covered with wooden pegs that held hats, belts, shirts, and vests. There was no chest of drawers. A small wooden table and a chair appeared to be multipurpose, used as a desk and as a washstand in the morning.

Parish put Josie's carpetbag down on the floor beside the bed. "Make yourself at home. As they say down here, *"Mi casa es tu casa."* That said, he left her alone.

"Mi casa es tu casa," Josie repeated. Plopping down on the bed, she stretched out, putting her

hands behind her head. For the first time in a long while she felt at ease and comfortable.

The heels of Rafe's boots made a staccato sound as he walked down the boardwalk toward the boardinghouse. He was determined. A week had gone by, enough time for Josie's feelings to cool off. It was time for a talk.

"Hello, Gwen." Pushing open the door, Rafe strode boldly inside.

"Long time no see, Rafe." Combing her fingers through her hair, Gwen fussed with her appearance.

"Just what do you mean by that?" Rafe wasn't in the mood for innuendos.

"Only that you have been as scarce as hen's teeth. Except for the day of your little gunfight fiasco when you asked me to give your lady love her gun and holster. You have been in hiding, or so it seems."

"I've been busy." A partial truth. "Helen Roberts just had twins, Ed Rawlston was down with the grip, Mary Gregory broke her leg, Jim Hendon cut off the tip of his finger with a saw, Frank Jenkins was bitten by a rattlesnake."

"How exciting," Gwen said sarcastically.

"Doctoring has its moments." He looked toward the stairs.

"She isn't there."

"What do you mean?" He frowned. "Has she gone out?"

Gwen shrugged. "You might say that!"

He scanned her face. "When did she leave?"

"Four days ago."

"And she hasn't returned?" His manner was curt.

"No." Gwen hesitated just a moment before she blurted out, "She left about four days ago with a young man. Parish Harper by name."

"Parish Harper? That young puppy?" He was in a foul mood, brought on partly by confusion and disappointment.

"Following at her heels, carrying her carpetbag. Looked to me as if she was planning to stay. Anyway, she gave up her room here." She seemed to take great delight in telling him that bit of news, but her attitude mellowed as she took note of his thunderous expression.

"Damn!" He hadn't counted on this turn of events. Josie had gone, vanished out of the blue. Terrible news made more upsetting by the fact that she had left with a young man.

Thirty-three

Rafe lay atop his bedcovers, several pillows cradling his head. For the last three days he had cloistered himself in his room, feeling irritable and sorry for himself. He was miserable. His nerves were shot, his head ached, every muscle in his body seemed to be rebelling. Not only that, but he couldn't be understood when he spoke because his nose was stuffed.

"Aaaaaachooooo . . . damchooo . . ." he swore, and sneezed at the same time. Of all the things he might have had plague him, this damned cold was something that he, despite being a doctor, couldn't do anything to cure. But then, what did it matter? He wasn't in a mood to go anywhere anyway. If that made him unsociable, well, so be it.

"All anyone ever talks about is that fool gunfight anyway." And Rafe just didn't want to be reminded. It was bad enough that when he could sleep he was disturbed by dreams of Josie. He didn't need the townspeople to remind him.

I'll just lie here and be miserable. What does it matter? And hope that in a week or so he would be as good as new again. Physically, that is. Emotionally he was in shambles, wondering if when all was said

and done he would lose Josie to that beardless nin-
compoop who had so eagerly played Sir Galahad
and swept her off to his . . . his . . . mother's
ranch house.

"Oh, for God's sakes!" He stifled another sneeze,
feeling thoroughly disgruntled, glaring at the door,
when he heard a knock. Whoever it was he just
wasn't up to any company.

"Rafe?"

"Go away!" he shouted out with unusual testi-
ness.

"No, I won't. Let me in. I'm worried about you."

It was Gwen. Undoubtedly she had come to gloat
about the turn of events in his life. "I don't wanna
see you!" Though he knew he was taking his frustration out on her for having been the messenger
of the unhappy tidings that Josie had gone off with
Parish Harper, he just didn't care.

"Rafe. Rafe, I'm sorry if you are angry at me.
But please, let me come in." There was a pause.
"I brought you something."

"I have the ague. I'm probably contagious." Oh,
what the devil. Knowing how insistent the woman
could be, Rafe gave up any hope of frightening
her away. "Cumb in. The door is oben," he snif-
fled.

He heard the door squeak, saw Gwen peek
around the half-open door. "Thought you might
need a little chicken soup." She smiled as she
spoke.

In spite of himself, his irritation at her was fading. Perhaps because he wasn't as satisfied being
all alone as he had thought. "Sounds like some-

thing any good doctor would prescribe." He eyed the bowl she had in her hand with upraised brows.

Boldly she pushed into the room, taking note of his unshaven face, uncombed hair, and generally disheveled appearance. "And from the looks of you, it seems I've arrived just in time."

Sitting up, Rafe combed his fingers through his hair, grateful that he couldn't see into a mirror. He supposed he probably did look pretty terrible. "I'b been sick" was all he could think of to say.

Her look was all-knowing. "Yes, I'd say that you were." She blurted out the words. "Lovesick, that is."

Her statement really riled him. "The hell!" He was just about to tell her to turn right around and leave, but before he could speak, he realized she had shoved a spoon into his mouth.

"Tell me to mind my own business if you want to, but I don't think it is only your sniffles ailing you right now. Why, I've noticed the way you have been acting." She dipped the spoon in the bowl and gave him another taste of her delicious soup. "In a manner that would make the word hermit sound cordial."

Rafe stiffened. "Hermit?"

"Keeping to yourself, not talking to anyone. Walking down the street as if you're in a trance. Standing out in the rain like a man who doesn't know enough to get out of a storm." She sighed. "Oh, Rafe. It's so pitifully obvious."

"Just what do you mean by that, Gwen?" Though he shouted, his expression was so downhearted and sad that she reached out and patted his hand.

"You really do love that girl, don't you, Rafe?"

"Girl? What girl?" he questioned sarcastically.

"You know perfectly well what girl I'm talking about." Now it was Gwen who was irritated. "Josie Smith, of course." Putting the bowl of chicken soup on a table near his bed, she began her earnest conversation again. "It's written all over your face how you feel about her, so don't try to act snide."

"It's none of your business." Rafe moved so suddenly, so violently, he nearly sent the bowl tumbling to the floor. Only Gwen's agility saved the day. Protectively she held on to the steaming vessel.

"No, I don't suppose it is, except that I hate to see you so depressed." Her own feelings glowed in her eyes. "I care about you, Rafe. I don't want to see you torturing yourself like this." Her voice lowered to little more than a whisper. "What's done is done. You can't change what happened. Nor can you keep punishing yourself for the ways things turned out. It wasn't your fault."

"It was." He was man enough to put the blame where it belonged.

Realizing she was tired, Gwen plopped down in a chair. "Oh, sure, you did kill the young woman's brother. But that was an accident, Rafe. And from that accident came a lot of good because of your decision to turn to doctoring."

Rafe walked slowly to his black leather bag. Opening it up, he took out a stethoscope and ran his fingers down the tubing. "I wish— "

"That things had turned out differently." Gwen

stirred the soup with the spoon absentmindedly. "I don't think there is a person alive who doesn't wish that about something." For a long time she didn't speak, then, looking up at him, she offered her advice. "Give Josie time, Rafe. Time to heal." She tapped her heart. "In here."

"Time?" He frowned. "It doesn't seem that I have any other choice." Josie had run away so that she wouldn't have to see him, wouldn't have to listen.

"No, perhaps you don't, but if you believe in fate the way I do, then you have to believe in happy endings." Her voice sounded so sad that now it was Rafe who was sympathetic.

"There hasn't been much happiness for you."

Gwen shrugged. "Oh, there have been times— " For a moment she had a faraway look in her eyes, then, as if to disengage herself from distant memories, she shook her head. "If Josie feels about you the way you feel about her, then she will learn to forgive you. Someday."

"Someday." Though Rafe knew she was trying to cheer him up, that word just didn't make him feel very hopeful.

Thirty-four

Josie opened the curtains to her bedroom window and looked out at the cattle grazing peacefully in the distance. Little by little she was beginning to feel at home. Certainly the Harpers had been very kind to her, though she knew that Parish's feelings went far beyond kindness. That was the only thing that made her uncomfortable. She liked Parish. Liked him a lot, but not in a romantic way. The problem was how was she going to get that through his head without hurting him and alienating his friendship.

Ever since arriving, Parish had hovered around Josie like an ant around a jelly jar. When she was doing the dishes, Parish was there to dry. When she was cooking, he was there to lend a hand. When she was sweeping, he showed up with a broom in his hand. When she was at the well, he carried the buckets. If her chore was doing the laundry, he helped her hang it out to dry. At dinner his place was always at her side.

As she stared out the window, Parish came into sight, riding around the corner of the barn, heading for the grazing cattle. Looking over his shoulder and seeing her through the glass pane, he took off his hat, brazenly showing off for her as he reined his horse from side to side, riding in a small arc to scatter the herd. Then, zeroing in on a calf, he methodically went about the job of roping and branding it.

Josie watched for a while, impressed with Parish's ability, then turned from the window. She didn't have time to lollygag around. There were a dozen things to do before midmorning. She had to light the stove and put water on to heat. There were eggs to gather, chickens to feed, cows to be milked, butter to be churned, bread to be baked. The Harper boys were hearty eaters. Later in the day there was laundry to do, dishes to wash, floors to be swept, candles to be dipped, soap to be made.

"Whew!" Just thinking about it made her tired. Going about those chores caused her to be dead on her feet.

Coming into the kitchen, watching Josie hard at work peeling potatoes, Nora Harper was concerned. "When I said I needed help around here, Josie, I didn't mean I expected you to be our slave."

"I know." Pausing, Josie wiped her shirt-sleeve across her forehead. It was hot in the kitchen.

"Then why don't you relax, dear?" Nora Harper picked up a potato and a knife to lend a hand.

"The busier I am, the less time I have to think. I want it that way." Hard work left her too bone-weary at night to feel sad, angry, or regretful.

"It's a man, isn't it?"

The question took Josie by surprise. "What do you mean?"

Nora wiped her hands on her apron. "I've been through it. I recognize all the signs. You don't eat very well, you nibble at even the most appetizing food, I hear you tossing and turning at night, your mind seems to be elsewhere, you seldom smile."

"It's Charlie's death. I . . . I . . ."

"You have had a difficult time adjusting to your brother's death, I know. That's why you got involved in that gunfight. But that's not what's troubling you now."

Josie couldn't lie. "All right. It is a certain someone."

"May I be so bold as to ask who?" Nora Harper's eyes were compassionate.

Josie's wounds were still too recent. "If you will forgive me, I just don't want to talk about it." She let out a long sigh.

"I understand. It took me a long time too." She looked toward the doorway where Parish stood, smiling. "But don't make my mistake. Don't give up on love. There are good men in the world too." Her eyes seemed to say, *Like my Parish.*

"I know." Josie concentrated on the potato in her hand. She tried hard to banish any thoughts of Rafe Gardner from her mind, but it was difficult. Just the smell of the coffee brewing on the potbellied stove reminded her of those blissful days together at his ranch.

"It's a nice sunny day, Josie. Not too hot, like some. Too beautiful to be cooped up in here."

She shrugged. "Can't help that, Parish, I've got work to do. Tonight we're having beef stew." Putting the peeled potato in a pot, she reached for a carrot.

"Which I am perfectly capable of preparing." Giving Josie a push, Nora Harper said, "Go on out and enjoy what's left of the day." When Josie hesitated, she said, "Shoo!"

Parish gestured toward the door. "Come on. Mom has just issued you a reprieve. Let's go for a long walk."

"A walk?" Josie was so used to riding on horseback that the idea of stroll was a refreshing one. "Okay."

It was a pleasant walk along the riverbank, where the grass and bushes were thick and flowers bloomed like a living rainbow. A warm breeze stirred the air and it felt good against Josie's skin.

"It's peaceful out here. A place where I go just to relax and think."

"It's beautiful." Josie sat down on a rock, contenting herself to just look out at the wildly flowing water.

"Josie . . ."

She turned her head and saw that Parish was staring at her.

"I don't think you really know just how much I like being with you."

"Yes, I think I do. And I like being with you too."

"No, it's more than just being in your company." His brows drew together in a puzzled frown. "Oh, hell, I just don't know how to say it."

"Parish . . ." Her voice was a mere whisper, but her eyes revealed her inner feelings.

"You still care about him."

"It's over." Yet just saying the words made her feel as if her whole world was crumbling at her feet. "At least in my mind it is."

"And in your heart?" He studied her keenly, his eyes searching her face for an answer. A silent minute passed, and then another and another. He reached out and took her hand, clasping it tightly. "I could make you forget." He sat down on the rock beside her. "Marry me."

His words stunned her. "You can't mean it."

"I do."

"No!" She picked up a rock and flung it into the river. "I'll never marry anyone, Parish," she mused out loud. "I opened up my heart to him. We . . . we were together. And all the while he killed my brother, only I didn't know— "

"And then you found out."

"And everything went topsy-turvy." She laughed bitterly. "And here all the while I had been harassing poor Clint Tanner, threatening to shoot him." She felt the pressure of Parish's fingers as he squeezed her hand. "Please understand. It's nothing against you."

"But it will take you a while to forget."

"Maybe a long time." If ever. The truth was, she felt in her heart that what happened with Rafe would haunt her soul forever.

He pulled up a weed, putting it to his mouth pensively. "I'll wait."

* * *

The light from the lamp was burning low, and Rafe reached over to turn up the wick, at the same time keeping an eye on the ledgers scattered before him. Josie had been a distraction for him for such a long time that he had let his paperwork go. There were bills to be paid, medicine to be ordered, and accounts to be brought up-to-date.

"Hmmmm."

By the looks of it, he had been much too lenient for too long. It seemed half the town owed him money. He couldn't settle for chickens, eggs, pigs, and homemade jellies forever. The truth of it was he needed some hard cash and needed it now. The problem was he just didn't like to be demanding because he knew that most of the townspeople were struggling financially.

"I suppose I could rent out my ranch down in Willcox." The truth of the matter being that since he and Josie were now estranged lovers, the very thought of the place made him sad. "Or I could sell that silly gun collection of mine." Just the very sight of it made him wince.

So Josie is living at the Harper ranch. Well, perhaps that is the best thing for her. Nora Harper is, after all, a good woman. Maybe she'll take her under her wing and help her get over the hurt I caused her. As to Nora Harper's sons, Rafe didn't feel the same. Ted, Ed, and Parish were all eligible men and no doubt Josie would be on the rebound. It was hard to tell what might happen.

"But whatever does, it's none of your damned

business," he said aloud, reminding himself for the hundredth time. And yet, how would he feel were Josie to fall in love with one of Nora Harper's sons? Perhaps even marry one of them?

Picking up his pen and dipping it in the inkwell, he forced the very thought out of his mind. Whatever happened, Josie deserved happiness. He couldn't be grudging or resentful, or worst of all, jealous.

"Let's see. Ben Archibald still owes me for setting his broken arm. Barnabas Hershel never did give me any payment for lancing his boils." And the list got longer and longer.

Leaning back in his black leather chair, Rafe stretched his arms over his head as he stifled a yawn. It was getting late. He had been working on his ledgers for an hour now and he was tired. Closing his eyes, he relaxed, nearly drifting off to sleep.

A loud knock at the door put an end to Rafe's solitude. "Open up! Hurry!" Tanner's voice.

"Okay. Okay. Don't break it down." He flung the door open to a strange sight. Clint Tanner was there all right, his tall frame and weight supported by one of his cronies. "Ed, what's wrong with him?"

"Drunk as usual. Jumped up on one of the tables to spout off about something or other and fell off. His leg went through the seat of a chair. Next thing I knew, he was grabbing at his ankle and screaming."

"Let me see." Rafe bent down.

"It's broke!" Putting his weight on the injured leg, Clint Tanner winced, moaning with pain.

"Maybe not. Could be sprained. We'll try to get your boot off so I can see."

Tanner took an uneasy step but almost fell as his leg buckled.

"Let me help." Going to Tanner's other side, Rafe helped Ed Crawley bring his friend in to Rafe's office. "Put him in that chair."

"Easy. Easy, Rafe. I'm injured." Clint Tanner looked more like a little boy than a man as he leaned on the other two men's shoulders, hopping all the way.

"Let's take off that boot and examine the damage." Pulling up a stool, Rafe hefted Tanner's leg.

"Ouch!"

His ankle was swollen, so swollen that Rafe couldn't get the boot over it. "I'll have to cut it off."

"Cut it off? These are my five-dollar boots. Calf leather. Cost a fortune." Tanner made a face. "Hell, I'd rather just wait and let my leg heal right in the boot."

"You can buy another pair, but you can't buy another ankle." Without bothering to listen to any argument, Rafe methodically went about cutting the leather with a knife, then peeled the boot away. "Hmm." Carefully be poked and prodded at the injured leg. "Sooooo."

"Bad?" Tanner muttered beneath his breath, "Shit!"

"Hope you weren't planning on doing any dancing." Ed Crawley started to laugh, then quickly sobered.

"Is it broke?"

Rafe shook his head. "You're not that lucky."

"What?" Looking down at his ankle, Tanner looked horrified. "Worse than that?" His eyes shifted to Rafe's instrument case with all its saws, pliers, and knifes. "You're not going to—"

"Amputate." Throwing back his head, Rafe laughed. "Of course not. But your ankle is badly sprained. It will take some time to heal properly."

"Which means?" Tanner was surly.

"You're going to have to take it easy." Rafe carefully wrapped the foot in a thick cotton bandage. "Stay off that leg for a week or two. Then favor it for at least a month."

"When will it be healed?"

"Come back in two weeks and I'll be able to tell you for sure."

"Two weeks. Damn. Just when he's really needed." Crawley went to the window and peeked out. "The Clayton gang has made their camp on a low, eroded mesa a few miles south of town. Could be trouble. Especially if word gets out that Clint here is holed up like a one-legged crow.

"The Clayton gang, huh." The four men were fiercesome, unlawful desperadoes who left a trail of bloodshed and havoc where ever they went. "We'll have to do all that we can to keep them out of Showlow." *And away from the Harper ranch*, Rafe thought, wanting to protect Josie.

Thirty-five

Rafe drummed his fingers on the large mahogany desktop, squinting against the dim lighting of the room as he concentrated on the letter spread out before him.

Dear Josie,
There is not a day that passes when I don't think about you. I miss you and regret very deeply the terrible deed that hardened your heart against me. Even so, I hope that someday you will find a way to forgive me and to—

"No!" As he read the words, Rafe was dissatisfied. He wadded the paper up and tossed it into the wastebasket. He tried again, this time making an attempt to sound less dramatic.

Dear Josie,
I hear that you are staying with the Harper family. I hope that makes you happy and that you are well—

Again he wadded up his scribbling and threw it away.

"That makes number ten." Ten attempts at putting his thoughts into words. Ten failures. "I'm certainly not any Mark Twain or Shakespeare," he grumbled, disappointed in his efforts.

Clutching his pen, Rafe gave it one more try.

Josie,
   There are so many things I need to say to you, so many words left unspoken. Though I know you have hardened your heart against me, I can only hope and pray that you will give me a chance to explain my thoughts and my feelings someday. That is all I can possibly wish for—

A loud thump announced a visitor. Putting down his pen, Rafe swore as he recognized Clint Tanner's woeful hobbling. "What is it now, Clint?"

"My damn leg hurts!"

"Of course it does, considering the fact that you haven't followed my advice." Like a father scolding a wayward child, Rafe shouted out, "Keep off that leg."

"I have." Tanner pouted. "You don't have to yell." Limping, he made his way to Rafe's medicine cabinet. "Give me something, doc, something to take away this constant throbbing. It's driving me insane." Opening the cabinet door, he reached for a bottle of laudanum.

"Put that back!" Reacting quickly, Rafe slammed the cabinet shut, nearly catching Clint Tanner's fingers in the door. "That's my last bottle. I'm saving it for emergencies."

"Yeah. Little old ladies with sleeping problems,

I suppose." Tanner wrinkled his nose and twisted his lips. "Well, I need it much more than they, old *friend.*"

"What you need is a good kick in the pants!" Rafe countered, feeling quarrelsome all of a sudden. Tanner's doing. "Old *friend!*" Softening his temper just a little, Rafe did concede a glass of his best bourbon. He crossed the room and fetched it from its hiding place in the broom closet.

"What's this?"

Rafe glanced up as he was pouring Tanner's whiskey, flushing as he realized that Clint had picked up his letter to Josie. "It's nothing!"

"Nothing?" Tanner seemed to sense otherwise. Holding it up to the light, he struggled with the words but made out enough of the letters to put two and two together. "Aw, Rafe. A love letter?"

"No!" Eager to retrieve the paper, Rafe charged across the room, reaching for the letter.

Tanner grinned like a devious imp. "Not so fast." Looking toward the medicine cabinet, he had the audacity to suggest there could be a trade. "I give you your letter and you give me the laudanum."

Rafe stood firm. "No!"

"Letter, laudanum. Letter, laudanum," Tanner teased.

Rafe wasn't one to give in to such a high-handed maneuver. He was just about to tell Tanner so, when the office door flew open. A tall, dark-haired young woman stepped briskly into the room. For the moment the letter was forgotten.

"Doctor, it's Nora Harper. I—I think she's ill."

"Ill?" Out of habit he reached for his black leather bag. "What is it?"

"I don't know. Or, at least, she just won't say. But it's obvious to see that she sometimes has trouble breathing." The young woman shook her head. "She works so hard. Too hard, it seems."

Rafe's eyes narrowed. "Hmmmm. Sounds like I need to take a look at her." Such things could never be taken lightly, particularly at Nora Harper's age. Picking up his hat, he followed the young woman to the door, pausing just long enough to shoo Tanner out. Carefully locking his office door, he followed the young woman down the street.

Pushing through the door, he was reminded of Josie and the time she had put starch in his underwear. Despite himself, he smiled. Though he had not realized it, everything had been so simple back then. If only he had known . . .

"Just put your bag on the counter, doc. I'll get Nora."

Setting his black bag down, Rafe nodded. It was late afternoon. A busy time with customers mulling around. Each of the girls was busy working the wringers and washboards. Was it any wonder that it was noisy? So noisy that it almost ruined his concentration as he mentally ticked off a list of questions he wanted to ask Nora while he examined her. Was Josie happy? Was she well? Was she settling in to stay at the Harper ranch for a long time?

"My letter!" Rafe clenched his fist, wishing he had gotten it back from Clint. He could have quickly finished it and brought it with him, could have given it to Nora Harper to give to Josie.

"Psssst. There's Dr. Gardner."

Hearing his name, Rafe slowly turned his head. Two of the young women were avidly gossiping, mentioning his name from time to time.

"Do you think that he and Josie McLaury were lovers?"

"Of course. I haven't any doubt."

"But she was going to shoot him."

"Oh, yes, at least that's what she said. But you notice that she couldn't go through with it."

"Could you? He's so handsome, and there are so few good-looking men in this town." Both young women giggled.

"Much better-looking than Parish Harper, I'd say."

"Even so, the rumor going around is that Parish Harper is Josie's beau. Why else would she be living at the Harper ranch."

Why else indeed, Rafe thought, his hopes for a reunion dampened. Now he was glad he hadn't finished that letter. All he would have accomplished was to have made a damned fool of himself. Talk to Nora Harper about Josie? Never. Josie was the one who had called him out, who had threatened to shoot him. If she wanted to make amends, she would have to come to him.

"Doc." The young woman who had called at Rafe's office looked sheepish. "Sorry to have troubled you, but it appears that when Nora found out from one of the other girls that I had gone to get you, she well . . . well . . . skedaddled."

"Left?" Rafe looked toward the door.

"She told Emily she didn't want to be a bother to you. That you had plenty on your hands as it was with all the sick people. She said she didn't want you being troubled by her. Said she was just tired. That she is as strong as a horse."

Rafe wasn't convinced. "Even horses, strong or not, can have maladies." Rafe picked up his bag. "So you tell Nora Harper that I won't rest until she's let me take a look at her." He walked toward the door. "You tell her."

"I will. But Mrs. Harper can be stubborn. Nearly as stubborn as Josie." The young woman followed after Rafe. "Doc, I'm sorry things didn't work out."

Rafe turned. "You mean concerning Mrs. Harper?"

"No." The gray eyes were wide, sympathetic. "I mean with Josie."

"Oh." Rafe swallowed the lump in his throat. "So am I." He didn't realize it was possible to feel so miserable.

Thirty-six

Josie stood before the mirror, trying to arrange her hair into something besides braids, but she was having difficulty with the task. Every time she tried to secure a lock of hair with a pin, several stubborn tendrils fell loose.

"Damn! I give up." Losing her temper, she yanked out all the pins, letting her hair fall loose, a tangle over her shoulders. Tying a ribbon around her head, she decided that hairdo would just have to suffice.

What does it matter? I'm not looking for a husband. To the contrary, however, she suspected that Parish was looking for a wife. Her. And because of that she was beginning to feel as if the entire family was trying to change her.

It was not that she was not contented there, or that the Harpers were not polite and kind to her, but they seemed to be trying to feminize her. At first there had been subtle hints— Josie's gun and holster had up and disappeared from her room, then hair ribbons had been laid upon her bed. A pink and white calico dress had appeared next, a gift from Nora Harper.

"I'm not sure I like this. I'm not sure at all," Josie muttered, staring at her reflection.

Nora Harper and Parish liked it, however. Josie knew that they meant well, wanted her to be happy. They insisted that it was like the metamorphosis of a caterpillar to a butterfly. Josie was willing to try being more of a woman but at the same time fearful that all too soon the old Josie would disappear and in her place would be one of those silly, chattering females she had always abhorred.

Even so, she had humored them as the days had settled into an established routine, perhaps because she just wasn't in a frame of mind to argue. Breakfast was precisely between six and seven, and Josie was usually the first one up, the one to put on the coffee. Afterward she busied herself with household chores. Lunch was usually sandwiches— ham, chicken, or beef. The early afternoon was spent riding or walking with Parish.

The late afternoon was a time for dinner preparation and finishing work left undone. But though the Harpers were being most hospitable, the fact of the matter was that most of the time Josie preferred to be alone. She needed time to heal. Parish was a good man, but she just wasn't ready for another relationship.

I have been such a fool. So naive. I'll never really trust again.

Josie had worked hard, hoping to keep her thoughts so occupied that she wouldn't think of Rafe, but no amount of toil could ease the ache in her heart. The truth was she all too vividly remembered how it had been between them. She mourned for the loss of the good times and secretly feared what the future held in store for her. One thing she had learned was that life was rarely fair. If it were, then Charlie would still be alive, she would be happy, and—

"Josie!" It was Nora Harper's voice, accompanied by a soft knocking. "Are you in there, dear?"

"Just a moment." Looking at her reflection one more time, Josie yanked off the ribbon, a gesture of rebellion, then opened the door.

"Oh, Josie, don't you look stunning. Parish was right. Pink is your color."

"Thank you." Josie wrinkled her nose. Personally, pink had always reminded her of a newly birthed baby's behind. And as to dresses, Josie really had no use for them. But could she be a tomboy forever, strutting around and doing just as she pleased? No. What had happened in town had proven that. She had been a willful child; now perhaps it was time to grow up.

"Before we eat I have a surprise for you." Whatever it was, Nora seemed to be holding it behind her back.

"A surprise."

Squinting her eyes, Nora Harper let her gaze sweep from the top of Josie's head to the toes of her boots poking out beneath her dress. "Shoes." She held out a small box. "The latest fashion. And if Parish measured correctly from your boots, just the right size."

"Shoes." Josie stared at them, hiding her distaste. Not only were they high-heeled and pinched at the toe, but they had laces. It would take her forever just to cinch them up. "I don't— " She started to tell Mrs. Harper that she didn't want them, but the glow in the woman's eyes changed her mind. "Thank you."

She reached for the present, putting them on a nearby chair. She hoped she wouldn't have to wear them too often. She was comfortable in her boots. They were old, but at least they were broken in.

"Put them on. Please."

It was a polite request that was impossible to refuse. Plopping down in the chair, Josie pulled off her boots and began the tedious task of lacing up the shoes, a task that took her fumbling fingers a long, long time.

"How do they fit?"

Standing up, Josie hobbled around, wincing as the shoes pinched her toes. Bravely, however, she smiled, saying, "Perfectly. Thank you." She didn't want to be beholden. "But you must let me pay for them."

"Pay? Pooh!" Nora Harper wouldn't hear of it.

Josie took Nora's hand in a rare show of affection. "But you have been more than generous already and— "

"Hush." She put her finger to Josie's lips. "With so many sons it gives me pleasure to at last have a girl to spoil." Nora Harper had in fact begun to act toward Josie as the daughter she'd wanted but never had. "But come . . ." Together they went in to the dining room.

A wolf whistle met Josie's entrance. Ted Harper appraised Josie with a look that bothered Parish. "Careful, little brother. I might give you a run for your money." Leaping to his feet, he pulled out Josie's chair, elbowing Parish in the ribs when he tried to interfere. A brotherly tussle erupted.

"Ted! Parish!" Nora Harper's anger was evident as she moved forward to pull them apart. "I will have none of that in this house. This isn't a barroom, boys."

"Sorry, Mother." Parish and his brother smiled sheepishly as they sat back down.

"Pass the gravy." Ignoring his brothers' quarrel, Ed was eager to eat.

"After grace!"

It was Ed's turn. Putting down his knife and fork, he said a quick prayer of thanks. Then with an impish smile he said, "Dig in."

Josie gazed avidly at the roast pork garnished with orange slices and parsley. It was the first time she had ever cooked a roast of any kind, and she could only hope that it was not overdone. And what about the gravy? Was it really supposed to be that lumpy? Oh, well!

"Perfect, Josie." Parish was quick to offer praise before he had even tasted it, a praise that was echoed all around the table. Silverware clinked, and there was the sound of chewing as everyone around the table partook of the food.

"Edward!" Nora offered another rebuke as she caught him eating with his fingers. "Your fork. Your fork!"

Guiltily he looked down at his greasy fingers. "Okay. Okay!"

Parish laughed as he cut a slice of pork roast and stabbed it with his fork. "See, it's easy, Ed.

And it keeps your fingers clean so that you don't get the tablecloth dirty." Parish's grin faltered as he looked at his mother. "Mom, you look tired."

She shook her head. "Well, I'm not."

Ted looked up. "You're working much too hard." He returned to the roast pork.

"A little hard work never hurt anybody!" For just a moment a shadow passed over her face. She put a hand to her throat, pausing for a moment before she said, "Besides, no matter what you think, I enjoy it."

"Enjoy it? Toiling over a hot tub of soap and water?" Ted was incredulous.

"I enjoy the people. My customers are my friends, Theodore." She picked up her fork, then set it down.

Parish interceded. "Well, we boys have taken a vote and we say you need to slow down."

"Right. You have enough girls to handle the work." Ed's voice was clipped and short. "And you have Josie now to help out here."

"But Mother is stubborn," Ted said in a whisper.

"Stubborn," they all agreed, then all conversation died. The only sound was that of the hearty eaters scraping their forks across their plates as they finished the food. Josie removed the plates and threw the bones to the two hounds outside. When she reached for Nora's plate, however, she stiffened. "Nora!"

The woman's eyes were staring. She was clutching at her chest. She was having difficulty drawing her breath.

"Nora!" At that moment Josie knew that something was very wrong. "Parish."

In a rare show of excitement Parish's voice exploded. "Mother! Mother!" Bending down, he grasped her by the shoulders. "Somebody ride into town and get the doctor. My God, something's happening to her."

"The doctor!" As Nora Harper's sons gathered around her, Josie knew that somebody would have to be her.

Thirty-seven

Rafe was in a somber, restless mood that no amount of work could alleviate. Pouring himself a glass of brandy, he sat down at his desk, fighting the feelings that threatened to engulf him. He just couldn't forget her. It was as simple as that. He remembered the first time he had kissed her, couldn't forget how soft her naked body was against his own. And yet it wasn't just the passion they had shared that made him feel such a great sense of loss. It was her companionship, her determination, her smile. The way she cocked her head, the way her eyes always sparkled when she looked at him. Hell, he even missed her stubbornness.

Always a man who valued his solitude, his privacy, it was the first time in his life that Rafe had really felt alone. Lonely. His office had once seemed to be so peaceful, a haven of quiet when other people were not there; now the silence troubled him. He missed her laughter, her conversation, her very presence beside him.

"God help me, I love her. Really love her." It was a fine time to find out.

Unfastening the top buttons of his shirt, Rafe

leaned back in his favorite chair, fighting the sudden insane impulse to saddle up his horse and ride out to the Harper ranch. What would it bring him but her scorn, her anger?

You've lost her. Better get used to it. Trying to drum it into his head, he said it over and over. "You've lost her." A cruel taunt that twisted and coiled in the pit of his stomach.

"But somehow you will survive," he murmured, sipping his brandy. Somehow.

A knock and then another knock sounded at the door. Loud. Urgent.

"If that's you again, Clint, I'll tell you for the umpteenth time, stay off that leg and quit bothering me. It's going to take time to heal, I told you. There's nothing more I can do. Nothing. Now, just go away."

The knocking sounded again. Louder. "It's not Clint Tanner," called out a voice. "It's me. Josie."

"Josie?" Rafe was up like a shot, moving to the door so quickly that he tipped over his glass. Brandy oozed over the papers on his desk, but he ignored the mess as he yanked at the doorknob. "Josie!"

Her dress was dirty, her hair tousled, her face pale. Breathing hard, rasping as she talked, she blurted out, "It's Mrs. Harper. Something is wrong. She's ill. At dinner she collapsed, clutching at her chest."

There was no time for questions or for accusations; still, it was obvious that the feelings between them had not died. Not for Josie and not for Rafe. Something nearly tangible crackled in air.

"I'll get my bag."

"Hurry." *I thought I could handle this,* Josie thought. But the mere sight of him knocked down all her carefully constructed emotional walls. Her heart was racing out of control; blood drummed in her ears.

Snatching up his black doctor's bag, hastily stuffing a bottle of digitalis inside just in case Nora Harper had suffered a heart attack, Rafe was ready. Gently, he pushed her out the door.

It took only a moment to ready his horse. "Let's go."

Ignoring her skirt, Josie swung up into her saddle. Nudging her horse in the ribs, she followed after Rafe.

Overhead the sky was already a deep purple umbrella, but luckily there were no clouds to block out the moon's light. It guided them as they rode through the darkness. Faster and faster they rode down the dusty red path that led to the Harpers'. There was no time for talk. Still, as she watched Rafe ride up ahead of her, Josie knew they would have to talk sometime. There were too many things left unsaid, too many recriminations between them. She didn't want that.

They arrived at the ranch in good time. Rafe quickly dismounted and handed his horse over to Josie just as the door flew open. Parish came flying out, grabbing the doctor by the arm without a word spoken. Josie tethered the horses, then followed the two men inside. Sitting on a chair in the corner, she watched as Rafe took out his instruments and examined the pale, rigid woman lying on the bed.

"She's had a heart attack."

"A heart attack." Parish was beside himself as he clutched his mother's hand. "Will she die?"

"No." Disengaging the son's hand from his mother's, Rafe felt her pulse." But she is going to have to stay in bed to recover and after that slow down. I would say that your mother has been working much too hard."

"She has. Pushing herself without any reason."

"Some people do." Rafe was known to do that many times out of habit, anxiety, ambition, or a need to forget. "But she will have to take it easy."

"I'll— I'll help out at the laundry." It was the least she could do, Josie thought, after they had all been so good to her. "And take care of things here." She would work mornings at the ranch and afternoons at the laundry. It would work out.

"I'll work at the laundry. You stay here with Mother." Ed was quick to volunteer. "Though I must admit I don't know a damned thing about washing clothes. Mother always did it. But somehow I'll manage."

"We'll all have to pitch in." Looking first at Rafe then at Josie, Parish seemed to be trying to judge what feelings there were between them. "You can count on me to do whatever is needed."

"Good. Then I'll give you these pills," Rafe answered, taking them out of his bag. "But they are to be used only if she has another attack like the one she had tonight."

Parish took the bottle, holding the amber-colored glass up to the light. "What are they?"

"Digitalis. A heart stimulant."

"Heart stimulant." Parish looked doubtful. Putting the pills on the table by the bed, he appeared to have reservations about the medicine.

"It's made from the dried leaves of the common foxglove. Known since the seventeenth century. Believe me, the pills will not harm her. To the contrary, they might save her life."

"Oh, well, then, of course."

Rafe straightened from his scrutiny of the older woman. "As to prescribing rest and giving you the pills, that's all I can do, I'm afraid. The rest is up to your mother."

"Then it doesn't look good?" Ted was concerned. He grabbed at Rafe's shoulder. "Does it, doc? Does it?"

"I didn't say that." Rafe's voice was stern. "But I will tell you that if your mother doesn't listen, if she gets out of that bed too soon or pushes herself again, it might have dire consequences."

"I see." Parish scowled, then gestured to his brothers. "Let's have a conference on it." Motioning to his brothers, he led them out of the room, leaving Josie and Rafe alone.

"How have you been, Josie?" Just being there with her made Rafe feel vulnerable. It was as if every nerve were exposed, as if his emotions were naked.

"I've been fine." Just the way he looked at her melted her heart, made it feel raw and aching. "And you?"

"Fine." His voice was cool and self-assured. "Fine." No, not fine, he wanted to say. I want you. I need you. I miss you. But everything he'd said to her before had been misunderstood. Would it be any different now?

"Rafe . . ." Josie sat in strained silence for endless minutes. Seeing him again, even under the circumstances, made her feel breathless, giddy.

He turned and caught her staring at him. "Are you content living here?"

"Yes. The Harpers have been very good to me."

"I'm glad." He fumbled with his stethoscope, using it as an excuse not to look at her. There was just too much pain in her eyes. He couldn't stand that.

"Rafe . . ." Suddenly she wanted to bury the past, wanted to forgive and forget. He had said it so truthfully the day of their aborted gunfight: "One death can't be vindicated by another." Likewise it was true that anger didn't vindicate a thing. All it did was destroy. She started to say just that, but her timing was bad. Before she had a chance to form the words, the Harper boys had come back.

"We've got it all settled among ourselves. Want you to know everything is under control, doc," Parish began.

"Even if we have to rope and tie Mother, she's going to slow down," Ed continued.

"Because we don't want to lose her."

"Good," Rafe answered as he was being pushed toward the door by the youngest son. An obvious gesture of dismissal.

"Thanks for coming out. We'll keep in touch."

Rafe wasn't fooled in the least. Parish Harper just didn't want him hanging around any more than was necessary. Another thing that was clear was that he cared a great deal for Josie. But did she care at all for him? Looking into her eyes, he didn't think so. Somehow he sensed that all was not lost. Somehow he thought he might still have a chance.

Thirty-eight

The room was cloaked in semidarkness, emphasizing the figure lying on the white sheets of the bed. Nora Harper's condition was unchanged in the three days following. Rafe had told the Harper boys to summon him immediately if their mother took a turn for the worse. She was neither better nor worse. That she wasn't worse gave everyone in the household hope, especially Josie. Nora had love on her side. That was enough to make anyone pull through.

Parish hovered anxiously over his mother's bedside, even when it wasn't his turn to watch over her. Mumbling under his breath, he damned Rafe and all physicians. "Quacks, all of them." He threatened to have the doctor's head if anything happened to Nora.

"I'm sure that Rafe knows what he is doing," Josie defended, remembering the professional way he had handled the matter. "I know when I got shot he fixed me up so well that I hardly even have a scar."

"Rafe! My, you are so familiar. Don't you mean the doctor?" Parish's jealousy was evident.

Blushing Josie caught herself. "Yes. Dr. Gardner."

Even after three days she was still thinking about their meeting. She wanted to see him again, wanted that very badly. The only problem was that Nora Harper's illness kept her tied to the ranch. She couldn't just go traipsing off, even for him. And yet Josie had been doing a lot of thinking lately. Parish had somehow changed. Instead of being warm and kind, he was becoming possessive, as if her staying at the ranch somehow made her obligated to him. Suddenly she realized that she couldn't stay there and have him think that there would ever be anything between them but friendship. It just wasn't fair or true. As soon as Nora Harper got on her feet again she planned to leave. It was time to strike out on her own again. She had always liked being independent.

Nora Harper liked being independent too. So much so that as she started to recuperate, she was, as Ted said, a handful. It was almost necessary to tie her to the bed to keep her from returning to her old ways. The words of caution to her to take it easy seemed to fall on deaf ears.

"I told you Ma was going to raise hell," Ed whispered.

"You bet. I want to get out of this bed." Nora shook her head, straining against her pillows. Quickly her color was returning, her voice was nearly as strong as it had been, and her stubbornness was just as fierce as before.

Much too soon it seemed she was up and around again, though her activity was at least being monitored by her sons. Whenever she walked around, one of them was always by her side to give her aid.

"Dammit, Josie, they're treating me like some fool invalid."

"Which is what you are," Ted chided.

"Says who?"

"Says Dr. Gardner."

"He wants you to take it easy, Nora. You don't want a repeat of what happened. It could be dangerous." Josie tried to say it as gently as she could.

"Well, he didn't say I had to lie in bed like a log."

"He said if you pushed yourself it could have dire consequences." Ted, the largest of the sons, physically kept her from walking for too long and too far. Picking her up in his arms, he carried her back to the soft padded chair next to the bed. "Now, stay put for a while."

"I got things to do."

"And other people who can do them," Parish replied. "Me, Ted, Ed, and Josie."

"And just what am I supposed to do with myself?"

"Read. Knit."

"Knit!" Nora Harper scoffed at that. "I don't want to be confined to my rocking chair just yet. I'm not some old woman." She patted Josie's hand. "But then, I think you understand. Woman to woman. That's why I'm so glad that you're here."

"Nora." Josie started to tell her of her plans to leave, but seeing the soft expression in the woman's eyes, she put it off. She would tell her tomorrow.

* * *

The door of the jailhouse squeaked, then slammed shut behind Rafe as he entered the cell block. Oh, how he hated jails. They reminded him of a cage. They were the ultimate punishment for those who had transgressed, for every man valued his freedom above all else.

"So, you two just couldn't keep the peace," he exclaimed, addressing the two young boys who glared at each other through the bars of their cells.

"He started it!"

"No, he did!"

"He hit me first."

Putting his hands up, Rafe did his best to initiate a truce but was unable to get the boys to stop squabbling for several minutes. At last having yelled themselves out, the boys quieted. Only then was it possible to tend to their wounds, a broken nose and black eye on one boy, a lacerated lip and sprained wrist on the other. Whoever had begun the fight, they both had suffered.

"I don't suppose either one of you was liquored up?" Rafe's eyes were all-knowing.

"Suppose we were?" Tommy, the elder of the adversaries, was belligerent. "It's none of your business."

"It is now," Rafe countered. "Unless you'd like to fix your own damned nose." Tommy instantly quieted, giving his panic away as he watched Rafe open his black leather bag.

"What are you going to do?"

"Try my best to put it back the way it was." Wiping away the blood, he carefully set the bone, then, using a splint, taped it securely in place. "There, it will take time, but you will be handsome again."

"Handsome?" The other youth laughed. "If you can make that wheyface less ugly, then maybe I need to have *my* nose broken."

Reaching through the bars, Tommy tried to grab his taunter. "Yeah, well, believe me, I'll gladly oblige you."

Only Rafe's timely intervention as he grabbed Tommy's shirttail avoided another confrontation. 'Hold it, boys. Violence doesn't settle anything. There won't be any more of this while I'm around."

"You?" Jimmy snickered. "Why? What are you going to do about it, doc. Shoot us?"

"Yeah." Tommy turned his head. "How are you going to control us, Mr. Gunfighter?"

"Maybe he'll call us out."

"Shoot-out at high noon."

"Yeah." Tugging the sheet off the jail cot, Jimmy put it around his waist like a skirt. " 'Course, it might not be as much fun with me 'cause I ain't female."

It was a brutal reminder to Rafe of that tragic day he had faced Josie in that stupid gunfight, and the repercussions. Though he had tried to push all thought of her from his mind, at least for the moment the image of her face hovered before his eyes. Seeing her again had been a bittersweet moment, but it had brought about a return of his sense of sorrow, loneliness, and futility.

"She's not any happier than I. It had been apparent by the look in her eyes, the downward slant of her

mouth. Was that what she was going to say to him?
Rafe shook his head. Perhaps he would never
know. That precious moment of their being together might never come again. That is, if Parish
Harper had his way.

"We know all about you, doc."

Tommy's voice was shrill, shattering Rafe's reverie. Angrily he leaned forward. "You don't know
a damned thing, you young punk! You've never
felt the chill of pure fear creep up your back.
You've never seen a man writhing on the ground
in agony. You've never smelled death and seen vultures circling overhead. You've never had to justify
in your mind the act of pulling the trigger. Nor
have you ever been so regretful over something
you have done that you would give your life to
undo it." Grabbing at the bars, he quickly calmed
himself. "No, Tommy, you don't know. You don't
know shit!"

"Doc!" Both boys' eyes were as wide as saucers.

"But keep on the way you are going and you
will. One day you'll feel as if your guts were ripped
apart and there won't be anything you can do."

Rafe said no more. He was deadly silent as he
finished tending to his patients, fighting again
the sense of emptiness that once again enfolded
him.

Thirty-nine

There was going to be trouble. Trouble with a capital T. Rafe read the account of the Clayton gang's antics over his morning cup of coffee in the hotel dining room. There had been robberies, cattle rustling, shootings, and antics just "for the fun of it." Antics like shooting up Contention City, taking potshots at the Indians on the nearby reservation. And they were moving closer. Showlow was next. He scanned the story with trepidation.

"Hell!" The Clayton gang was wanted for everything from tripping little old ladies to murder. "Whew!" He gave a low whistle. Oh, they were something all right.

Rafe looked at the sketches of the men and shuddered. The outlaws were an unkempt-looking group. Shabby. Mean-looking. Disheveled. All of them had scraggly beards, mustaches, and long hair. One had black-stained teeth and another had a tooth missing. All in all, they were frightening to look at.

He read the names and studied the sketches just in case he saw them loitering around. "Abe Jackson." He was the oldest. His dark hair was streaked with gray, his thick brows held a perpetual scowl.

"Billy Clayton." The baby of the group and the only one with blond hair. "Bart Terrill." The most brutal of the gang. A cold-blooded killer. "Frank Clayton." Handsome in a frightening sort of way. But his eyes were as cold as ice. "Eli Russell." He was the one with the missing tooth, said to have been knocked out while he was escaping a hanging. "Henry Clayton." The rotund, beady-eyed mastermind of the gang. The scar across his nose made him look like a frontier pirate.

Rafe took a sip of his coffee, reading further. The gang was slowly working their way from town to town. It wouldn't be long. Trouble was, who was going to stop them? Clint was still suffering with his sprained ankle. There was a marshal in the area, but he always seemed to be anywhere but in Showlow. As for the citizens of the town, there were few of them, if any, who would be a match for the Claytons. Except for him, nobody could even stand a chance.

"Oh, no!" He didn't want any of that. As far as he was concerned, he was never picking up a gun again. That part of his life was over. Finished. Dead.

"Morning, Rafe!" Hobbling over, Clint Tanner struggled to sit down in the chair opposite him. Placing his cane on the arm of the chair, he leaned forward to take the pressure off his left leg.

"Morning." Rafe looked up, folding his paper. "How's your leg?"

"Sore as hell. But then, you said it would be. He picked up the discarded paper. "Anything interesting?"

Knowing that Clint couldn't read very well, Rafe

related, "Story about the Claytons. I don't think it will be long until they are sitting right on our doorsteps."

"Oooooh!" Tanner made a face. "Makes me glad I've got an excuse to back down from them." He pointed at his foot, then whispered behind his hand. "Truth of the matter is, old buddy, I don't think I'm fast enough to beat them to the outhouse."

"Not if you're going to have to run." Rafe laughed, then ordered his breakfast. The usual. Two eggs over easy and smothered with hot sauce, sausage, flapjacks with plenty of butter and lots of strawberry jam.

"Ha-ha!" Clint Tanner looked worried as he ordered his scrambled eggs and ham. "I just hope I'm not forced to take part in any showdown. I wouldn't want to look, well—"

"Old?"

Tanner brushed at his temples, where his ginger-colored hair was turning silver. "Well . . . yes."

"Let's hope it doesn't come to that. I'll send a telegraph to Marshal Evans warning him what's up."

"He probably knows."

"Probably." But it wouldn't hurt. Rafe thought about Josie. Even though she was pretty good with a gun, she just wouldn't be able to protect herself against a bunch of blood-hungry wolves like the Claytons. She would be like Little Red Riding Hood. Swallowed up. "And then again, the town could take precautions by forming a posse."

Clint thought a moment. "Good idea. You could head it up."

Rafe shook his head. Well, what had he expected? "I was thinking about you doing that. I'm busy."

"Delivering babies."

"Among other things."

Clint grinned. "Heard from that little spitfire yet?"

"Yes." Rafe didn't want to elaborate. His meeting with Josie was something he wanted to keep private. Clint was just too insensitive to emotion to share his feelings with.

"Oh. Still angry with you, huh?"

"Still angry." No, he had thought that she was softening in her attitude. In fact, he sensed that she might have even told him that if the Harper brothers hadn't come in at that moment. But they had, and just like some watchdog, Parish Harper had hovered protectively over her. Rafe had gone out to the Harper ranch several times to check on Nora since then, always to be told that Josie was elsewhere. It was frustrating. As if they didn't want her to see him, or maybe it was her idea.

"Well, that's a woman for you."

The food was brought out from the kitchen. Stabbing at his eggs with a fork, Clint Tanner was soon too busy eating to talk. Rafe wasn't complaining. He relished the silence as he ate. It gave him time just to think. How was he going to see Josie if the Harpers conspired to keep them apart? Should he send up fireworks? Push his way in? Send her a secret note? No, under the circum

stances he couldn't take the chance of making a
nuisance of himself and upsetting his patient. He
would just have to hope that eventually he and
Josie would run into each other again.

"Doc! Doc!" The loud tramp of boots across the
hotel's wooden floor and the frantic voice of Rufus
Danner caused Rafe to look up.

"Rufus."

"Come quickly. Tucker's been shot. In the stomach."

"Shot? By who?" Dropping his fork, Rafe
grabbed his suitcoat off the back of the chair and
struggled into it.

"Claytons, I suspect. At least that's what he was
mumbling."

"Claytons." So they were closer than he had first
thought.

"He's in his wagon out front. Went into Contention City for some special supplies and ran into
the gang. They were on a rampage."

"I see." Rafe stuffed several napkins and a knife
into his pocket just in case there wasn't time to
retrieve his black bag from his office, then, snatching a bottle of bourbon from the hotel bar, he
followed after Rufus. Climbing into the wagon, he
bent over the wounded man.

The wound turned out to be much worse than
he thought. Tucker was lying in a pool of his own
blood, holding his stomach. "Gut shot. The worst
kind." The odds of survival were slim. "Damn."
The man had a pretty wife and three children.

"Doc . . . Doc . . . something for the pain.
Please . . ."

Rafe didn't have to do a very thorough examination to know that Tucker was going to die. It was just a matter of time. Either his death would be mercifully quick or ruthlessly lingering. "Rufus, run to my office and bring me back a bottle of laudanum. Hurry."

"Ohhhhhh, God!" Tucker shrieked his pain.

"Easy. Easy." These were the moments that Rafe so hated. The times when he knew that no amount of skill could save a patient. That Tucker was only twenty-four made it all the harder. When a man had so much to live for and yet had to die, it was tragic. Yet all he could do was to make Tucker comfortable, at least for a time.

"Here's the laudanum, doc."

Rafe lifted up Tucker's head, feeling an overpowering compassion as he eased the liquid into his mouth. He pulled the bottle back when the dying man choked.

"Am. . . . am I going to die?"

It was the kind of question a truthful man hated to have to answer.

"I am." Tears filled Tucker's eyes. "Get me a priest."

It was a request that Rafe obeyed, sending Rufus after the holy man while he stayed behind to offer what comfort he could. "Tucker, was it the Claytons?" He had to know.

"Yeah. They . . . they rode up on me. Shot me. No reason." He coughed up blood. "No reason."

It wasn't the first man Rafe had seen die, nevertheless, it didn't make it any easier. He watched as the priest gave Tucker last rites, watched the gray eyes glaze over in an endless stare, heard the death rattle.

"The damned bastards!" Senseless. Brutal. But probably not the last man to die at the gang's hands. Closing Tucker's eyes, then covering him over with a canvas tarp rolled up in the back, Rafe stood in silence for a long time. At last he made his decision. He couldn't just stand by while the Claytons terrorized Showlow. No, if it came down to it, if he was the only one who could stand in their way, he would strap on his gun again.

Forty

Usually Josie had no trouble falling asleep after a long and weary day, but tonight was different. Long after midnight she found herself tossing restlessly on her bed, staring up at the ceiling. She knew in her heart that she had to leave the Harpers, but it would be one of the most difficult things she had ever done. Nora Harper and her sons had been very good to her. Still, it was time to move on. Time to establish her independence. Time to get on with her life and see to her future. The trouble was, how was she going to tell them?

"I can't put it off much longer." Now that Nora Harper was slowly regaining her strength, the time seemed right. A few more days, a week, and then she would tell them.

If I don't leave soon, I'll be trapped here by my feeling: of gratitude and of being needed. One day will pass and then another and another and with each day I'll find i harder to break away. I have to say good-bye. There i. no future for me here. I don't want what they want. don't want to be a member of this family, not if it mean by marriage.

"And that is just what Parish and Nora have ir their minds."

It was as obvious as the trunk on a circus elephant. Worse yet it seemed to be some sort of conspiracy among them all. Just that morning Josie had learned that Rafe had been out to the ranch several times, that he had tried to see her. And yet not one of the Harpers had told her. There could be only one reason.

"They see Rafe as a rival, but— "

Josie sat up in bed. There was the splitting crack of a rifle in the distance, then more shots farther away, a strange cacophony of sounds. Unusual, for it was always quiet at night at the ranch. She heard the shots again.

"I better go see."

Getting out of bed, she leaned toward the window and glanced out. Pressing her nose to the glass, she squinted her eyes, trying to distinguish a strange silhouette. At last she realized what it was. A group of men riding together. But what men? Not the Harpers surely. It was too late to be outside working.

"One. Two. Three. Four." She counted six riders in all, three moving to one side of the corral, three moving to the other. That they were armed, that some even held their revolvers in their hands, alerted her that there was going to be trouble.

She heard the sounds of voices whooping and yelling, horses hooves, the bellows of panicking steers, trampling hooves as the animals bolted in different directions. Someone was stampeding the cattle.

"Ed! Parish!" They would be asleep in the bunkhouse. Surely the noise would send them after the intruders. What about Ted? Josie ran through the house trying to find him, but though his bedcovers were askew, he was nowhere to be seen. No doubt he had heard the disturbance too.

Once again she ran to the window, stiffening as she saw that two of the shadows were moving toward the house. Coming here! Men whose motives surely were no good.

"Nora!" Josie felt the need to protect her. To protect herself. "My holster. My gun." She was frantic. Frustrated. Oh, where had they put them?

Searching through the house as best she could in the darkness, she looked in every nook and cranny, fumbling through drawers, closets, and cupboards. At last she found them hanging on a hook, tucked away in the broom closet like some unnecessary souvenir. Without bothering to dress, Josie strapped the holster on and stuck her Peacemaker in its cradle.

Suddenly there was a loud thud as the back door was kicked in. She heard the click of metal, saw the movement of a shadow.

"Let's see what's in here, Billy."

Josie took a deep breath. She fired three warning shots in rapid succession toward the intruders. Two shots missed their target, the third tore the hat from one of the men's heads.

"Shit! What the hell was that?" a hoarse voice swore.

"Josie! Josie, what's going on?" Nora's voice. Bad timing for such a question.

"Nothing, Nora. Just stay put," Josie called out, inching toward the woman's bedroom.

"Well, well, Abe, women!" There was the sound of malicious laughter, laughter that chilled Josie to the very bone.

One of the men stepped in front of the hall window, revealing his dark hair streaked with gray. "Shall we have some fun, Billy?" The meaning was very clear.

The dark was a close and terrifying enemy. Josie turned away, trembling, but at the same time knowing she could depend on no one to save them but herself. For if she didn't, the alternative could be tragic.

God help me. Courage. Easy. Easy. Slowly she crouched to a sitting position, then rolled to one side. Getting up on one knee, she took cover behind a chair. She didn't want to make any hasty moves and give herself away. Listening, watching, she waited for the men to make the first move.

"Hey, girlie!"

The man's rough growl echoed in the stillness, nearly destroying her calm. He was closer than she had thought. Then suddenly he was upon her, standing just a few feet away.

Apprehension squeezed at her so hard she could barely breathe.

"Well, well, well . . ."

In an instant she had her gun pointed at him. "Don't move!"

Josie stared at the man. She knew by the look of him that he was dangerous. No prankster or thief this one. He had the cold eyes of a killer.

"Well now!" He grinned at her, his teeth a flash

of white in the darkness. "What have we here? Give me the gun. You might hurt yourself."

Josie leveled the gun. *Don't show your fear.* "Hardly. I know how to use this."

Minutes passed slowly as he scorched her with his eyes. Then it was as if the world froze, then moved in slow motion. Josie saw the man take a step forward, then reach for his gun. At that moment she fired, watching as his face formed an inhuman grimace. Then he fell.

Josie's heart hammered. She didn't take time to see if he was dead. Bolting to her feet, she started running toward Nora's room. There was another man. She had to get to Nora before it was too late.

"Nora!" She gasped as she came to the doorway and saw the woman lying on the floor, her nightgown spread around her as she struggled with a blond-haired man. "Nora!"

At the sound of her voice the man turned around. Seeing that she was armed, he pulled away. "Now, now, I don't want any trouble."

"Then get the hell out of here!" Her voice was shrill and threatening. "I mean it. I just shot your friend and I'll shoot you right between the eyes if you don't do as I say."

"Okay. Okay. I'll leave peacefully." That said, he inched toward the door, passing through it, but then suddenly he popped his head back in. Josie took aim and shot, hitting the door frame. She put her finger on the trigger to shoot her last bullet, but he was gone.

"Nora. Nora."

Bending down, she saw that Nora was having a

difficult time breathing. The excitement had been too much for her.

"Your pills!"

Hastily Josie darted to the bedstand and reached for the bottle. Her hands shook as she poured the tiny pills out. Returning to Nora, she reached for her, frantically putting her arm under her head to gently lift her up. Dear God, she was so still.

Her heart was thundering. "Nora. Nora. Answer me."

There was only silence.

Forty-one

Long, dark shadows stretched over the pathway.
Rafe rode at a fierce gallop toward the Harper
ranch, disregarding the lateness of the hour. He
had to warn Josie. The Clayton gang had been
spotted moving toward the ranch, causing mischief
to everything in their path. He wanted the Harper
brothers to be ready, just in case trouble occurred.

"Dear God, I wouldn't want what happened to
Tucker to happen to any of them." The young
man's death bothered Rafe. It had been so senseless, so meaningless. A waste of a good man. He
didn't want to have to attend to any more dying
victims of the Claytons.

*Oh, how I wish I could convince Josie to move back
to Showlow, where she belongs. Where I can watch over
her. Anything can happen way out here.* Ranches like
the Harpers' were sitting ducks for the Claytons.

Rafe was startled by his horse's sudden erratic
behavior. "Easy . . ."

Nostrils flaring, the horse reared, nearly unseat-
ing him from the saddle.

"What on earth!" Something was troubling the
animal. It seemed crazed, and only with the utmost

skill was Rafe able to get the horse back under control.

In a moment he learned why. A wall of billowing dust, the pounding of hooves, thundering in the dark stillness, told of a stampede. That and the sound of gunshots alerted Rafe to the fact that something was wrong.

"Come on!" Seeking a firm grip on the reins of his horse, he guided his mount toward the ranch but away from the cattle. Tricky business under the circumstances. Meanwhile, the hooves sounded louder and louder. Urging the stallion toward an area where there were trees, Rafe sought to get out of the path of the steers.

Reining in his mount, Rafe rested behind a tall, stout tree. From his position he could watch as the steers passed by. Steers followed at a distance by horses ridden by men with rifles and revolvers in holsters that were tied to their thighs. Gunslingers, by the looks of them. To his horror Rafe recognized the six disheveled men. Vermin. Bastards. It was *them*.

"Hell!" Cold rage mixed with fear filled Rafe. The Claytons were coming from not going to the Harper ranch!

The pounding of his horse's hooves thundered in Rafe's ears as he guided the animal at a frantic pace over the uneven road. It was a wild ride down the hill as he imagined the worst.

"Oh, Josie." Time, he thought in exasperation. It seemed to be something he usually had in full measure, except tonight. Now, though his horse galloped as fast as possible, it seemed that he was moving in slow motion.

Though the sun had long faded, it was hot. Sweat trickled down his forehead and into his eyes, blurring his vision. Reaching up, Rafe wiped the perspiration away, squinting his eyes as he rode.

I should have warned Josie long before now. I should have ridden to the ranch and carried her off kicking and screaming if need be. Any way to have kept her safe. Now he didn't know what he might find. All he could do was to hope and to ride.

Rafe's blood surged angrily in his veins with the obsession of saving Josie. Long shadows crept from the hills as the moon slid from behind a cloud. He was tired, but dared not rest, disheartened, yet dared not lose hope. Even so, as he saw the silhouette of the Harper ranch in the distance, he felt as if a fist suddenly grabbed his insides and twisted them upside down and inside out.

All of Rafe's senses were on alert as he rode closer. The thick walls of the ranch house were painted a light shade of tan, blending with the desert sand and the dirt. He reflected that it was a dangerous hue, for it would clearly define the shadowy outline of anyone approaching.

Dismounting, Rafe gripped his pistol tightly. Heading toward a clump of cottonwoods, he secured his horse to one of the trees. Breathing deeply, he tried to calm his nerves and force himself to think logically and clearly. He had to be careful. There was no way to know if the Claytons had left any of their gang members behind.

There were several doors that led inside, a front

door, one that led inside the large kitchen, one to the drawing room, and one that led directly from the stables. Rafe chose the door to the kitchen. Crouching low to listen for the sound of any voices, he slowly crept up the steps and pushed his way inside.

Forty-two

The light from the oil lamp illuminated Nora Harper's pale face, her eyes closed forever in death. Bending down, Josie smoothed the woman's hair from her face, once more whispering her regrets. "If only I had been able to come to your side sooner. Perhaps . . ." But it was too late. All too quickly life can ebb away, leaving behind just a lifeless shell.

Death can be so cruel, so agonizing, so soul-wrenching. It made a person feel so helpless, so powerless. Once the woman lying on the bed had been so full of life, now she was so still. Like a big china doll. The violence of the night had caused her death. Her struggle with the intruder had just been too much for her heart.

"May God rest your soul," Josie prayed, trying to somehow return to some semblance of calm. It had been a terrorizing evening. Frightening. Tragic. Josie remembered how she had chased the two intruders off, only to find out that any heroics she might have enacted had been done too late to save her friend. All she could do for her was to lift her up by her arms, drag her to the bed, and wait until her sons returned.

"Poor Parish." And Ted and Edward. Wherever they were right now, and Josie suspected that must be off chasing outlaws and cattle, they would return and find that their mother was dead. *If they all return, that is.* The thought that they were in mortal danger, that they might not return, hadn't entered her mind until then. But what if one or the other of the sons didn't come back?

"I won't even think about it." Still, she didn't want to be caught unawares. That was why she was wearing her holster. The two men had fled from the house, but if they dared to return, she would be ready.

Josie was determined to be prepared, but her nerves were on edge. She was more than a bit jittery. It was suddenly so eerily quiet that she found herself jumping at every little sound. The walls of the house seemed suddenly so confining, as if they were closing in on her. But she dare not go out. Not yet. Not until she knew what had happened.

"Now, Josie McLaury, keep calm!"

It was good advice that she gave herself, yet harder and harder to follow as the minutes dragged on. She was alone in the house with a dead woman. There were gunmen running around the ranch. She didn't know what was going on outside. Had the six men been run off? Were the Harper boys still all in one piece? The unanswered questions were deeply troubling.

Sitting down on the edge of the bed, she tried to calm her tense nerves but her inactivity only made the situation worse. Likewise, pacing up and down didn't help the matter. She wanted answers. Wanted to know what was going on. Needed—

A sound! Josie jumped to her feet, her eyes darting this way and that. Her whole body stiffened as she reached for her Peacemaker. Someone had opened the door, then closed it again, she could hear the hinges creaking. The whisper of boots on the wood floor warned that someone was sneaking inside.

Josie blew out the lamp, staring through the gloom as she left Nora's bedroom and walked slowly down the hallway. A man was searching the house, a tall man whose face she could not make out. She swallowed hard, positioning her finger on the trigger.

"Josie!"

She jumped at the croaked cry of her name, searching out the identity of the speaker.

"Josie," the man said again.

Their eyes met and held, and at that moment Josie knew she had never been so glad to see anyone in all her life.

"Rafe!" She felt an overwhelming sense of joy and relief. As if it were the most natural thing in the world, she dropped her gun and ran to him, flinging herself into his arms. "Dear God, am I glad to see you. Rafe. Rafe."

He opened his arms wide to accommodate her encircling arms. "I rode out to warn you about the Clayton gang. But as I was riding in I saw them riding out and knew my warning was going to be too late. Are you all right?"

She shuddered as she remembered her close call, but said only, "Yes, I'm fine."

He was achingly moved by the sight of her and reached out to stroke her hair. "Thank God. The Claytons are killers. I was so afraid—" As if to reassure himself that all was well, he tipped her chin up and looked into her face. "Oh, Josie."

His voice was a soft, deep rumble, sending a shiver through her. Pressing herself closer to him, Josie closed her eyes, trying to forget for just a moment what had happened. It was, however, impossible.

"Nora Harper is dead," she gasped.

"Dead?" Rafe assumed the worst. "They shot her! The bastards!"

"No." Josie's words stuck in her throat as she tried to explain. Her face was etched in pain as she relived the moment once again. "Two . . . two men barged in. I wounded one, the other pushed his way to Nora's room." Her fingers tightened on his shoulder as he held her closer. "When I got there, she was lying on the floor. I shot at him to scare him off, but it was too late. Her heart."

"Are you sure that's what killed her?" For just a moment the doctorly side of him took over. "No bullet wound?"

"She wasn't shot. When I bent down she was gasping. I tried to give her one of her pills, but it was just too late."

"And you are sure she is dead?"

"Quite sure. She's been dead for at least an hour." She shivered again. "She's so stiff. So cold. So white. Just like a ghost."

Rafe hated the idea of losing any patient. It deeply troubled him, though he knew it wasn't his fault. "I wish I had gotten here sooner." He knew ways in which Nora Harper might have been revived. But as Josie said, it was too late now.

"So do I." A well-remembered tingle shivered along her nerves at the feel of his body pressing so intimately against hers. The feelings she had for him hadn't altered one iota. "But I'm so grateful that you're here now."

"Are you?" He touched the soft curve of her cheek with one finger, tracing the lines of her face, then her neck. An arousing touch.

Josie responded to the gentle caress by looking up at him. She could feel the heat of his body, the hardness of his chest, could hear the loud thud of his heart. It was pounding nearly as fiercely as hers.

"Oh, Josie." Involuntarily his hand came to rest on her shoulder, then her hip. He slid his fingers up her back as he pulled her closer. Gently, he brushed his lips against her hair. Ignoring the jab of her gun belt, he was conscious only of the way her full, soft breasts felt against his chest. Conscious of the sweet way she smelled. Conscious of how right it felt to hold her in his arms. Passion tempered with a great tenderness rose up in him.

Josie lifted her eyes to the potency of his gaze. "Now that you are here, I feel safe."

For just a moment he regarded her, then, with a strangled exclamation, bent his head to claim her mouth in a startling, gentle kiss. It was a chaste kiss they shared, yet it made Josie achingly aware of her body and how alone she had been without him. She was glowingly conscious of the warmth that spread over her, a pleasurable tingle that tightened in the pit of her stomach.

"Mother! Josie!"

At the sound of Parish's voice, Josie pulled away. "Over here, Parish. Near the bedrooms."

There was the flash of a match, the flooding light of the lamp as it was lightened. Holding it aloft, Parish strode down the hall. "Dr. Gardner!" That he was surprised and not the least bit glad to see Rafe was evident. "What on earth are you doing here?"

"He came to warn us about the gang," Josie said quickly, somehow feeling guilty at his presence. Their kiss no doubt.

"The Claytons," Rafe put in.

Parish scowled. "Well, you *are* too late. They have already made themselves known. We've been chasing the results of their mischief. Hopefully that is all that they are guilty of."

"Parish . . ."

Possessively he put one arm around Josie's shoulder and drew her toward the kitchen, ignoring Rafe. "Let's have a cup of coffee and I'll tell you all about it."

She pulled free. Her voice was cold. "To the contrary, let me tell you." She tried to maintain her composure. "Two of the men broke in here."

"Broke in?" His face paled as he at last noticed her holster.

"I shot one, wounded him."

"And the other?" His eyes widened as he looked

toward his mother's room. He sensed then that something was very wrong. "Mother?"

"Parish . . . she's . . . she's—"

Before she could get the words out, he was running, heading toward his mother's room. Barging through the door, he cried aloud.

Josie found him kneeling at Nora's side, his head bowed, his hand gripping tightly to hers, sobbing.

"Parish, I'm so sorry!" So deeply sorry. Yet it was one of those moments when words could not express one's true emotions. "Parish." She moved to stand beside him, placing her hand on his shoulder.

"Why?" He looked up, his eyes misted with tears.

"It's . . . it's just one of those things that happen." Like her brother's death, she thought. Just something that happened.

"How?"

Briefly Josie explained. "When I got here she was lying on the floor, struggling with the blond-haired gunman. I shot at him and scared him away, but the terror of the moment was just too much for your mother, I guess. She was gasping. I fumbled for her pills but I—I was just too late."

"The pills. Those damned pills." As if needing someone to blame, Parish's eyes lit on Rafe's form in the doorway. "Well, they didn't do a damned bit of good!"

"Parish!" Despite the circumstances, Josie was annoyed. "It wasn't his fault. He didn't barge in here. He didn't harm your mother." She took her share of blame. "If you want to be angry at anyone, be angry at me. I was the one who was with her. I was the one who might have saved her had I been quicker, or wiser."

"Josie." Parish shook his head. "It wasn't you."

"If you want to blame anyone, blame the Claytons," Rafe cut in. "They have been terrorizing the whole territory, like some incurable plague."

"The Claytons," Parish repeated. Clenching his fist, he banged it on the top of the nightstand. "Well, they'll pay! They'll pay for this!" It was a threat and a vow. Pulling the sheet over his mother's body and face, he stood up, pushing past Josie.

"Parish! Where are you going? Don't— " She started to go after him, but Rafe blocked her way.

"Let him go. Let him work his anger out in his own way."

"But he can't even think of going after those men alone."

"Why not?" Rafe's eyes were sad. "You went after your brother's killer all by yourself." And became the judge and jury, his expression seemed to say.

"Yes, I did, but— " The way he was looking at her somehow seemed to interfere with her breathing. The rhythm of her lungs was thrown off as she stared up at him. At that moment Josie realized for the first time how very much Rafe was also hurting because of her brother's death. And at that moment she found it in her heart to truly forgive him.

Forty-three

It was a cloudy day. Bleak. Dark. The kind of day that added a somber mood to Nora Harper's funeral. Still, it was peaceful on the hillside as the preacher dutifully read from the scriptures. " 'The Lord is my shepherd, I shall not want. He maketh me to lie down in green pastures. He leadeth me beside the still waters. He restoreth my soul . . .' "

Clothed all in black, wearing a dress of Nora's that had been altered, Josie stood beside Parish and his brothers as they said their final good-bye. Then the dark wooden coffin was lowered on ropes into the recently dug hole.

"Damn those Claytons. Damn them to hell," Parish said under his breath. "They killed her just as surely as if they had pulled a trigger."

"But they will get theirs. I'll see to that." Ted clenched his fists as he made the vow.

"Ditto," Ed mumbled, equally upset.

Josie stood with her hands folded tightly, hoping that the Harpers wouldn't be rash. Still, she couldn't blame them, especially after hearing the story of what had happened that night. The meeting with the Claytons had become a violent bloody spectacle. Bullets from behind the barn had sprayed the wooden wall of the bunkhouse as the brothers had made themselves known one by one. Viciously the Claytons had not only let out the cattle but had planned a deadly ambush. "Target practice" as they had called it. It had been a harrowing and dangerous time for the Harper brothers, and only by the grace of God was there just one newly dug grave.

"The bastards were even going to set fire to the place," Ted had informed her, holding up his injured hand, severely burned when he had fought hand to hand with the culprit holding the torch.

"But we showed them a thing or two," Ed had crowed.

Actually it had been more subterfuge than prowess that had saved the Harper ranch. Following Ed's plan, the boys had circled around, shooting the Claytons from different positions, convincing the outlaws that there were twice as many men guarding the ranch as there really was. A clever ploy.

" '. . . rest in peace, amen,' " Josie heard the preacher say. She watched stonily as shovelfuls of dirt were thrown on the casket.

" 'For dust thou art, and unto dust shall thou return,' " she whispered, remembering what the Bible said. *But not the soul.* Like a dove the soul soared upward toward the heavens, or so Nora Harper had believed. Lifting her eyes toward the sky, Josie wondered if Charlie was up there somewhere watching her now. "Oh, Charlie!"

Josie listened as the preacher said another prayer, then, walking by the grave, she said a final good-bye to the woman who had been such a good friend to her. Nora Harper had been there when she had needed someone. She would never forget that.

"Come on, Josie."

She felt the pull of Parish's hand on her arm. She started to walk with him until she saw a familiar figure out of the corner of her eye. It was Rafe, staring at her from across the crowd. *Rafe.* Their eyes met and held, and for just a moment it was as if no one else existed, now or ever.

"Josie!" Parish's tone was more insistent. Elbowing his way through the throng of sympathizers, he led her to the buggy. "We want to get back to the ranch house before the others."

Neighbors and friends had come in a steady stream, bringing dishes of food and expressing their sympathy. Parish expected a few more and wanted to be there to meet any who might come.

"So, Parish, is this the woman you've been telling me about?" A tall, gray-haired man blocked their way, showing a keen interest in Josie.

"This is the one, Uncle Albert." Familiarly Parish enfolded her into his embrace.

"Well, there is something about her that reminds me of your mother. The spark in her eyes perhaps." He extended his hand to Josie, taking hers warmly. "Well, you will have some big shoes to fill, but if intuition is of any use, and I for one think that it is, then I think you will deal just fine taking Nora's place."

"Taking her place?" Obviously there had been some kind of misunderstanding. Josie started to converse on the subject, but Parish hurried her along.

"We have to get back," he said sharply, giving her a hand up onto the seat. With a crack of the whip he set the horses in motion for a wild and bumpy ride.

Only when the landscape had leveled out and the horses had slowed down did Josie have a chance to make her opinion on the matter known. "Parish, I don't know just what your uncle meant back there, but I don't have any intention of taking your mother's place. No one could."

"If anyone could, I think it would be you. Even Mother often said that," Parish answered. He patted her hand. "I guess that's my way of asking you to marry me."

"Marry you?" Josie was angry with herself for not realizing that this was coming. Hadn't Nora herself been working on a union between Josie and her son for several weeks before her death? She had.

"I was going to propose to you a little later, but Mother's death hurries things up a bit." Parish flushed. "To but it bluntly, it could set tongues to wagging with you living up here with all of us. So I intend to make you a member of the family. An official member." The buggy lurched as he stared at her, losing control for a minute.

"I can't." Josie shook her head, moving away from him.

"Can't." He cocked his head. "Can't what?"

Josie took a deep breath, broaching the subject that needed to be talked about. She could not live a lie. Couldn't pretend. "I can't marry you and I can't stay." There, it was said.

Parish looked at her, trying to absorb what she had just said. "Well, of course you can, and you will, Josie."

"No." She knew her own mind. Nothing he could say would alter that.

Parish laughed. "It's the only sensible thing to do." His voice became louder, more insistent. "You need me and I need you. It's as simple as that. Besides, you know how I feel about you."

"I do. And . . . and I'm very fond of you too, Parish." She enjoyed his company, liked talking with him, walking with him, but there was someone else that she loved. And always would love, her heart told her.

"Fond." He didn't seem to like the word.

"I'm in love with someone else. It wouldn't be fair to become your wife knowing that." She sighed regretfully. "I'm sorry."

"Sorry?" Parish looked as if she had just struck him. "Sorry."

"Yes, sorry. From the bottom of my heart. You are the kind of man any woman would be proud to live her life with, Parish, but— "

"But Rafe Gardner beat me to your affections." He thought a moment. "I guess I can understand that, and respect you for your honesty, Josie." His eyes were veiled. "But a guy can wish."

"I'll always be your friend, Parish." She hated to destroy the feelings that they did have for each other.

"Friend." He sighed. Suddenly he was the old Parish, the one she remembered. "I can settle for that." He thought about it awhile. "Yeah, I can settle for that and be thankful. Real friends are hard to find."

"Yes, they are." Josie smiled sadly, her eyes watering. Parish was a friend, but so was Rafe, only she hadn't thought of him in that way before. A friend and a lover. She remembered the good times between them, hoping that it wasn't too late.

Forty-four

It felt good to be back in Showlow, Josie thought as she walked briskly down the main street. She felt at peace with herself. She felt free. Gone were all the resentments that had come so close to poisoning her. For the first time in a long while she had truly come to terms with Charlie's death. Though she would always love him in her heart, she knew she had to go on with her own life, her own happiness.

"Life is just too short to spend it being angry," she whispered, passing by the general store. Nora's death had taught her a lesson.

Reaching into her pocket, Josie withdrew all the money she had left and counted it. Five dollars. Not much to establish a new life for herself or secure her independence, and yet she wasn't worried. Somehow she would make it. The really important thing was her newfound tranquility. Gone was the old belligerent Josie and in her place was a Josie with more maturity. A Josie who realized that life was to be fully lived.

Walking down the street clutching her carpetbag, her steps were lighter and she was smiling. She nodded to the men congregated on the boardwalks and said good morning to the women passing by.

Though more often than not she was snubbed, she now knew it was far better to treat them as friends than as enemies. She'd win them over eventually.

"Good morning. I'd like a room, please." Seeking out her old boardinghouse, Josie was cheerful, unprepared for the hostile reaction she would receive. It seemed that Gwen did not share her new philosophy on life.

"I've no room. I'm filled up," she snapped.

"Filled up?" The keys hanging on the wall said otherwise. It appeared that there were several rooms.

"That's what I said." Turning her back on Josie, Gwen dismissed her without another word, though she did pause to sneak a peek at her once or twice as she walked away from the desk. At last she called out, "If I were you I'd go back to that ranch house with that Harper boy. A bird in the hand, as they say."

So, that was it, Josie thought. Gwen wanted her out of the way, far away from Rafe Gardner. Well, she just didn't care. There were other places to stay, other boardinghouses. Like the one across the street from the doctor's office.

That boardinghouse proved to be neat and clean, with windows that overlooked the street. Run by a gruff but seemingly kind middle-aged widow, it soon began to look to be the perfect place. Best of all, it was cheap.

"There will be kitchen privileges. You'll have to do your own cooking or eat elsewhere. I refuse to spend all my time standing over a stove."

Josie shrugged. "I think I can make do."

"You'll have to wash your own bed linen."

"I'm experienced with that." Josie laughed.

"And there are no bathing facilities. My boarders have to use the public bathhouse."

"No bathtub here?" Josie hesitated. She had become spoiled at the ranch, relishing the warmth and soap bubbles every Saturday night. Still, she would just have to do without, at least for the time being.

It was the first time the widow had any trace of a smile on her face, yet she smiled now. "But don't worry that the bathhouse will be crowded. Most of the men hereabouts avoid that place just as surely as they would a woman's quilting bee."

"Then count yourself as having a new boarder." Josie stuck out her hand. "I guess I'll take a room. But please. The least expensive."

"Follow me!"

Josie did, climbing three flights of stairs to an attic room that was charm personified. Furnished with a Victorian-style foldout bed, a nightstand, tiny table, white, blue, and pink flowered wallpaper, and a small window that opened to allow fresh air, it was like being in a doll's house. Tiny, to be sure, but comfortable.

"I call it the best-wishes room. It seems to be good luck. The young woman who lived here just up and married her beau. And the girl before that moved out to become a missus. And the one before that—"

"How much?"

"Seventy-five cents a week."

Josie patted her pocket, striking a deal. "Since

I have to cook, wash my own sheets, and go without a few amenities, how about settling on fifty cents?"

"Seventy!"

"Fifty-five."

"Sixty-five and not a penny lower."

"Agreed." Josie was pleased with herself for making such a good bargain.

"Good." Holding out her hand she took Josie's money, then headed for the door, but she paused and turned. "My name is Eve. Eve Hennessy. My late husband's name was Adam."

"Adam and Eve." Josie smiled. "I'm Josie. Josie McLaury." She waited for any sign that the woman recognized her as the girl who had antagonized the town, but there was none.

"Pleased to meet you." Eve eyed Josie quizzically. "How about you. Do you have a fella?"

"I used to." Her eyes held that faraway look as she remembered.

"Hmmmm. Well, a young woman as pretty as you will have one again, I would warrant." Eve Hennessy reached for the doorknob, but once more hesitated before leaving. "If you are lonely, we have a square dance once a week. A good way of meeting people." The way she said "people" meant men.

Josie shrugged. "I'm not very good at dancing." Besides, there was only one man she was interested in. "But thank you."

"Sure." The door closed almost silently.

And so, here you are, Josie. On your own just like you wanted. What now? As if to answer her own question, she walked to the window, leaning over the sill as she looked out, her eyes focused on Rafe's door. He was so close. So very close and yet she wanted him even closer. The only problem was, she wasn't sure how to go about it. After all, the rules of courtship clearly stated that the man was the one who was supposed to take the initiative.

"But then, when have I ever followed the rules?"

Forty-five

Aches, pains, a broken thumb, a case of indigestion. It looked to be the usual sort of day and the usual kind of complaints, Rafe thought as he handed Ida Mae Watson a bottle of Hostetter's Stomach Bitters.

"Now, *just* a tablespoonful this morning and then again this afternoon if your problem doesn't go away," he cautioned her. The medicine was fifty proof and the alcohol could really pack a wallop for those who weren't used to it. But it always seemed to do the trick, soothing indigestion better than anything else he could have given her.

"Just a tablespoonful," she repeated, smiling sweetly.

"And keep it away from your husband. Last time he drank the whole bottle down before you had a chance to use it, as I recall."

"I'll hide it away." Dutifully she stuffed it in the big pocket of her apron, then rose to her feet. "And thank you, doctor."

Watching as the sweet-tempered gray-haired woman walked to the door, Rafe could only hope that she followed his instructions. It wouldn't be the first time that some strictly disciplined matron

who would not dare be seen near a saloon succumbed to the temptation to use a prescription the
wrong way.

"Good day, Mrs. Watson." Turning his back,
Rafe busied himself with putting away his stethoscope, tongue depressor, and laryngoscope, and ti-
dying up his office. He was preoccupied for just
a moment, that was why he didn't know Josie was
in the room until she spoke to him from the doorway.

"Hello, Rafe."

He whirled around. "Josie!" There hadn't been
a day that passed when he hadn't thought about
her, wondered how she was doing. Now here she
was. His blue eyes shone with undisguised joy at
seeing her again, yet he couldn't think of a thing
to say. All he could do was to stare. She looked
especially pretty with her hair reflecting the sunlight that streamed through the windows, but there
was a worried look on her face.

"I— I came to thank you for riding out to the
ranch to warn us about the Claytons that night."
Remembering that he had also kissed her, Josie
smiled.

"It was the least I could do." And an excuse just
to see her. "I'm only sorry that things ended up
the way they did. I had a lot of respect for Nora."

"So did I." She paused. There was something
magnetic about his eyes. She felt as if she were
caught in them, drowning in their depths. "She . . .
she was the main reason I stayed out at the Harper
ranch."

"She was?" Rafe digested this information, then boldly asked. "And what of her son?"

"Parish." She detected something in his voice that she couldn't quite discern. "Parish is— " she hesitated, wondering just how to explain "— a kind and gentle man and— "

"In love with you," he interrupted. A troubling reality under the circumstances. Undoubtedly Josie would sympathize with him now that he had lost his mother. She would be just as vulnerable in her way as Parish to what had occurred.

"He is, I know." Josie didn't like the direction the conversation was going. She hadn't gone there to talk about Parish.

"And why not," he said aloud. Josie McLaury was everything a man who liked spice in his life could ask for.

Suddenly Josie felt incredibly awkward. Oh, why wasn't Rafe making this easy for her? Her breath caught in her throat as she tried to speak, then her words came out in a whisper. "But I don't love him." I love you, she wanted to say but didn't. "I'm fond of him."

"Fond." A twinkle danced in the depths of his eyes. He chuckled.

"Yes, fond." Was there anything wrong with that?

"Fond," Rafe said again. He felt strangely triumphant.

She was stung by his mood, didn't like his laughter at all. Perhaps she had said too much, told him more than he needed to know. In a huff she turned and started to leave, but his hand on her arm held her back.

"Don't go, Josie. Not yet. Not until my eyes have had their fill of you." With a downward sweep of his eyes he fully appreciated the lush curves of her feminine beauty. "I was hoping to see you again. At least before Parish Harper staked his claim." He felt the compulsion to ask, *he hasn't already, has he?*

She was conscious of his hard, strong body as she turned around slowly. They stared at each other for a poignant moment. Josie felt the irresistible tug of her feelings for him. She couldn't look away, couldn't move, couldn't lie.

"He has tried. . . . " She searched his face, trying to denote his feelings. The lines of his face drew her eyes. The line of his eyebrows, the angle of his jaw, the thickness of his hair where it waved at his temples. She wanted to touch him, hold him. "But I said no."

"No." His sigh of relief was audible.

"And. . . . and I have moved back into town."

"Moved back!" It was like a Christmas present and a birthday party all rolled into one, the best news he could ever have received.

"That's one of the things that I stopped in to tell you." Taking his hand, she led him toward the window, pointing. "I now live right over there. The Hennessy boardinghouse."

"Eve Hennessy's place." His voice was low, husky, a seductive rasp in her ear. As if already he were making plans.

"Do you know her?" She purposefully leaned

against him, remembering so many pleasant things. The touch of his lips, the way his hands had brought her body to life, the way he had felt inside her. And afterward, the tender way he held her in his arms.

"A patient of mine. A favored patient now." Taking her hand, his fingers closed around hers. Bending his head, he pressed his lips against the palm. "Because of you." His arms closed around her waist, holding her close. "Welcome back to Showlow, Josie."

He had been given a second chance! Watching as Josie crossed the street, that was all that Rafe could think about, and the thought made him feel like a boy with his first case of puppy love. Opening the door, wandering out in the street, he found himself staring after her until she closed the boardinghouse door behind her. With her out of sight, he headed straight for the barbershop. After all, a man had to look his best when he went courting.

The snip of scissors, the clink of hair tonic bottles being jiggled together, and the murmur of men's voices mulling over the latest town happenings greeted Rafe as he stepped through the door.

"Shave and a haircut, doc?"

"Just a shave." He smiled. "Like Samson, I like to keep my hair long."

"To please your Delilah?" The barber winked knowingly. "I hear Josie Smith is back in town. I hear she came to see you."

There was a smile in Rafe's voice. "She did."

He leaned back, closing his eyes as the barber
stroked his face with lather. "And believe me,
Tom, this time I'm going to make sure that I don't
give her any reason to go gunning for me."

Forty-six

Josie hugged the pillow, wishing it were Rafe instead. Still, today had been a start. Now he knew all the important things. That she was back, that she didn't want to marry Parish or live at the ranch, that she wanted to rekindle what they had once had. But could she bury the past and start over again? She knew she had to try. The feelings that stirred inside her breast for Rafe were certain to plunge her into turbulent waters, and yet wasn't he worth the risk? He was.

Right from the first I noticed him, was attracted to him, but my anger and obsession for revenge blinded me. Determinedly she shoved aside the dark misgivings that entered her mind and clung to her gentler feelings. She did love him. Right now that was the only important thing. Her mind, her heart, the very core of her being, longed for him. Only him. Closing her eyes, that was the thought on her mind as she at last fell asleep.

She was awakened by the insistent sound of knocking. Bounding out of bed, she answered the door and was surprised to see Eve Hennessy standing there, a bouquet of wildflowers held tightly in her hand.

Looking toward the unmade bed, then at Josie's white nightshirt, she said apologetically, "I hope I didn't disturb you, Josie dear."

Rubbing her eyes Josie hurried to assure her. "Oh, you didn't. I wanted to get up. You see, I have to find a job." Something with a future. Something promising. Something to sustain her in Showlow so that she could stay.

"Good." Eve Hennessy held out the bouquet which had been obligingly put into a vase. "These are for you. A welcome back to Showlow."

"Ohhhhh." Josie was touched. "Why, Mrs. Hennessy, you shouldn't have." She buried her nose in the petals of the yellow and lavender blossoms, breathing in the fragrant odor.

Putting back her head, Eve Hennessy gave vent to her mirth. "I didn't."

Josie raised her head. "Then, who . . . ?" It was then she spied the note that Mrs. Hennessy had quoted from. " 'Welcome back to Showlow. I missed you. Love Rafe.' " Of course. Who else?

"And I thought you told me you didn't have any beaus." Putting her hand to her throat, Eve rolled her eyes. "Dr. Rafe Gardner. The most eligible bachelor in town."

"I know." Oh, the exhilaration. The wild, sweet triumph.

Bidding Eve Hennessy adieu and closing the door, Josie sat up in bed, hugging her knees. When all was said and done, it seemed she had the same soft streak as other women had for green leaves and bright petals. She was pleased that Rafe had sent her flowers. It made her fee happy and content. The world was a much happier place now that she was in love and sensed that her feelings were returned.

Love. It was not tangible, yet Josie had thought at times that she could nearly reach out and touch it. It enfolded her, warmed her. Though she had always valued her independence, there were times when she was overcome with a fierce desire to follow Rafe Gardner to the ends of the earth if necessary. To tread in his footsteps, to share in his dreams.

Though she'd always prided herself on having her feet firmly on the ground, unless she was riding, that is, Josie seemed to be floating now. "Moonstruck" she called it, recalling the happiness of the past few days. *But it can't go on forever. Nothing did. How will I feel when it ended. If it ended.*

It wouldn't end. There was no reason for what was happening between them to end now. Not after what they had been through. The anger and the bitterness were well behind them. She was content. And Rafe? If actions could be translated into words, she knew he was just as optimistic as she.

Getting out of bed, Josie's hand trembled as she brushed her hair a hundred strokes so it would shine. Padding on bare feet to the table, she poured water into the basin to wash her face and brush her teeth. This done, she dressed in her blue shirt, blue denim pants, and brown boots. Then, critically, she assessed herself in the mirror. She was ready to go job-hunting.

Surely someone in Showlow needs help. If not, then she could always find work at the laundry.

And yet, she wanted, needed, something else. Something she could sink her teeth into. Something with a future.

She could hear footsteps coming up the stairs.

"Morning." It was Rafe's voice that called from the other side of the door.

A pleasant surprise. "Morning."

Opening the door, Josie noted that there was a sparkle in his blue eyes that made him all the more handsome. Moreover, he made a striking picture standing there dressed in a gray suit with a royal-blue cravat. As always, his suit showed off the perfection of his physique, the width of his shoulders, the slimness of his well-proportioned frame. He was the very picture of the successful doctor, which was all the more reason she was determine to be successful in what she did too.

"Thank you for the flowers." She pointed to their place of honor on the table by the bed.

"I wanted roses, but I couldn't find even one in all of Showlow." He brushed past her, appraising her room. "This is nice." He eyed the single bed.

"Cozy." Pulling up the quilt, she fluffed up the pillow. "I like it."

"So do I." Particularly its proximity to him. "I thought I would take you to breakfast," he offered, explaining his early morning visit. Strange. They had been antagonistic toward each other at first, then lovers, then adversaries, yet he had never felt as self-conscious around her as he did then. Perhaps because this newfound truce between them was so fragile. So important to him.

"Oh?" She picked up her hat. "And did Eve Hennessy bribe you?"

"Bribe me?" He looked puzzled.

"To keep me from burning up the kitchen."

He laughed. "No, she didn't. I just wanted to get away from aches and pains and grumbles for a little while." He held out a small picnic basket. "Nothing fancy. Just fresh fruit. Doughnuts from the bakery. Hard-boiled eggs. A carafe of coffee."

Josie took his arm. "I accept your invitation."

The ride up the canyon was a pleasant one. For a time Rafe forgot his troubles as he basked in the warmth of Josie's passionate soul. She had a zeal for living, a knack for sharing laughter, a passionate nature that charmed him. A side she hadn't revealed to him before. Not really.

"Oh, look, Rafe. How beautiful it is up here."

Taking his eyes off her, he looked around. "Beautiful?" Strange, the various shades of brown earth, the red of the rocks, the sparse vegetation, had not seemed beautiful to him before, but it did now. Perhaps because he had someone to share it with. Breathing deeply of the fresh air, he paused to listen to the song the birds were singing and hummed a similar tune himself.

Josie sat proud and tall on the saddle, her face framed by wisps of wheat-colored hair that the breeze whipped into her eyes. Rafe's gaze caressed her, realizing just what a rare young woman she really was. Most women would have been tempted to stay at the Harper ranch, where there was a measure of security. But not her. Josie had wanted her independence. Even if it meant incurring hard-ships.

"Josie, what you are going to do?"

"Do?"

"Now that you've moved into town." He found himself wanting to be her protector but knew she would not hear of it. Still, he knew how hard it could be for a woman on her own. Particularly out west.

"Oh, that." She shrugged, trying to hide her concern. "Don't worry, Rafe. I'll be all right."

Her body language stated that she wanted to drop the subject, thus he did, contenting himself with idle chatter and talk about his doctoring as they rode along. At last, reaching a grove of trees, Rafe paused. "How about here?"

"Perfect. Besides, I'm hungry." She started to scramble down, but, sliding from his horse, he put both hands around her waist and aided in her de-scent. Josie was giddily conscious of the warmth emanating from his hands. Her stomach fluttered like the wings of a butterfly, but not because she hadn't eaten.

"Come on, I'll show you the place I used to go when I first came to Showlow," he said.

Rafe picked up the lunch basket as he started up the slope of a hill to a meadow, a secluded spot near a stream shaded by an old gnarled oak tree. It was there he set down the basket. Taking out a small red and white checked linen cloth that Mrs. Hennessy had given him, he spread it upon the ground and began laying out their food.

"I'm afraid the coffee is cold." Starting a fire,

he warmed it up. "Just for the memories," he explained, thrusting a cup into his hands. "Remember—"

"How we always drank a cup of coffee together before target practice," she said with a half-smile, recalling those strangely blissful days. She had been so intent on learning how to shoot that some of the simple pleasures had escaped her attention at the time. Now they came back to her.

The breeze carried the scent of wildflowers and sun-baked earth. Rafe shaded his eyes against the sun's glare and appraised the scenery. It was a truly romantic setting with cottonwoods, ash, and box elder trees growing thickly along the stream. As he watched, a flock of birds winged high overhead and swooped to make the trees their resting place.

"Beautiful." A word that could have been used for her as well.

"Like being in the Garden of Eden." She laughed. "Arizona-style."

"Like Eden. . . ." He hunkered down beside her, trailing his fingers over her hand and up her arm. "I should have thought to bring a blanket."

"I don't mind sitting on the ground."

"Nor do I." He lay down on his side, leaning upon one elbow, watching as she finished unpacking the basket. He didn't say anything for a long while, and Josie honored his silence, though wondered at his mood. Reflective. Sorrowful. She sensed a certain tension in the way he held himself, although he was trying to hide it from her with a mask of false good humor.

"Are you hungry?" she asked at last. Her gaze

moved slowly over his face, longing to see him smile.

"I am!" He poured himself a cup of coffee, clicking his cup against hers. "But first a toast. That we will never be parted again."

"That we will never be parted." They drank to that hope, then ate in silence, but she was aware of his gentle scrutiny.

"I missed you, Josie," he said at last.

She watched as he unfastened the top three buttons of his shirt, revealing his dark, curling chest hair, and rolled up his sleeves in an effort to make himself more comfortable. Josie's eyes were pulled in his direction. His virile presence was always exciting.

"I needed time to think. Time to come to terms with my feelings."

"And have you?" His shoulders tensed as he raked his fingers through his hair.

"Yes."

Rafe's gaze moved down over her breasts. He wrapped his arm around her. Josie snuggled against him, curled into the crook of his arm. She pressed her face against his shoulder.

"Josie. . . ." He moved her hand around to his lips and gently kissed the palm. He stared down at her face somberly. "Is there hope for us?" If only he could bring her brother back, but all he could do was to share his pain. "Can you for— "

She knew what he was going to ask. "I already have." Her eyes seemed to burn his with green light as they misted with tears. "As far as I'm concerned, all the anger, all the . . . the hostile things between us, the hurtful words, are behind us."

"You're crying. Don't cry, Josie." He groaned and caught hold of her, tangling his fingers in her hair, his mouth hovering just inches from her own.

"Kiss me. I want you to, Rafe."

He didn't need another invitation. Bending his head, he moved his lips gently but insistently from the nape of her neck to her mouth, uttering an imprecation as his mouth claimed hers in a lingering kiss. His heart stopped, then surged with a liquid heat. He wanted her, God knows, but he held himself back. This time he would woo her. Besides, it was more than lovemaking he wanted. Understanding, love, gentleness, and a sense of permanency were what he longed for.

For endless moments they lay locked together. Time stood frozen as they explored each other's mouths. This was what she wanted, Josie thought. To be with him like this. For now, for a lifetime.

Suddenly a shot rang out. They sprang apart.

"What was that?" Warily Rafe left Josie's side and went to investigate. When he returned, the frown on his face alerted her to some sort of danger.

"Rafe?"

"It's those damned Claytons. Down over the hill. One of them was shooting at a jackrabbit."

"The Claytons." She shivered, remembering. "So they're still hanging around."

"Like a bunch of vultures." And they were much too close to Showlow for his liking.

"Shall we go?" Damning herself for not being

armed, Josie felt helpless. If there was any trouble, she would be useless.

"No. Let's wait awhile and watch." Taking her hand, he guided her to a point overlooking their camp, where their waiting and watching paid off. As the six riders mounted up and headed off to the south, Rafe knew immediately just where they were going. "Come on." He pulled her to her feet, running along, taking her with him. "We've got to beat them there. We've got to warn them." At last the danger he had feared for so long was at hand. The Claytons were heading toward Showlow.

Forty-seven

If horses had wings, they couldn't have moved any faster. Hugging the necks of their mounts, Rafe and Josie urged them to a breakneck speed as they headed back to Showlow.

"I wish I had my gun!" Josie called out. It would have been tempting to engage the Claytons in gunfire. As it was, all she could do was play messenger.

"Don't go getting any ideas!" As Rafe looked over at Josie he knew just what was on her mind. But he didn't want her getting in the line of fire. "When we get back I want you to stay in your room behind a locked door. Do you hear me?"

Josie tossed her long hair. The very idea was infuriating. Besides, if there was going to be trouble, every able-bodied person who could shoot would be needed.

"And just what makes you think that you can give me orders, Rafe Gardner?" She glanced over her shoulder. She had no idea where the horsemen had come from, but they were like black specks coming closer and closer.

"Because . . . because . . ." There was the sound of gunfire. Rafe looked behind him. Lead was splattering the ground. "Damn. We've been

spotted." And all he had with him was a rifle.
Even so, he fumbled with it as he rode, trying to
pull it free of the saddle. At last succeeding, he
reined in for just a moment and fired.

"You missed," Josie exclaimed, watching as two
of the Clayton gang turned toward the rise to cut
them off. "Quick. This way." Josie urged her horse
to the left and Rafe followed. Gunfire echoed behind them.

"Josie, here. Stay in the shadow of the trees. At
least where there are any." Rafe led her along the
stream, looking behind him from time to time to
check on his pursuers. Their horses were galloping
disjointedly, careening in a strange, uneven pattern
as the Claytons whooped and cursed.

Looking over her shoulder, Josie noted the way
the horses were being led and knew in an instant
why. "They're drunk."

"The horses?" Rafe wasn't under so much pressure that he couldn't make a try at some humor.

"Of course not." Josie laughed. Still, as a bullet
whizzed over her head she knew just how deadly
serious the situation was.

"Josie, come on. Faster."

Feeling the stark realization of fear, she forced
her horse into a killing pace that didn't stop until
they had reached the town. Sliding wearily out of
the saddle in front of the Hennessy boardinghouse,
she hurried up the stairs to get her Peacemaker,
wearily raising a hand to her brow. It had been a
long, hard ride.

"Now, remember what I told you. Keep the door

locked and bolted," Rafe called after her, then he was gone.

Taking the stairs two at a time, Josie moved as fast as if the Claytons were on her heels. But she didn't lock the door. And she didn't stay behind. Instead, she strapped on her holster, grabbed a handful of bullets, slammed her gun into its cradle, and ran back down the stairs, just as the Claytons were riding around the bend.

"They're coming. They're coming," yelled out a little boy just before his mother grabbed him by the hand to pull him inside the general store.

Josie caught sight of them, staring in dismay. The Claytons were an unkempt-looking group. Despicable. Mean. Disheveled and sneaky. All of them had scraggly beards and mustaches. Long hair. Some had black-stained teeth and one had a tooth missing.

All in all they were frightening to look at. Even their perspiration and dust-covered denim trousers and wide-brimmed Stetsons were grimy. This gang had the reputation of being fast on the draw, Rafe had told her. They could fan their revolvers and fire their repeating rifles with tremendous speed. Would Rafe and the townsmen stand a chance?

"Hide. They're here," cried out an old man, pushing through the door of the saloon.

As the Clayton gang approached the town, everyone scrambled behind closed doors. They were afraid. Windows slammed shut and doors were bolted by the time the outlaws rode through the dusty streets, shooting and swearing. They fired their pistols into the air as they rode up and down.

Splinters of glass and wood flew everywhere. Even the planking of the boardwalk was bullet-riddled.

One of the gang, a rotund rogue with a scar across his nose, roared with laughter. He called out, "Where are you going? Isn't anyone going to send a welcoming committee?"

"Naw, I don't think they like your looks, Henry," yelled out the youngest of the lot, the yellow-haired skinny kid that Josie had encountered at the ranch. Seeing him again, she paled, ducking behind the corner of the store before he recognized her.

"Hell, I don't like his looks neither." There was a loud guffaw.

"But say, how about we have some fun. How about it, Frankie?"

"Not yet, Bart. We're gonna mind our manners for a while."

"Like the devil, we will."

"Hey, Eli, come on and join me. I'm gonna get liquored up, find me some women, rob me a bank, and kill a man or two. And that's just to warm up." Again there was laughter.

Peeking from behind the corner of the general store, Josie's eyes widened as she saw the outlaw she had wounded coming her way, his shoulder bandage showing beneath his torn shirt. Flattening herself against the wooden building, she tried to make herself invisible. All the while she wondered, where was Rafe? Gathering up a posse, she supposed.

Meanwhile the Claytons were easily taking over the town. The six dust-caked men were arguing among themselves, pushing and shoving. Leaving their horses to cool off and assuming an aggressive stance, showing it was obviously their intention to get ready for a fight, they headed toward the saloon. The door was locked, but it didn't do the owner much good. They shot off the lock and pushed the door open.

There was the sound of gunfire, of glass and furniture breaking, screams and hollering. And all the while Josie felt helpless. She held no illusions about being invincible. She couldn't be a fool. Wouldn't dare tangle with the Claytons alone, and yet how could she just stay quiet while they bullied and battled their way through Showlow, she thought soulfully as the men reappeared. Stalking down the street, whiskey bottles in their hands, they were heading west.

"First the whorehouse, then the bank, then we'll have ourselves a little target practice," she heard one of them say.

"Oh, no, you won't," she yelled, getting one of the outlaw's attention, the one who was the biggest target. As he drew his gun, she dropped to her knees, leveling her pistol.

"Josie!" She turned just as Rafe dove toward her, taking her to the ground. "I thought I told you to stay put." A bullet flew over their heads.

"You did. But I don't see you doing anything to stop them." She struggled in his embrace, at last breaking free.

"I will." That said, Rafe loosed three shots at the Claytons, drawing back as they returned the fire in a quick, ragged volley. The sound of gunfire pierced the air.

"You need some help." Bracing her gun atop a rain barrel, Josie took aim and hit one man right above his belt buckle. She watched as he fell. "One down, five to go." Her shot had been as accurate as she had been taught.

Rafe and Josie stayed crouched low behind a stack of barrels as bullets ricocheted off buildings and rocks. She looked at Rafe as vehement words fell from the outlaws' mouths.

"What the hell!"

"Somebody got Frank."

"Oh, now they'll have to pay."

The four gunmen scattered, trying to find a vantage point. Slowly and cautiously Rafe and Josie changed their positions from the barrels to behind an overturned wagon as sizzling lead splattered bits and pieces of stone and other debris all around them. Josie's ears rang.

"Run for it."

They did, running as fast as their feet could carry them, amid gunfire. Josie felt a moment of anguish as Rafe seemed to disappear behind a cloud of smoke. But soon they were together again, well protected behind an old stable at the end of the road.

Rafe's shot downed another. He weaved and staggered, finally falling in a pool of blood. "Two down, four to go." As menacing a foursome as had ever existed, who were now forewarned that they had adversaries lurking in the shadows. Brains clouded with liquor or not, the Claytons gathered together for a fatal showdown.

"I'm afraid we're in for some real trouble." Rafe's exclamation was an understatement. "It's four against two, Josie."

Then the worst thing possible happened. Rafe's gun had jammed, rendering him virtually helpless. A spray of bullets sent the dirt dancing up as he tried to work himself away from his antagonists, darting from building to building while Josie covered him. Soon the entire valley was reverberating with shots and Josie found herself in the middle of the melee.

"Four against three," she proclaimed as she saw a horse and rider approaching. To her mortification, she saw that it was Parish. Staring, she watched as a bullet sent his hat flying from his head. "He's going to get killed."

Parish's horse was in a full galloping stride as he drew his gun and fired, but the animal was shot out from under him. A shrill, high-pitched whinny of pain, and the horse was down. Parish fell sideways and rolled clear of the flailing horse.

"Damn!" Rafe stared in anger. "The young fool!"

Josie stared in horror. Slipping from her place of hiding, she ran to Parish as his doomed horse lay on the ground, hoofs pawing at the earth in its death run. Mercifully she put the animal out of its misery.

"Drop flat, Josie!" Rafe's command reminded her of how vulnerable she was, and she dropped to the ground. Rolling to one side, she got up on a knee behind a horse trough. Temporarily blinded

by a blast fired right beside her, Josie triggered off
an unaimed shot from her Peacemaker.

"Here, lean on me!" She had to get Parish to
safety. Putting her arm around his waist and loop-
ing his arm over her shoulder, Josie acted as a
human crutch, helping him hurry to safety as fast
as he was able. All the while bullets sprayed around
them as she looked over her shoulder.

"I'm fine now, Josie." Hiding behind an overturned wagon, Parish returned the gunfire.

"Okay." Then, as if in the very midst of a horrible nightmare, she saw that one of the Claytons
had reared up from behind a packing crate and
had Rafe in his sights. Fear for Rafe's life hit her
with a violent force. "Rafe!" she screamed just as
his eyes met hers.

She saw him take cover just before a string of
rapid shots struck the very spot where he had
been. Josie knew the tricks of evading enemies.
She did not get to her feet, but crawled on hands
and knees toward him. His gun was useless. She
had to protect him.

But Rafe could take care of himself. Moving
with astounding quickness, he darted toward one
of the fallen Claytons as Josie kept the other outlaws occupied. Wrenching a Winchester from the
dead man's hand, he was soon back in the fighting.

"Three down, three to go," he called out.

"Rafe. Need help, old buddy?" Riding down
Main Street, Clint Tanner added his gun to the
fighting.

"It's about time!" Rafe called out. "Josie and
have done all the work."

"Better late than never," Clint retorted, shooting as he rode. But it was Josie who downed another Clayton.

"Four down, two to go," she said, keeping a tally.

"Shit, let's get the hell out of here!" The blond-haired Clayton and the big outlaw with the scar made for their horses. Amid cursing and the pounding of hooves, the two remaining outlaws had it in mind to get out of town.

"What do you say. Shall *we* follow them?"

"We?" Josie raised her eyebrows in question.

"We," Rafe repeated, then said under his breath. "I'm proud of you, Josie. You've done what most of the men in this town feared to do." But his full praise had to wait. Mounting up, he and Josie headed through the town in pursuit of the escaping Claytons.

"Might as well get them all," she exclaimed.

"Might as well." Seeing them up ahead he called out, "You take the first one, Josie, and I'll get that skinny bastard behind him."

What happened next moved in slow motion, started when the largest member of the gang took aim at Rafe, instigating Josie's fury.

"Oh, no, you don't." The pupils of her eyes narrowed to mere pinpoints as Josie fired. He tumbled off his horse in a heap. Rafe's shot was just as accurate. The last outlaw fell on his back, unmoving, eyes staring up at the sky.

"By God, it's over." Rafe let out a sigh of thankfulness. He hadn't liked this carnage, hadn't liked it one bit, and yet it had been necessary to protect the people of his town, those people who depended on him to save their lives. He *had* in more ways than one.

"Rafe, are you all right?" Riding up behind him, Josie got down off her horse. He followed suit.

Taking Josie in his arms, he lifted her off her feet and spun her around. "We did it, Josie. You and I kept this whole town from a brutal attack without any help from anyone. Just you and me. That's a good omen, Josie, that you and I are a good team. A great team."

"An unbeatable team," she repeated, hugging him tightly.

"We did it, and I love you." That said, he rewarded her with a kiss that reverberated throughout her whole body. A kiss that reaffirmed both life and love.

Forty-eight

The aftermath of the shoot-out with the Clayton gang was gruesome and grisly, as if a cyclone had whipped through the town. They had left a path of death and destruction that would take Showlow a long while to recover from.

"Like a bull in a china shop," Josie whispered, fingering a large indentation in the general store's front door.

"Six bulls. Violent and brutal," Rafe breathed, crouching near the water trough. He was totally exhausted. Dipping his hands in the water, he splashed it on his face. "Whew. I'm glad we don't have to deal with this every day. I'd rather take my chances with fevers, sprains, and warts and chills."

Bullets holes had peppered the boardwalk and pitted the buildings, both adobe and wood; glass had been broken, doors kicked in, wagons and barrels overturned. The Golden Cactus Saloon was totally demolished. The worst toll, however, was in human life. Eleven of the citizens of Showlow had been caught in the crossfire, three of them killed.

On the other side, when all was said and done, Frank Clayton, Bart Terrill, and Eli Russell had been killed. Billy Clayton, Henry Clayton, and Abe

Jackson had been wounded and hauled off to jail to await the marshal.

"Doctor. Doctor, come quickly."

As Rafe was beckoned to tend to the wounded, it became obvious that his role in the day's happenings was just beginning. Planting a quick kiss on Josie's cheek, he hurried off.

"Quite a little turkey shoot." Limping toward Josie, Clint Tanner seemed eager to bask in the glory of the Claytons' demise.

"A turkey shoot indeed." She started to ask him where he had been when the melee had started, then thought better of it. There was already so much bad blood between Tanner and herself that she didn't want to fan the flames any longer. He was arrogant, yes, stupid at times, obnoxious when it came to some issues, but he was after all Rafe's friend.

"Yep, a real turkey shoot." Ignoring her retort, oblivious of her scorn, Tanner pounded Josie on the back. "Thanks for helping Rafe and me out," he exclaimed, striking a pose for the photographer who was taking pictures for posterity, both of the victors and the vanquished.

Laying the deceased members of the Clayton gang on doors that had been pulled off their hinges, posing them in lifelike poses complete with their guns, the photographer intended to visually prove that the ultimate payoff for outlaws was death. It would serve as a graphic warning to any would-be gunslingers on the wrong side of the law. It was to be a grim reminder, a lesson for any who might seek out a life of crime.

"Helping?" Josie held up her Peacemaker and forced a smile as the photographer posed her for a picture.

"Yep." His grin was like that of a self-centered child. "For a woman, you handle a gun pretty damned well."

"For a woman!" Not wanting to make a scene in front of the photographer, Josie bit her lip against the scalding comment she really wanted to make. Instead, she said simply, "Thanks." After all, she knew what she had done. That was the important thing.

Parish on the other hand, was eagerly complimentary, looking at Josie as if she were an angel. "You saved my life, Josie," he said, hurrying to her side. "I'll never forget that. When that horse went down with me, I was sure that my life was going to end right then and there, but you—"

"Did only what had to be done. I saw that bullet strike your horse and knew I had to save a very dear friend."

His eyes bored into hers. "I wish I could be more." He brushed at his pants. "But seeing you with Rafe Gardner makes me realize that will never be. You love him, Josie, and he feels the same about you. It was as plain as the nose on my face. What's more, the two of you belong together."

"Parish." She took his hand. "I hope that some-day you find someone too."

"I will." Reaching out, he touched her face, wiping a spot of dirt away. "But no one like you. Be happy, Josie." Turning on his heel, he silently walked away with a finality that told her he was also walking out of her life.

Sadly Josie watched him go. "Good-bye, Parish." . She wished him well.

"There she is," a voice behind her yelled out. "She's the one. Shot those Claytons dead!"

"She and the doctor saved this town."

Slowly the townspeople came out of hiding, cheering Josie like some wondrous avenger, looking upon her with awe.

Strange, Josie thought, how quickly one's life could change. Once she had been ostracized by the citizens of Showlow. Now she was being welcomed with open arms as a heroine. The woman who had saved the town from the Claytons. Her reputation as a sure shot, as a woman with cool nerve, was assured. Now when she walked down the street she was greeted by both men and women as a special personage. Someone of value.

"Hello, Miss Josie, you are sure one hell of a brave woman."

"Morning, Josephine, we thought you might want to attend our quilting bee next Tuesday."

"Howdy, ma'am, heard you won a hefty reward for what you did. Well, it was most certainly deserving."

It was true. There had been a reward for the Clayton gang. Josie's share added up to six hundred dollars, a fortune. A nest egg to secure her future, at least for a little while.

"So, I've got myself a wealthy woman," Raf teased, seeking her out as soon as his patient wounds were well on the road to healing.

"Not wealthy exactly, but not poor." Just enough to assert her independence until she made up her mind what she wanted to do with her life. Not be a gunfighter, that was for sure. Seeing those outlaws stretched out like trophies was a real guarantee of that.

"Well, rich or poor, all I know is that you were very, very brave." He nuzzled her throat. "And that you remembered everything that I taught you."

"Welllll, maybe not everything. There are a few things I wish you would refresh me on." She winked, making her amorous meaning clear.

Rafe tugged at her arm. "Come on. As I recall, we were interrupted right in the middle of our breakfast. If the ants, jackrabbits, and lizards haven't already devoured it, I say we go back."

Oh, how he wanted to be alone with her, to give full vent to the passion he had been keeping so tightly in control. Despite the tumult of the morning, he knew it to be the perfect spot to initiate their lovemaking again. And indeed it was, a perfect lovers' nest. Taking a blanket from his saddle, spreading it down, he pulled her beside him.

"Rafe?" His name was smothered by a deep, leisurely kiss as his mouth claimed hers. Her mouth opened to him as she closed her eyes. His kiss left her weak and filled her with that familiar tingling sensation, a heat that centered from the womanly core of her and spread all the way down to her toes. It was the kind of kiss she had been so hoping for, the kind that was a prelude to the wonders they had shared at his ranch in Willcox.

Rafe drew a rasping breath as he lifted his mouth

from hers. "That's just to show you how much I care. How much I've always cared, despite everything." Rafe realized that what he had always wanted was someone who really cared about him. Josie did. Despite what had happened in the past, he knew it now. He had seen her crawl on her hands and knees to try to save him when his gun was jammed.

"Strange, how peaceful it is now." Despite the fact that their breakfast had been devoured, she was enjoying the moment of quiet. "The quiet after the storm of the morning."

Josie leaned her head against his shoulder, wishing so very much that he would make love to her. They had spent the past moments kissing, caressing, and cuddling, but she wanted more.

"A storm that at least put an end to the Claytons. But let's not talk about it anymore." His lips caressed her forehead, then moved down her temple to kiss each closed eyelid in turn. He lifted her hair from the nape of her neck with stroking fingers, tracing a path to her ear. The touch was followed by warm, exploring lips that sent shivers up and down her spine. They lay side by side, looking up at the wispy clouds. The ground was hard, the blanket prickly, but they hardly noticed.

"Rafe. You know that day of our gunfight. I never could have shot you. Not even in the foot. I—"

Rafe brought his mouth down to capture her lips again, muffling her words. The past was behind them. He wanted to think only of now.

Slowly he unfastened the buttons at her throat.

She arched toward him as he moved closer, caressing her. His lips traced a fiery path down the curve of her neck to her just-bared shoulder.

"Mmm. Oh, Rafe, don't stop what you are doing. . . ." His touch warmed her as surely as did the sunshine.

"I won't. You taste good." Deftly he removed her shirt and brought his head down to kiss the soft mounds of her breasts, gently taking a rose-tipped peak in his mouth, savoring it. Soft moans of pleasure floated around them, and Josie suddenly realized that they came from her own throat. Her hands clutched at his hair as she pressed against him.

Unmindful of the rocks and twigs, they lay side by side, contenting themselves in the pleasure of touching, of kissing. Weeds tangled in her hair, but she shook them loose with a vibrant toss of her head. Then her arms went around his neck, answering his kisses with sweet, wild abandon.

"Oh, my darling gunfighter." Rolling over on his back, Rafe reached for her hand, drawing her up to her knees. A quiver of physical awareness danced up and down her spine as he brushed his lips against her hair. "This means I love you." He nuzzled her throat. "And this." His mouth traced a path from her collarbone to the tip of her breast. "And this."

Josie removed her boots, wiggling her toes. It felt so good to get them off. It was Rafe, however, who slipped off her shirt and pants, making no secret of what he desired. Her. When she knelt in just her underwear, he ever so slowly removed those too.

"You have the most beautiful body, Josie. I could just lie here and look at you forever." He patted her on her now-bared bottom. "But I won't. I have other things on my mind."

"Oh?" She watched as Rafe stripped off his own clothes, couldn't take her eyes off him, the broad chest with its matting of hair, the flat stomach, the lean, taut flanks from which sprang that part of him that gave her such ecstasy. His muscles rippled with strength as he moved, radiating a virility that was very stirring. "And just what is that?" she breathed.

"I think you know." His eyes were drawn to the soft swelling of her breasts, and he bent his head to kiss her there.

"I think I do."

"And you?"

She shivered with the pure pleasure of being near him. "I have the same thing in mind."

They blended their bodies in an intimate caress. He stroked her belly, her thighs, then moved to the soft hair between.

Lifting her arms, she encircled his neck, wound her fingers in tousled dark hair. For an endless time they clung together, their naked bodies touching intimately. Rafe's probing maleness replaced his hand, slipping hotly against her thighs, then teasing the entrance to her softness. He held her to him for moments while spasms of exquisite pleasure sent rippling waves through her, a feeling mirrored in Rafe's expression. She stared into th depths of his dark blue eyes. Glorying in the closeness with him, it seemed to Josie that her heart moved with love.

"Ah, Josie! You're the only woman who has ever touched my heart, my soul, my body this way. With liquid fire."

The moments that passed were a soul-ravaging maelstrom of kissing, caressing, and touching, culminating in an unstoppable tidal wave of desire. A desire every bit as heated as the danger of the morning had been. Wrapped in each other's arms, they gave vent to the all-consuming passion that steamed between them.

Josie felt dizzying sensations course through her blood, like the sparks of a radiating fire, consuming her as she felt the firm touch of his hardened flesh entering her moist womanhood. She writhed under his touch, arching up to meet him as he rose over her, seeking the softness of her body. When he glided into her, it seemed to be the most natural, blessed thing in the whole world. She clung to him, her arms around his neck, her legs locked around his waist, answering his movements with her own. Rafe was her mate. The lines of separateness blended. She was incapable of holding any part of herself from him. She had to love him with all the strength of her devotion because she could give him no less than her whole self.

With her hands, her mouth, her body, she demonstrated the full potency of her love and he returned her affection in full measure. On the un-washed earth she gave her heart to him and found a haven of passion and love. In the peaceful silence of the clearing they loved each other, their bodies joined, their hearts touching. He knew just how to touch her, how to bring her to the peak of pleasure again and again.

Josie knew as they lay naked together that she was indeed a fortunate woman. She had soared above the clouds and she was racing toward the sun, there to burst into a hundred tiny sparks of flame.

Rafe gazed down upon her face, gently brushing back the tangled hair from her eyes. "Josie." She was his now as surely as if they had already spoken vows. Whispering words of passion, he made gentle love to her once more, watching her eyes as he brought himself within her once again. He saw the wonder written upon her face that anything could be so glorious, and at that moment he was filled with a complete sense of contentment. The world was theirs for the taking.

Forty-nine

The streets of Showlow had never been so crowded with out-of-towners most of them newspapermen. They had come from all around to get the story on the capture of the Clayton gang and on the woman who had brought them down. Interesting reading for most, exciting for all, but nerveracking for Josie, who at the moment was holed up in her room at the boardinghouse, trying to avoid detection and escape from the uproar. The truth of the matter was she just wasn't in the mood to handle this newfound fame.

"Oh, damn!" she swore, looking out the window to the scene below. The street near the boardinghouse was crawling with men lugging big black cameras and tripods or carrying notebooks and satchels.

Frowning, she put her hand on her stomach, trying to quiet the hungry rumbling. She was trapped. She didn't dare unlock her door and go down to the kitchen for fear of being swarmed.

"This is unbearable. Silly."

So much turmoil over a necessary deed. The Claytons had invaded the town and she and Rafe had merely defended it. It was as simple as that.

How was she to know that her actions could so complicate her life? And just when things had been going so well. She had been accepted by the town, she had reward money in her pocket, and best of all Rafe Gardner had told her that he loved her.

Rafe! Being with him made her happy. Content. Loving him had changed her life, so much so that there were times when she had to pinch herself to make certain she was not dreaming. Well, this morning certainly wasn't a dream. With all the newspapermen thronging the streets, it seemed like more of a nightmare. And all of them wanting to ask questions, questions, questions.

Even now she heard an insistent pounding on her door. Well, she just wouldn't answer it. She wouldn't let them violate the privacy of her room. There had to be some limits, after all.

"Josie. Josie, let me in." Eve Hennessy's voice. A welcome sound.

"Eve?"

"I've brought you some breakfast, child. Thought you might need it before you faint."

"Breakfast." Josie opened the door, stunned to see that Mrs. Hennessy's clothing was askew, her hair messed up, and that she was out of breath. "Eve? What on earth happened?"

"I was ambushed. I had to fight my way past five newspapermen who wanted to talk to me about you!" Closing the door behind her, she set a tray down on the ledge by the windowsill. "Land-sakes, child. It seems that at the moment you're nearly as famous as Wyatt Earp." Eve's eyes shone with pride. "And just think, you're living in *my* boardinghouse."

Josie shrugged, not letting her take all the attention seriously. She was more interested in what was on the tray. Coffee, sliced apples, scrambled eggs, potatoes, and homemade bread. "I thought you said you didn't like to cook."

"Well, I wouldn't do it for just anybody." Eve grinned. "Besides, circumstances alter cases, dearie. I suspected you were in hiding."

"I am." Josie was so hungry that for the moment all she wanted to concentrate on was eating. She chewed and swallowed as Eve rambled on.

"Oh, those Claytons. Seems they were quite the ones. A dangerous lot. Just awful. Horrible. Why, it scares me just to look at their pictures! Killed just about anyone who got in their way. Shot good folks just for the fun of it. At least that's what this morning's *Gazette* says."

Josie had to be truthful. "They were scary all right." Seeing the newspaper under Eve's arm, she was curious. "Can I read it?"

"Of course! That's what I brought it up here for. So that you could read it with your morning coffee." She handed it over, a faraway look in her eye. "That's what my Adam always did."

Unfolding the paper, Josie nearly choked as she read the account. It was fantasy pure and simple, magnifying Clint Tanner's part in the episode. He was quoted as saying that it was "all in a day's work." But why not. He was the personal friend of the *Gazette's* editor. Despite that, however, the

Gazette was accurate in portraying the part she and Rafe had played.

Eve Hennessy read over Josie's shoulder. "Mmm. So romantic. You being with the doctor and all. Fighting beside him, saving his life. Just like in a book."

Remembering the harrowing moments all over again, Josie shivered. "Not exactly." But what had happened after the shoot-out had been. Closing her eyes, she remembered how glorious it had been lying beside Rafe after their lovemaking. Their being together like that had been the only thing that could have calmed her soul after the violence of the morning.

"Are you going to marry him?" It was a bold question.

"Marry?" Sipping her coffee, she thought about it. After all, when two people loved each other, *really* loved each other, that was what was expected. The trouble was, Rafe hadn't asked. "I don't know." And if he asked, what would her answer be?

Yes, if things could be like they were at the ranch in Willcox. But would it be like that? Remembering the way her father had treated her mother, Josie could only wonder. She didn't want to be any man's mother or slave. She loved being with Rafe, eating with him, sleeping with him, and the passions that accompanied their togetherness. The trouble was, would he let her be herself? Or would he try to change her? Remembering how Parish and his mother had tried to feminize her, Josie frowned. She would just never be the kind of woman who would be contented with stitchery, cooking, and cleaning.

"Landsakes, child. How could you say that you don't know." Eve Hennessy was flustered as she spoke of all the other women who would be waiting in line were Josie to say no. "Including me, were I a few years younger."

"But marriage—"

"Can be downright hard work at times. Not all roses and laughter and kisses. Living with somebody else, even a man like Dr. Gardner, just isn't always heaven. It takes patience, understanding, and compromise. But if you love someone, really love them, then the good times outshine the hard times. And you wouldn't trade one minute of being with them for anything else in the world." That she was thinking of her late husband was apparent by the look in her eyes. "Anything."

"But if only I could be sure." When Josie did anything, it was always with her whole heart. What if she were disappointed? What if the heartache she had felt once before because of Rafe happened again? Love could be so turbulent. Joy and at the same time pain.

Eve Hennessy snorted. "Ha. Life is about taking chances, just like you did when you tangled with the Claytons. There aren't any guarantees in life, child. No such thing as security. If there were, I'd have my husband beside me now instead of sleeping in a cold bed."

"I see." Silence hung in the air as Josie digested what Eve Hennessy had just told her. It was true. There weren't any guarantees.

"Why, I—" Hearing shouting down below and gunshots, Eve ran to the window. "What on earth?" It was obvious that something was happening.

"What is it?" Josie ran to the door, then thought better of it. She didn't want to be cornered by the newspapermen waiting below.

"I'll go and see."

Eve Hennessy was gone for quite a while as Josie paced her room. When she returned, it was plain to see that something was very wrong. "Josie, you had better sit down."

"Better sit down?" Those were exactly the words her mother had used that terrible day she had heard about Charlie's death. Was it any wonder, then, that her face turned ashen? "What is it? What's happened."

"It's that Clayton boy. Billy. He's escaped."

"Escaped!"

"Seems he complained of stomach pains. Dr. Gardner was called into the jail to see what was wrong and—"

"And?" Josie's blood ran cold.

"And ended up being taken hostage."

Fifty

Rafe couldn't remember when he had ever been so angry with himself. He should have known better. Should have been cautious. Instead, he had fallen for the oldest trick in the book. Playing possum. Now he was the hostage of one of the nastiest men he had ever had the misfortune to meet up with, Billy Clayton.

Blame it on his sense of nobility or the young outlaw's skill at acting, Rafe had been suckered in. Falling for the outlaw's groans and moans, he had taken his black medical bag into the jail cell to heal a human being. His reward had been to end up at the wrong end of a gun, a gun hidden beneath the outlaw's pillow, no doubt. Now, with his hands tied securely behind his back, he was sitting across a campfire, looking the youngest Clayton in the face.

"Yep, I'm gonna get real satisfaction out of killing you," the outlaw was saying. "Then I'm gonna go after that yellow-haired bitch. One of you killed my brother, Frankie, but I don't know which one. So I'll get you both."

"*I* killed him," Rafe exclaimed, thinking to protect Josie. "Leave her be. I'm the one you wanted, I'm the one you have."

"You killed him." The ice-blue eyes narrowed to slits of hatred. "Well, mister, you'll pay. I'll kill you nice and slow."

"And lose your ticket out of Arizona Territory," Rafe said coolly. "Face it, Billy, you'd like to shoot me or worse, but you can't. Not yet. Not if you're smart."

"Argh!" Though he leaned forward, put the gun to Rafe's head, Billy Clayton didn't pull the trigger. He needed Rafe, at least for the time being, and he knew it.

"So, at least you do understand." Rafe breathed a sigh of relief, thankful the skinny outlaw wasn't as much of a simpleton as he looked. Still, at the back of his mind was the worry of what would happen later, after his presence was no longer needed.

"Yeah, I got it. But don't feel too secure. Your time is coming." Keeping his eye on Rafe all the while, Billy Clayton fumbled in his saddlebags for the necessary supplies, then threw a skillet on the ground. "I always come prepared. My brothers taught me that." He also filled a pot with water from his canteen, measured out some coffee, then put the tin utensil over the fire. It made a sputtering sound as it came to a boil.

"Coffee. The smell is tantalizing," Rafe said, trying to make conversation and hoping he would be offered some.

Billy didn't answer, nor did he share the beverage. Taking the coffeepot from the fire, he filled a tin cup, then stared at it for a moment. He clenched his jaw. "Why'd you have to kill him? He was the only one of my family I could stomach."

"Why?" Surely he couldn't be serious. "Because you were causing havoc in town. It was either that or watch him hurt everyone else."

Billy raised her head. "He only was playing, that's all."

"Playing?" The way he talked about it, one would have thought Frank Clayton to be just an innocent child.

"We was just having a bit of fun. You gunned him down." His tone was accusatory.

"If you are trying to make me feel guilty, you can just save your breath. I don't. Any man does what he feels he has to do sometimes."

"Yeah? Well then, I guess you'll have to be just as understanding when I put a bullet through your brain."

Rafe refused to talk about the matter further. If he did, all that he was going to accomplish was to bring Billy Clayton's wrath down on himself. Thus he just contented himself by watching the fire.

The flames danced and sparked, creating shadows. The expression of anger on the outlaw's face took on a demonic cast as the shadows danced over his nose and chin. Well, Rafe wasn't afraid. Not of him. Not of any man. Still, he was cautious, watching Billy Clayton's every move. He didn't trust him, now or ever.

I have to get free. Somehow, I've got to get away from him before it's too late. With that thought in mind, Rafe fumbled around on the ground behind him, searching desperately for something to cut his bonds. At last he came up with what he needed. A jagged-edged rock that was as sharp as a knife. Now all he needed to do was to wait.

Fifty-one

The angry murmurings at the tavern echoed through the door. It was an ill-humored crowd to be sure, each one eager to place the blame for what had happened to Rafe on someone else. The prime someone being the marshal, who as of yet had not made an appearance.

"There's no law here in Showlow. No law at all. Up until now we've been lucky, but this Clayton affair could start a precedent," the owner of the Golden Cactus Saloon was saying.

"Yeah, this may not be the last time we have to put up with such dangerous shenanigans," a banker added.

"Trouble is, Clint Tanner just isn't the watchdog he's supposed to be. Otherwise this whole thing wouldn't have gotten out of hand," the proprietor of the general store grumbled.

"He's past his prime," the undertaker said aloud.

"Why, hell, if it had been up to him, the Claytons would be running this town by now. Truth is though, we weren't well informed."

"Yeah!"

"Took a woman to set things aright and open our eyes!"

"Quite a woman."

There was a rumble of laughter. "Mayhap we ought to put her in Tanner's place."

"Maybe."

From the back of the room Clint Tanner had stood silent, listening to the comments. At last he could stand it no longer.

"The hell!" Turning bright red in the face, Clint Tanner pushed through the crowd, hurrying to defend his reputation. "I done my part even though I've got a bad ankle. Besides, I didn't see any of you toting a gun and joining in the fracas." His point was made. "And I don't see any of you hurrying to be deputized so that you can save poor old Rafe's bacon either."

It was at that moment Josie chose to appear, pushing through the swinging doors of the saloon as if she owned the place. "If you're looking for volunteers, you can deputize me." That she meant it was obvious by the expression on her face.

Normally a woman wouldn't be allowed in this part of the saloon unless she worked there, but after what she had done, they couldn't keep Josie out.

"You're on." The cry was unanimous. She would ride with the "posse." Joining with Clint Tanner, Zeke Caldwell, Tom Bradley, and Zebulon Owens, she stormed from the saloon, saddled up and rode out of town.

"Nope this won't be like looking for a needle in a haystack," Zeke Caldwell, a balding man with a long nose, declared.

As time wore on and they traveled farther and

farther, one by one the men talked about returning to their homes.

"We're never gonna catch up to them" seemed
to be the general opinion.

"And the thought of trailing Billy Clayton is
scaring the hell out of you, isn't it?" Josie questioned. That was all she needed on this trip
through outlaw country, a bunch of cowards.

"That ain't it," Zeke Caldwell added, trying to
defend his reason for wanting to give up. Still, they
all looked sheepish as they followed after her.

"Look, about every so often the foliage is tram-
pled by a horse's hooves. Like some sort of sign."

"After all, you have to admit that Billy Clayton
would not be purposefully leaving a trail for us to
follow," Zebulon Owens put in.

"No, but Rafe might." Josie thought to herself
that was just something he might do. It was a
hunch that proved to be right.

A sign that they followed. Now, after several
hours of riding, Josie's hunch seemed to pay off.
They could see the smoke of a fire in the distance.

"Come on." Josie spurred her horse into a faster
gallop, then upon reaching the outskirts of the
camp, motioned for the men to dismount and go
on foot the rest of the way. Heading off in different directions, they silently, slowly, closed in.

Rafe! Seeing him sent a spurt of hope through
her whole body. For a moment all she could do
was to stare at him as she hid behind a rock. They
had to move carefully. She didn't want to risk anything happening to him.

"Slowly."

He looked up, catching sight of her in a fleeting glance, a moment that she could only hope would give him courage.

The minutes that followed seemed to affirm that it did. Josie saw Rafe move, hesitantly at first, then with the speed that did him proud. Breaking his bonds, reaching for the coffeepot, he threw scalding coffee in Billy Clayton's face just as Josie made herself known.

"Ouch! Gawd damn!" Leaping, turning around and around, grabbing at his face, Billy Clayton acted like a wildman.

"Get his gun, Rafe!" Josie held the Peacemaker trained on the outlaw, her finger poised on the trigger just in case he got any ideas. "Don't try anything, Clayton!"

It was at that moment that the others made their appearance. "You're covered."

"Reach for your gun and you're dead, Billy."

"Tie him up."

There was a scuffling sound as the "posse" hurried to take Billy Clayton into custody. As for Rafe and Josie, they had eyes only for each other. Smiling broadly, they made no secret of just how they felt. Then without another word they were in each other's arms.

"Why, look at that." Zeb poked Zeke in the ribs. "Lovebirds, pure and simple."

"Oh, Rafe. When I heard what happened I thought I was just going to—" Her words were muffled as he covered her mouth with his own. A heated kiss, nearly as hot as the coffee had been.

The minute they drew apart, Rafe declared his

intentions. "Let's get married right away, Josie. That is, if you'll have me," he said, realizing he had not yet asked her properly.

"Married?"

He put it to her boldly. "There is just no reason to wait. This little episode with Clayton made me realize how precious every day is. I want to spend the rest of my days with you."

"And your nights?" She tickled him behind the ear.

"Especially those."

It sounded like a dream come true; still, Josie was hesitant. "I love you, Rafe. I really do. But to tell you the truth, the idea of marriage scares me." There, she had admitted it.

"Scares you?" He smiled. "The woman who nearly fought the Clayton gang singlehanded?"

She nodded. "I . . . well, I've always been free to do as I please. I'm not certain that I could be happy being the prim and proper wife of the town's doctor."

"Prim and proper?" The very idea of those words describing Josie almost made him laugh, but not wanting to hurt her feelings, he held back. "Does that mean you'll expect to run wild?"

She thought a moment. "Not exactly. But it does mean I want more in my life than cooking, cleaning, and sewing." She smiled impishly. "You know, I've been thinking. This town really does need a sheriff. I thought that since *I've* proven myself more than capable of—"

Rafe's smiling mouth covered hers again, hot, warm, sweet. Time stood frozen, like a dream in slow motion as his mouth traced a pattern of longing on hers.

Watching from a short distance, Clint Tanner elbowed Zebulon in the ribs. "Did you hear what she had the nerve to suggest? Imagine that. A woman sheriff. Why, that would be the day." Putting back his head, he laughed uproariously.

Zebulon wasn't laughing, however. He cocked his head and winked in Josie's direction. "Yes, Clint, you're right there. That would be the day. A lucky day for the town of Showlow, or so I'd be thinking."

"What?" Clint Tanner started to argue and make a fuss right then and there, but Zebulon took him by the arm. Dragging him off, he headed in Billy Clayton's direction, leaving the two lovers locked in each other's arms.

Fifty-two

Showlow buzzed with the news. There were to be not one but two ceremonies today, both newsworthy events. First, Josie McLaury, a woman, mind you, had just been sworn into office as sheriff, a happening that made the women smile as they were gossiping.

"A female wearing a bronze star. And why not? She deserves it."

"Braver than a lot of the men in this town, if you ask me."

"Braver than most."

"Won the election fair and square." Though the women couldn't vote, their gentle persuasion had tipped the scales in Josie's favor. Besides, most of the men had already decided that there really wasn't any reason that a woman couldn't handle the job. At least this woman.

Secondly, the town's most eligible bachelor, Dr. Rafe Gardner, was all set to tie up with that newly appointed sheriff.

Hearing the conversation twittering about, Rafe looked at Josie as they walked up the steps of the church. He winked. "Never thought I'd be the sheriff's husband. But then, something tells me being married to you, there are going to be quite a few surprises in my life."

Josie winked back. "Pleasant surprises, doctor."

For one hushed moment Rafe looked into her eyes. "The most pleasant thing in my life will be marrying you. And even though he knew that in all probability his life would never be the same again, that it would be exciting, never dull, possibly hair-raising, he knew that he would never want to be without her. She was a one-of-a-kind woman, the kind he had spent his entire life wishing for.

They were married in a simple, brief ceremony in the church right down the street from the Hennessy boardinghouse, the chapel of which was packed with people. Shoulder to shoulder and elbow to elbow they had come to assuage their curiosity and to give the heroes of the town a rousing sendoff.

"They make a handsome couple," more than a few were heard to say.

Indeed they did. Rafe in his dark brown coat and trousers, a white lace cravat, Josie in a simple but stylish dress of white pique were living replicas of the tiny dolls that stood atop many a wedding cake.

" 'Dearly beloved, we are gathered here today to join this man and this woman in holy matrimony,' " the bespectacled reverend began.

The reverend's words flowed over them like honeyed wine, warming Josie through and through. Her cheeks glowed with happiness as she looked at Rafe. Thinking about their first meeting the day he had swept her up in his arms, she smiled. If only she had known then what she knew now.

"Do you, Josie Marie McLaury, take this man to be your lawful wedded husband?"

She didn't even have to think twice. She nodded. "I do."

Rafe answered the same, reaching down to squeeze her hand.

" 'For richer, for poorer, in sickness and in health, till death do you part.' "

"I love you, Josie."

She leaned toward him, touching first the sheriff's star on her bosom, then the thick gold band he had just placed on her finger. "I love you too."

For a timeless moment he looked at her, that is, until he heard someone yell out, "Well, don't just stand there. Kiss the bride."

Rafe didn't have to hear that request more than once. Drawing Josie into his arms, he caressed her lips gently in a passionate kiss that took her breath away. Strange, she thought, how kissing him always made her heart flutter so. Even more so than it had that day of the shoot-out with the Claytons. Until then she had only dreamed of such feelings. Now, as she stood beside her new husband, she knew that such dreams really could come true if you believed in yourself and in love.

"The doctor and the sheriff," she heard someone say, "what a pair they will be."

TODAY'S HOTTEST READS
ARE TOMORROW'S SUPERSTARS

VICTORY'S WOMAN (4484, $4.50)
by Gretchen Genet

Andrew—the carefree soldier who sought glory on the battlefield, and returned a shattered man . . . Niall—the legandary frontiersman and a former Shawnee captive, tormented by his past . . . Roger—the troubled youth, who would rise up to claim a shocking legacy . . . and Clarice—the passionate beauty bound by one man, and hopelessly in love with another. Set against the backdrop of the American revolution, three men fight for their heritage—and one woman is destined to change all their lives forever!

FORBIDDEN (4488, $4.99)
by Jo Beverley

While fleeing from her brothers, who are attempting to sell her into a loveless marriage, Serena Riverton accepts a carriage ride from a stranger—who is the handsomest man she has ever seen. Lord Middlethorpe, himself, is actually contemplating marriage to a dull daughter of the aristocracy, when he encounters the breathtaking Serena. She arouses him as no woman ever has. And after a night of thrilling intimacy—a forbidden liaison—Serena must choose between a lady's place and a woman's passion!

WINDS OF DESTINY (4489, $4.99)
by Victoria Thompson

Becky Tate is a half-breed outcast—branded by her Comanche heritage. Then she meets a rugged stranger who awakens her heart to the magic and mystery of passion. Hiding a desperate past, Texas Ranger Clint Masterson has ridden into cattle country to bring peace to a divided land. But a greater battle rages inside him when he dares to desire the beautiful Becky!

WILDEST HEART (4456, $4.99)
by Virginia Brown

Maggie Malone had come to cattle country to forge her future as a healer. Now she was faced by Devon Conrad, an outlaw wounded body and soul by his shadowy past . . . whose eyes blazed with fury even as his burning caress sent her spiraling with desire. They came together in a Texas town about to explode in sin and scandal. Danger was their destiny—and there was nothing they wouldn't dare for love!

Available wherever paperbacks are sold, or order direct from the Publisher. Send cover price plus 50¢ per copy for mailing and handling to Penguin USA, P.O. Box 999, c/o Dept. 17109, Bergenfield, NJ 07621. Residents of New York and Tennessee must include sales tax. DO NOT SEND CASH.

DISCOVER DEANA JAMES!

CAPTIVE ANGEL   (2524, $4.50/$5.50)
Abandoned, penniless, and suddenly responsible for the biggest
tobacco plantation in Colleton County, distraught Caroline Gil-
lard had no time to dissolve into tears. By day the willowy red-
head labored to exhaustion beside her slaves . . . but each night
left her restless with longing for her wayward husband. She'd
make the sea captain regret his betrayal until he begged her to
take him back!

MASQUE OF SAPPHIRE   (2885, $4.50/$5.50)
Judith Talbot-Harrow left England with a heavy heart. She was
going to America to join a father she despised and a sister she
distrusted. She was certainly in no mood to put up with the in-
sulting actions of the arrogant Yankee privateer who boarded her
ship, ransacked her things, then "apologized" with an indecent,
brazen kiss! She vowed that someday he'd pay dearly for the lib-
erties he had taken and the desires he had awakened.

SPEAK ONLY LOVE   (3439, $4.95/$5.95)
Long ago, the shock of her mother's death had robbed Vivian
Marleigh of the power of speech. Now she was being forced to
marry a bitter man with brandy on his breath. But she could not
say what was in her heart. It was up to the viscount to spark the
fires that would melt her icy reserve.

WILD TEXAS HEART   (3205, $4.95/$5.95)
Fan Breckenridge was terrified when the stranger found her near-
naked and shivering beneath the Texas stars. Unable to remember
who she was or what had happened, all she had in the world was
the deed to a patch of land that might yield oil . . . and the fierce
loving of this wildcatter who called himself Irons.

*Available wherever paperbacks are sold, or order direct from the
Publisher. Send cover price plus 50¢ per copy for mailing and
handling to Penguin USA, P.O. Box 999, c/o Dept. 17109,
Bergenfiled, NJ 07621. Residents of New York and Tennessee
must include sales tax. DO NOT SEND CASH.*

Taylor—made Romance From Zebra Books

WHISPERED KISSES (3830, $4.99/5.99)
Beautiful Texas heiress Laura Leigh Webster never imagined that her biggest worry on her African safari would be the handsome Jace Elliot, her tour guide. Laura's guardian, Lord Chadwick Hamilton, warns her of Jace's dangerous past; she simply cannot resist the lure of his strong arms and the passion of his *Whispered Kisses*.

KISS OF THE NIGHT WIND (3831, $4.99/$5.99)
Carrie Sue Strover thought she was leaving trouble behind her when she deserted her brother's outlaw gang to live her life as schoolmarm Carolyn Starns. On her journey, her stagecoach was attacked and she was rescued by handsome T.J. Rogue. T.J. plots to have Carrie lead him to her brother's cohorts who murdered his family. T.J., however, soon succumbs to the beautiful runaway's charms and loving caresses.

FORTUNE'S FLAMES (3825, $4.99/$5.99)
Impatient to begin her journey back home to New Orleans, beautiful Maren James was furious when Captain Hawk delayed the voyage by searching for stowaways. Impatience gave way to uncontrollable desire once the handsome captain searched *her* cabin. He was looking for illegal passengers; what he found was wild passion with a woman he knew was unlike all those he had known before!

PASSIONS WILD AND FREE (3828, $4.99/$5.99)
After seeing her family and home destroyed by the cruel and hateful Epson gang, Randee Hollis swore revenge. She knew she found the perfect man to help her—gunslinger Marsh Logan. Not only strong and brave, Marsh had the ebony hair and light blue eyes to make Randee forget her hate and seek the love and passion that only he could give her.